AGE OF RESOLVE

THE E.V. CHRONICLES

ILENE GRYDSUK

iUniverse

AGE OF RESOLVE
THE E.V. CHRONICLES

iUniverse books may be ordered through booksellers or by contacting:

iUniverse
1663 Liberty Drive
Bloomington, IN 47403
www.iuniverse.com
844-349-9409

ISBN: 978-1-6632-4477-2 (sc)
ISBN: 978-1-6632-4479-6 (hc)
ISBN: 978-1-6632-4478-9 (e)

Library of Congress Control Number: 2022916068

Print information available on the last page.

iUniverse rev. date: 10/05/2022

For my children. There is good in this
world; you are the living proof.
Above all else, stay true to yourselves.

PROLOGUE

> Dostoevsky once wrote: "If God did not exist, everything would be permitted"; and that, for existentialism, is the starting point. Everything is indeed permitted if God does not exist, and man is in consequence forlorn, for he cannot find anything to depend upon either within or outside himself. He discovers forthwith, that he is without excuse.
>
> **—Jean Paul Sartre, 1946**

EVERY ERA MUST COME to an end so that a new era can be born. And every era has that pivotal event that seals its fate. The Stone Age gave way to the Bronze Age, and then came the Iron Age. Ancient history gave way to the Age of Discovery in the fifteenth century. Civilization was introduced to rudimentary globalization through overseas exploration, planting the seeds of twenty-first century capitalism. Before the annihilation. Fast-forward through the machine age, the atomic age, the space age, arriving at the information age, complete with the digital revolution and the birth of multimedia. And left to your own devices, what has been the outcome of this human and social evolution?

My instructions were simple, clear, succinct. I created a clear guide for humankind, an enduring missive that extends to the far reaches of the human race, in one form or another. Through the centuries, you have added and interpreted and made the stories your own, but the underlying message has *never* changed. The hypocrisy is nauseating. Have I not been patient? Have I not been benevolent? But like any good parent, I have my limits. World wars, famines, genocide, crime, poverty, violence, homelessness, addiction, corruption. Nuclear armament, exploitation, terrorism, environmental destruction, abuse, torture, false gods. You were made in my image, yet you stray more from my likeness with each passing day.

You have lost your way. The human existential crisis has reached monumental proportions. You have forgotten what a gift I have given you in life on earth. The seeds of impiety have been cast far and wide. The honorable and the righteous among you must now pay for the sins of the many wicked. You have been weighed, measured, and found wanting. No more survival of the fittest, no more reaping what you sow, no more legacy of chaos and wretchedness for your children.

The path to Armageddon stops now. Welcome to the real Age of Atonement. The Age of Resolve.

Behold, the day of the Lord cometh, cruel both with wrath and fierce anger, to lay the land desolate: and he shall destroy the sinners thereof out of it.

—Isaiah 13:9 (New International Version)

CHAPTER 1

How can a man know what is good or best for him, and yet chronically fail to act upon his knowledge?

—Aristotle, Ethics

IT'S BEEN ONE HUNDRED years since the Correction, the great reset that wiped out the misguided ideology and spurious intentions of an ancient civilization seemingly bent on destroying itself. One hundred years since the Biodome replaced all the tyrannical, monocratic regimes and phony democracies as our one true panglobal leader. And with it, the existential virus, EV for short. Our modern-day exterminator of all things wrong with the world. The keeper of moral universalism. I don't know how she became a "she," but her matronly anthropomorphosis is now an established fact.

She is not contagious, she is not airborne or waterborne or foodborne. I was literally born with her, just like everyone else. Unlike for her ancient predecessors, there is no vaccine, no antivirals; medical intervention is pointless. She is not interested in children. *Learning* right from wrong as a child, after all, is not the same thing as *knowing* right from wrong. But since I just turned seventeen, she is awake and free will now come with a price. I still have freedom of choice, of course, but I intend to choose wisely. For at least the next fifty years or so, when she will once again fall dormant.

I've listened to the debate about what exactly she is countless times now. Is she a coronavirus, a calicivirus, an astrovirus, an arenavirus, a flavivirus? I say who cares. It doesn't matter what she is; as long as you live by the Biodome decree, EV is just along for the cellular ride. No harm, no foul. Like Mom says with her cheeky "be HIP" chant. Harmony. Integrity. Purpose.

So much has changed. The world that has been spun out of the Correction is so evolved, yet some things endure. Like high school. *Ugh.* Like this particular high school. No amount of paint can mask the weariness of this tired old building. This year we got robin's egg blue to replace last year's sunray yellow.

As my eyes wander around the room from classmate to classmate, I am struck by how much we have all grown over the last four years. My childhood friend Jenny sits front and center of Mr. Pietra's ancient history class. Her wavy brown locks have gone from long to short and back again. The braces she wore through our two years as juniors are gone, leaving a brilliant smile in their wake. Harriet sits to her left, exotic as ever with her deep brown eyes and dark complexion. She's grown into a long, lean, athletic frame with legs that go on forever. I look over my peers one by one. Crop cuts, flat hats, jeweled backpacks, friendship bracelets all fading to distant memories. We are on the threshold of adulthood here. This is the graduating class of 100 PC.

And then I think of my own transformation. To my great relief, little Everett Steele has shed her gawky thirteen-year-old body. My little stick figure-self, all elbows and knees, has been replaced with warm curves. The spray of freckles across my nose is long gone, and my rounded chubby cheeks have given way to a more refined and mature countenance. I have been described as a porcelain doll more than once. Mom calls me her little sprite. I'm Dad's pint-sized dynamo and Evander's spunky big sister. I might roll my eyes, but the monikers fairly depict my willful nature.

My ears register an abrupt change in tone and cadence. The interruption brings me back to the present.

"Come on, Mr. Pietra. You can't be serious. There's no way this kid created this social media empire that infected 220 million people in one shot! That's impossible!"

That's Marty Jansen, all-around good guy, never one to hold back with his adorably naïve perspective on all matters of historical import.

"It sounds preposterous, I agree, Mr. Jansen. However, in the pre-EV era, millions of people could be found on these social media platforms, indulging in wanton misconduct all hours of the day and night. And hardly victimless crimes. Cyberbullying, gambling, drug trafficking, propagating lies, rumor, and inuendo. Thank our stars that EV straightened out that mess before the point of no return," Mr. Pietra responds.

I remember the story of this particular correction well. Incorrigibles afflicted with EV6, the "avian flu," a nasty little righting protocol that included fever, aches, chills, nausea, and headache that persisted for weeks. Most folks recovered, but the righting protocol did claim more than a million miscreants, according to Biodome records.

Before the Biodome, self-governments exhausted countless resources playing cat and mouse trying to root out incorrigibles and bring them to justice. Sadly, for every incorrigible they took down, three more sprang up. It was a losing battle right from day one.

"Well, EV is nothing if not efficient."

This from my maybe, could be, kind of boyfriend, Matthew "Matt" Colby.

"I mean, there is just no escaping her."

Matt is the perfect combination of intellect and physical prowess. At six feet with a nicely tapered V frame that accentuates his powerful shoulders, a clean-shaven jawline, close-cropped deep brown hair, flawless olive skin, and the most interesting hazel green eyes ever, he is definitely not hard to look at. As the star quarterback of our football team, his deeds on the field are legendary. He is also a straight A student with real ambition.

I am so hoping he chooses the same department next week at the initiation ceremony. He has talked about animal welfare before, but with his technical, mathematical brain, I am worried he is going to veer toward community infrastructure and engineering. Definitely no place for me. So much for hanging out at lunch and our long walks to and from school every day. We are just so new that we haven't even made it official yet. I hate feeling insecure like this. Well, we can still make it work. We only live eight houses apart, after all.

The talk of incorrigibles sticks with me through lunch and into third period math class. For some reason it's left me a little unsettled. My knowledge of the fall of the ancients comes from a combination of classroom learning and Sunday morning sermons at the breakfast table with Grandpa. Before the existential virus, the ancients relied on a man-made judicial system in which people decided the moral obligations of people through doctrine then known as the criminal code. How truly bizarre.

EV was first discovered in facilities housing hundreds of thousands of people who violated, or allegedly violated, their moral obligations to one another or to society. Prisoners, as they were known, developed hemorrhagic fever and organ failure. If I recall correctly, it was thought to be some ancient virus known as Ebola. The Biodome archives claim that 11.13 percent of the inmate population recovered from the attack, while, oddly, a fraction of persons caring for these individuals also succumbed to this first documented wave of EV.

It was later determined that those who recovered were the wrongfully convicted; they were then rehabilitated. This period in history has become known as the Correction. And so began the Postcorrection Era, a global reset, 1 PC.

In the three hundred years before the Correction, the population of the planet swelled from one billion to more than nine billion people. The Correction wiped out more than 20 percent of the Earth's population in a matter of months, ridding the entire planet of the incorrigibles, the most foul, corrupt, criminal elements of ancient civilization. Scholars and scientists alike christened her the existential virus, and she has since evolved into her newest form, EV31, so named for her thirty-one known variants that serve to remind and correct abhorrent behavior and rid the Biodome of incorrigibles.

Grandpa reminded me that before the Correction, there were more than 220 viruses known to infect humankind. EV probably has more in her back pocket, but we haven't seen a new variant in more than thirty years, a testament to her effectiveness as a crime fighter. Crime is virtually nonexistent in the Age of Resolve. Back when EV was first being studied, scientists developed a matching game that persists even today. EV23 has the molecular makeup of what was once known as the Zika virus. EV4 is often compared to the pre-EV SARS virus, although I have no idea what that stands for. EV9 is a really bad one, apparently akin to the ancient human immunodeficiency virus. EV11 likes to hang around my school; Dad says she was once called the rhinovirus. Last week, Tiffany Belamus came to school with a runny nose and a headache that lasted for two days. She's not talking, but my guess is she missed curfew again.

And so, as time marches on, we become better citizens, better neighbors, and better stewards of the planet. I thank my lucky stars that I was born in the Age of Resolve. I've had seventeen years to think about my purpose, my part in the AOR. Now it's time to deliver.

CHAPTER 2

Free will can also be understood to be given for this reason: If anyone uses it in order to sin, the divinity redresses him [for it]. This would happen unjustly if free will had been given not only for living rightly but also for sinning. How would God justly redress someone who made use of his will for the purpose for which it was given? Now, however, when God punishes the sinner, what does He seem to be saying but: "Why did you not make use of free will for the purpose for which I gave it to you?"

—Saint Augustine, *De Liberto Arbitrio*
(On Free Choice), AD 388–395

MOM SHRILLS FROM THE bottom of the stairs, "Everett, honey, today is the day! Don't keep the Biodome waiting!"

I groan and peek over at the red LED display on my bedside table. Six minutes before the alarm was set to go off. I feel robbed.

"I know, Mom. I'm coming."

I know she can't hear me. I better move before she goes again. I stretch and plant my feet a little too harshly onto the hardwood. That she will hear. Funny, I've heard so many stories from older friends about the moment they knew EV was settling in all her latent glory inside every cell in their bodies. I guess everyone is different, because I can't say I've felt my moral awakening. Maybe it's more subtle than I imagined it would be. My seventeenth birthday was last month; she never misses that birthday.

As I step into the shower, I can't help but feel a twinge of excitement. Back before EV became part of our DNA, society was riddled with incorrigibles: the unemployed, uninspired, and uninitiated; deviants, dissidents, and rule breakers; and so much mundane existence without purpose. With EV came the Age of Resolve, and today I will become an official disciple of the new order. Okay, so it's a little more than a twinge ...

I head downstairs, ready for the big day ahead of me. Mom is hovering, arranging and rearranging breakfast settings, alternating between opening her mouth and pursing her lips in an effort not to ask what I know she wants to ask. The same question she's been asking for weeks now. I giggle. She reminds me of a puffer fish from a cartoon Evander and I used to watch on Saturday mornings. I save her the torment.

"Mom, I am not going to change my mind. Ever since I was like, I don't know, eight years old, I knew I was going to join AW. Animals are my life, and animal welfare is where I belong."

We have had this conversation a million times now. It doesn't help that my little brother, Evander, has pledged himself to the Department of Environmental Restoration with Mom and Dad, Mom in Fisheries and Oceans and Dad in the Climate Restoration Division. Evander's only twelve. He could change his mind yet. Then again, I never did.

Mom sighs and smiles, a real smile. Although she was hoping our purposes were aligned, she is not disappointed in my choice. She is as proud as a parent can be. It's our special connection that she is afraid of losing. More than mother-daughter, we are the best of friends, each other's anchor. If I am perfectly honest, it scares me a little too.

"So what division are you applying for then, honey?" Dad glances up from his e-news broadcast through the fog of his steaming coffee.

"I'm working that out, Dad. I am not quite there yet."

I think I would like to try the Regional Species Restoration Division. I might even get the chance to get in on a habitat reintroduction mission. But then again, I need to learn more about the equine gene pool stabilization program first. I'm not sure I could turn down the opportunity to work in the barn every day. I've been drawn to horses from a very early age, first through picture books and toy animals and eventually with riding lessons and then my own horse. The unshakable bond I have with Robbie, my now eighteen-year-old red bay quarter horse, has only grown stronger in the seven years since my parents surprised me on my tenth birthday when they brought me for my regular riding lesson at the Gray River Ranch.

Mom says the look on my face was priceless when I walked down the aisle of the barn and noticed the bright red banner draped across the top bars of his stall with the words *Happy Birthday Evey* splashed across it in white. Stunned, I had rubbed my eyes, thinking I must be dreaming, but when my vision cleared, he was still standing there with his strong jawline, soft angelic eyes, and not one marking to distract me from his perfect face. It was, as the ancient saying goes, love at first sight.

Yet I've always been fascinated with wolves, and Central Division AW has a big lupine rehabilitation program. So many choices, so many opportunities—I just can't decide. As my brain splinters in four different directions, I start to feel overwhelmed. Mom picks up on my mental overload and attempts to placate me.

"You don't have to decide right this moment. I'm sure there are thirty-one neighborhood kids feeling the same way this morning."

"Er, no, Mom. Actually, there's only twenty-nine."

That has both my parents' attention now. I go on to explain that two students from the other senior class have been withdrawn from the agent initiation ceremony. Since we as a society have dispensed with idle gossip and rumormongering, favorite pastimes of the ancients, I have no insight into their transgressions. However, the existential virus always doles out her sentences commensurate with the offense. And judging by the righting protocols dispensed, I can say with no uncertainty that they missed the "what to expect when you turn seventeen" memo: EV is not to be trifled with. She is judge, jury, and—when need be—executioner.

Matt takes hold of my right hand and pushes the panic bar on the gym door. PDA still makes me nervous, even small gestures like this one. Matt seems to enjoy my discomfort. I guess we are official now, although it's an unspoken official. I don't want to jinx it; I'll stick with the assumption. The gym has been converted to our own personal career center.

Before the Correction, kids used to go to college after high school or sometimes universities. We studied this in institutional history class. They would spend thousands of dollars on "diplomas" or "degrees"—I can't remember which is which at the moment—but anyway, they would spend all this money and years in these post-secondary programs, and so many of them would end up without a purpose just the same. Even worse, lots of them did literally nothing, sometimes for years after high school. Gosh, I can't image life before the Correction.

I glance over at Jenny. She's holding her head very still, but her gaze is darting around the room and back again. So, still undecided. My gaze, on the other hand, lands on the Department of Animal Welfare in the far left corner of the gym, and that's where it stays. Corinne and Tony are making their way over to the Department of Environmental Restoration. The gym might be transformed for us, but the telltale squeak of Tony's sneakers as he shuffles across the high-gloss floor reminds me that we are still at school.

I see Tamara and Connor chatting it up with the representative from the Department of Elder Care, I can hear tidbits of their conversation with the handsomely bearded representative in the cute black vest worn over the rolled-up sleeves of his neatly pressed white shirt.

"Seniors are the most coveted members of the new society. They are celebrated and honored for their lifelong contributions to the Biodome. After giving fifty years to the Biodome, they are the most esteemed members of society. As an elder care attendant, you will be assigned to families with post-EV family members."

Grandma's EC, Charlie, is amazing. He is always there just when she needs him. He helps her with her groceries when Mom is working, takes her to her favorite café to meet with her friends, and tends to her cats when she is with us for the weekend. Even when Grandpa passed on three years ago, Charlie stayed with us and now he is part of our family. And I love his kids. They make Grandma so happy. It's a great purpose, for sure. An honorable contribution to the Biodome. But I just don't think I can be swayed.

The Department of Health Promotion is not here today, which is not totally surprising. Since the Correction, EV has eradicated most of the man-made diseases that plagued the ancients and absorbed every virus into her genome, eliminating any and all transmissible infections. Incorrigibles involved in drug cartels and crime syndicates succumbed to some of EV's nastier righting protocols, like EV 3, the Marburg mutation. Before the Biodome, capitalism reigned large, bringing with it big polluters and manufacturers of disease-inducing products. And then, of course, unhampered human behavior allowed people to engage in all kinds of reckless and thoughtless pastimes. Before EV straightened out this mess, hospitals were everywhere, filled with car crash victims, unwanted and complicated pregnancies, drug overdoses, cancers, heart disease, gunshot wounds, domestic abuse, mental illness, not to mention infection upon infection upon infection of one sort or another. I will never forget the videos Mr. Pietra showed in class. I didn't sleep for three nights.

Since the Correction, the Department of Health no longer consumes Biodome resources like it once did. Sure, people still get injured and accidents still happen. Of course, labor and delivery agents are still required. Health promotion agents are always in high demand. It's not like it's going to disappear like those ancient police departments or anything. It's just that the Biodome doesn't need as many agents as it once did, and senior agents rarely, if ever, transfer out, so agency spots are limited. I think Jenny is disappointed. She always talked about the DHP. She can always get on the reassignment list. Lucky for me, I was never destined for health promotion, so no skin off my nose.

Still hand in hand, Matt and I approach the Department of Engineering and Infrastructure. I can feel him tense up as he slows his pace. Well, here it is. I don't know why I thought this would end any differently. He must sense my sudden shift in mood, because he pulls me closer.

"Hey, nothing is going to change. We still have weekends. Don't forget. curfew will be extended. We will have some evening time too."

I muster up as much cheer as I can. "Of course. I mean, I knew you would choose the DEI. With that math brain of yours, your purpose would be wasted on anything less."

Matt stopped walking and turned to face me. "Hold on there, Evey. Don't you dare minimize your importance. I could never do what you do with those horses. Who's that vet for the AW, Dr. Reisman or Reimans? He says you're a natural. And what about that litter of puppies you helped raise last year? I could never do that! I get to build roads, but you get to save God's creatures."

I let Matt's words sink in. "OK, I have to admit, when you put it that way, I guess my purpose is pretty special. And so are you, Mr. Colby. You always know exactly what to say."

I take his hands in mine. Suddenly PDA isn't so bad.

I leave Matt at the DEI, talking projects with the very loquacious department ambassador. The agent is gesticulating wildly as he describes a new initiative around the reconfiguration of pre-Correction urban centers that were once megacities with eight-lane highways running straight through and so much pollution that people wore masks when they went outdoors. I am so thankful to be born and raised in my little rural Midwestern town surrounded by nature. Even with one hundred years of urban rehabilitation, I would not do well in a big city. But with guys like Matt, those behemoths will be rebalanced in no time and harmony restored.

On to my purpose. I approach the Department of Animal Welfare and am warmly greeted by Kylie, a bubbly redhead with a slight Southern drawl. The freckles splashed across her nose and cheeks make her look younger than her thirty-something years. Her soft blue eyes greet me, along with her perfect smile and dazzling white teeth.

"Hey there, Everett." She says, glancing at the name tag pasted to my blue blouse. "Are you thinking the AW might be right for you?"

I glance over at Matt across the gym and two booths over, still chatting with the animated DEI representative. I'm not sure if he's even noticed I have left yet. I look back at Kylie and the backdrop of images of recovered species, photos of restored wildlife habitat, and a giant group shot of smiling AW attendants standing arm in arm under the banner of the Midwest AW campus, exactly where I will be stationed. I imagine myself in that photo, celebrating the contributions of the AW to the Biodome. It feels right. I know this is where I belong. I never really doubted my choice, but this seals it for me.

"Actually, not thinking at all, Kylie. I am ready."

CHAPTER 3

In the first place, all would agree that, if we led our lives according to the ways intended by nature and the lessons taught by her, we should be intuitively obedient to our parents; later we should adopt reason as our guide and become slaves to nobody.

—Etienne de La Boetie, *The Politics of Obedience: The Discourse of Voluntary Servitude*, 1552–1553

I'M A BUNDLE OF nerves mixed with excitement and wonder. I hardly remember getting dressed this morning. My thoughts had been racing as I prepared for my first day at the Department of Animal Welfare, Midwest campus. My feet automatically take me downstairs, where my family is already seated for breakfast. The butterflies scampering around in my belly dampen my appetite, so I settle on plain oatmeal. I'm not really going to be tasting anything anyway.

Cosmo sits staring up at me from the foot of my chair, pressing his wet nose against my shin. I reach down and brush my hand over his little white head, much to his content. He calms the churning in my gut.

Mom decides to drop me off today. She won't admit it, but she really wants to see where I will be spending my time now that high school is behind me and I am officially a Biodome agent. She is a respected senior agent in the Fisheries and Oceans Division with more than twenty years of service to the Biodome. She has never applied for reassignment; she is as content as a DFO agent now as she was at my age.

Reassignment protocols were explained during orientation. The Biodome would never expect us to serve a department if our interests changed. "Purpose without happiness and personal fulfillment is simply servitude." That had been the message from the new agent orientation director last week. That was the last time Matt and I would sit together in class. Today marks the first weekday in four years that I won't see my childhood peers or spend my day in the easygoing banter that comes with years of familiarity.

I climb in the passenger seat, still on autopilot. My face looks back at me in the tiny mirror as I pull on the visor to block the sun. I turn my head left and right, not in vanity, but to make sure I haven't left any breakfast on my chin. I push the hair back from my face. It slides down my shoulders halfway to my elbows. Although Evander and I share the same golden hair color, where his curls at the temples in the humidity, mine is poker straight even in a downpour.

Mom throws her purse in the back seat and plops herself in the driver's seat. While she navigates us through the neighborhood, I conjure up memories of birthday parties, slumber parties, play dates, and backyard barbeques in many of the homes that pass by my window. It seems like only yesterday. As we hit the highway and head north for the compound, the bonds to my childhood sever with each passing mile.

We pull into the compound. When I glance over at my mother,

she is gushing with pride. I see tears threatening to spill over her bottom lashes.

"Mom, you're fussing for nothing. I am fine. I can take the shuttle tomorrow. Now you have to come all the way back here to get me."

I won't admit it out loud, but it's really nice that she still dotes on me.

"I know, honey. You've just grown up so fast. I want to cherish every moment."

She hugs me fiercely. With that, I say good-bye, get out of the dark blue sedan, and stand in the parking lot as I watch her drive away. I feel the tether that binds us growing a little bit longer as her taillights disappear around the corner.

The campus is huge, and I mean huge. Two hundred acres of forested land dedicated to the rehabilitation and repopulation of all forms of native and nonnative species. In a few weeks, I will get to pick my specialties. Of course, I am leaning toward equine welfare, with lupus programming a close second. But for now, the sixteen new agents, myself included, will be focused on becoming familiar with the compound, the different programs, and the senior agents, who will be our mentors.

Only Marlee Cross from my school joined the AW with me. The other new agents are not hard to spot; we are all looking around in wonder with campus maps in hand, trying to take it all in. We have the next two weeks to explore, pop into different program buildings, observe, and ask questions. The senior agents are so welcoming and encouraging. I just know I am going to love it here.

I spend most of my first afternoon around the central complex, reading up on the different programs, pinpointing them on my campus map, and planning my program visits. My first official program visit on Tuesday morning is at the equine rehabilitation center (no surprise there), and I am instantly in love with every one of the twenty-three horses in the program. Well, twenty-four, actually. I get to witness the birth of a colt, a little thoroughbred with long spindly legs and a classic brown bay coloring who wobbles and trembles while I hold my breath until he finds his footing. They name him Eddie after one of the senior agents who assisted in his delivery, but he's already being dubbed Steady Eddie. Gregory Pines, the head of both the equine and canine gene pool expansion programs, is pleased with my interest.

"By diversifying the thoroughbred gene pool, we are seeing a gradual decrease in the genetic load. Less harmful genetic mutations mean healthier horse populations. Our results are being duplicated across our canine program."

"Wow, Dr. Pines, this is so exciting. After the campus orientation, I will definitely be back. My purpose is here with you."

Dr. Pines nods at me and smiles.

"Glad to hear it, Ms. Steele. We'll look forward to officially welcoming you to the team. In the meantime, do enjoy your time with the other programs. There is great work being done all around this campus."

With that, Dr. Pines turns back to Eddie, who is checking the vitals on the mare who delivered Eddie the colt just a short time ago.

Because the wolves are isolated on the far northeastern side of the campus, a compound within the compound from what I can tell on the map, I decide to wait until I can dedicate a full day to visiting the program. Next on my list is the avian program. The northern owl and barn owl population restoration missions are my absolute favorite.

At the time of the Correction, before EV demanded that humans live in harmony and in balance with nature, the ancients had decimated more than 41,000 species, some 16,000 to the brink of extinction. The facts from that biology class are burned into my brain. One in four mammals, one in eight birds, one-third of all amphibians, 70 percent of the world's plants, and worst of all, more than eight hundred species were wiped off the face of the Earth before the Correction. I think that was the day I knew I belonged with the

Department of Animal Welfare. But now that I'm here, I want to do it all, all at once. I am bursting with purpose. Suddenly fifty years of service does not seem nearly long enough.

The first week of department orientation is behind us. It's a beautiful sunny Monday morning, with a light southerly breeze and a horizon rimmed with big fluffy cumulus clouds. Today I will visit the lupus compound on the southeastern corner of the compound. I could take the shuttle bus across campus, but today I think I will walk and take the opportunity to decompress from last week's whirlwind of program visits and maybe plan my life on the way. I grab my gray AW ball cap and an elastic from my backpack and get to work sweeping my hair up of off my neck.

Oddly, the hat makes me think of Dad. He loves to share tales about the department's climate restoration projects. They are his version of bedtime stories. When the Biodome officially reached three hundred parts per million of atmospheric CO_2, Dad went on for days, recounting milestones from the time of the Correction when EV stopped corporate polluters in their tracks and we set about restoring balance and harmony, one ppm at a time. I pull my ponytail through the back of the hat and thank my lucky stars I live in the Age of Resolve, when a hat is just a hat and no longer a man-made medical imperative.

Map. Check. Water. Check. Snacks, cell phone. Check and check. OK then. I should be at the lupus compound well before lunch. All afternoon with those glorious wolves. I am so spoiled.

No sooner am I out of the parking lot and heading for the walking trail than the shuttle driver pulls up to the end of the lot and beeps to get my attention.

"Good morning, Everett. Can I help you get where you're going this lovely day?"

"Good morning, Tobias! I am headed to the lupus program, but I will enjoy the walk today. I am in no hurry."

"Oh my! I don't know anyone who walks that trail. That's clear across the compound! Are you sure I can't give you a lift?"

"Thank you, Tobias, but I will truly enjoy my time and it gives me the opportunity to reflect."

"Well, that does sound like a blissful morning. But do you have your telephone in case you change your mind?"

I pat the pocket of my backpack and smile warmly at Tobias. With that, I set off on the walking path.

Along the way, I see an elephant with his trunk curled high above his head. A little farther along the path, I spot a dolphin jumping out of the sea of white rimming the sky. I used to spend hours with Grandpa, lying on our backs in the grass, shape hunting in the big white fluffy clouds just like the ones running along the horizon today. The memory brings an involuntary smile to my lips.

Twenty-three minutes and eight cloud creatures later, I come across a fork in the path with a sharp right onto a smaller path. Huge hardwood trees crowd the entrance to the little trail. I reach for my backpack. I don't remember seeing this trail on the map. Better double-check. I unfold the map and follow my path with my finger. No, I am not lost. I know exactly where I am, and there is definitely no trail marked on this map. Huh. That is odd. Very unlike the Biodome to produce anything that is not absolutely perfect.

I am just about to make my way past the mystery trail when I hear the distinct whinny that can only come from a horse. It is coming from that trail. What? Now that doesn't make sense at all. The equine program is on the north side of the compound. I should know. I've already been there four times in the last week. There it is again. OK, now I have to check this out. I step onto the small trail and am making my way through the overhanging boughs of a gigantic hickory tree when I spot her, a cute little chestnut mare with a white blaze and two white socks. Her name is Gracie, if I recall.

And then I spot him. I have not seen him before. He's tall, at least six feet, and bulky in an "I'm used to hard work" kind of way. I can see that even underneath his baggy white T-shirt and loose-fitting jeans. He has shaggy dirty blond hair just a shade darker than my own; it pokes out in all directions underneath his ball cap, which is an identical match to mine. He has childlike facial features complete with sky blue eyes and a slightly pouty bottom lip. A wayward ray of sun makes its way through the trees and catches his profile. I see long, perfectly curled eyelashes that are slightly darker than his tousled head. Geez Louise ...

Gracie is presently walking him in circles in that telltale way horses have when they are anxious. She lets out another whinny.

"What are you doing, woman? Would you please just stop already?" the boy tries to reason with Gracie, not in an unkind way but in frustration.

"She's calling to her herd. She doesn't like being alone," I chime in.

The boy spins toward the sound of my voice. Clearly, I've taken him by surprise. The most adorable flush blooms across his cheekbones and makes it way down to his collarbone.

"Oh, hey. Uh, I didn't see you there. I was just, uh, just, well, talking to this here horse." He shrugs and looks toward his feet.

"I talk to my horse all the time. He's a good listener."

At that, he looks up, and his chagrin is replaced with a warm smile.

"Where did you come from?" he asks.

"I'm headed toward the lupus compound."

"On foot? No one walks to the lupus compound," he replies.

"Yeah, that's the second time I've heard that today. Where are you taking her anyway?" I look over to Gracie. "This is so far from the paddocks."

I walk up to Gracie and rub her neck. She calms instantly.

"May I?" I ask, pointing to the lead line.

He hands me the lead rope. I loosen it, back Gracie up a few steps, and then walk her forward and ask her to stop. Her tension melts away.

"Don't have a lot of experience with horses, do you? She's already upset about being alone, and you being nervous is only adding to her anxiety."

"Oh," the boy replies sheepishly as I move Gracie so she can reach the grass at the trail's edge. I let her graze. "I guess that makes sense. I'm just a transporter."

"A transporter?"

That position is not listed anywhere in the department literature.

"Are you with Dr. Pines in the equine program?" I ask.

"Uh, no. Not exactly. I move animals from all the programs."

He sounds a little nervous now.

"Move them?"

This isn't making any sense.

"Move them where?"

Oh my gosh. Where are my manners? I offer him my free hand.

"I'm Everett, by the way, Everett Steele. I just onboarded from Grand Leigh High."

He takes my hand in his. Just as I thought, his hands match his frame. They're calloused and rugged. Working hands.

"Jacob. But my friends call me Jake. Been with AW going on two years now."

"Well, I would have been a junior, but I knew most of the seniors. I don't remember you, Jacob, uh, Jake."

He chuckles. "Jake works. I went to Brantwood."

"Brantwood? Wow. You don't really look like a city boy."

He pulls his ball cap from his head, tries to smooth back his hair, and then proceeds to start tucking in his shirt.

"Gosh, Jake. I'm so sorry. I didn't mean it like that. You look great. I mean, you look fine. I mean ..."

What in the Biodome is wrong with me? I feel like my head is full of marbles. Jake graciously lets me off the hook.

"Well, I better be getting going. I have to drop this little lady off before lunch."

He extends his hand. I almost take it in mine until I realize he is waiting for the lead rope.

"Oh, right."

I gently lift Gracie's head from her patch of grass. Jake brushes my hand and takes the lead rope.

"Just loosen your grip. Don't hold the line so close to her face. She just needs a little space," I offer.

"OK. Well, I'm willing to try anything that is going to make this easier on both of us."

With a nod and a small smile, he and Gracie set off down the mystery trail. Wait. He forgot to tell me where he is taking her.

CHAPTER 4

Now the serpent was the most cunning of all the wild animals that the Lord God had made. He said to the woman, "Did God really say, 'You can't eat from any tree in the garden'?"

—Genesis 3:1 (Christian Standard Bible)

WHAT'S THE WORST THING that can happen? EV4 maybe? Runny nose, a cough, a headache? EV7? A little pink eye? The problem is how to explain it to Mom and Dad. And it's only Monday. How could I possibly get through the rest of the week on campus without people asking questions? I need to turn around, get back on the main trail, and get to the lupus compound. I can still make it there before lunch. It doesn't matter that I didn't really feel EV awaken on my seventeenth birthday, not the way I expected. I know she's in there, and she doesn't miss a beat. I turn half a dozen times, but my feet are still planted in the same spot. Jake and Gracie disappear around a bend in the trail. A transporter? Who moves animals? Why? Where? For whom?

This is so wrong. I know it. Yet I also know I am going to do it anyway. I'll deal with whatever EV dishes out later. I wait another minute or two and start to make my way down the trail after them. I don't have to go far. Less than ten minutes later, I hear Jake ahead of me. He must have stopped. I slow and move off the trail, sliding from oak to ash to basswood, thankful for their protection.

Then it comes into view. What in the name of the Biodome? I have never seen anything like it. Sitting right there in the middle of what is supposed to be one of the Biodome's crowning achievements in forest-scaping sits an enormous concrete oval. Blacked out windowpanes wrap around the first level of the structure, followed by what looks like two more levels of pure concrete blocks, engineered to geometric perfection. A smooth flat black roof dotted with vents and a concrete ring at ground level completes the otherworldly architecture. It's old. No, ancient. Built before the Correction. I'm not sure how I know this. It's more of a feeling.

It's not supposed to be here. If the ancients didn't destroy their own work, which they were prone to do according to Matt who loves to talk everything infrastructure, it should have been dismantled as part of ecorestoration. According to my AW compound map, all department administration facilities are centrally located a half hour behind me up the main trail, and there is no animal program here, what this peculiar structure is doing here is beyond me.

There are three concrete ramps that I can see. I image there's a fourth on the back side.

I spot Jake and Gracie climbing the eastern ramp. I weave my way through the trees to get closer. I am within earshot; I hear clipped pieces of conversation Jake strikes up with a young woman with a smart dark brown bob cut framing an equally smart face with large brown eyes and sharp cheekbones. She is tapping away on a tablet. She looks up as Jake approaches.

"Hi, Ashley. She was a little put out about coming here. Took me a bit longer than expected."

"Oh, hey, Jake. No worries. She's going to the Hendra lab, southeast corridor. Security is waiting for you."

Security? The word almost drowns out the more important word in that exchange. Hendra. I pronounce the word slowly in my mind. I know that word. Why do I know that word? I snap back to the moment as an overhead door opens on a track and Jake starts to walk Gracie into a concrete tunnel. Gracie stops and turns her head in my direction. No. She turns her head directly at me. She knows I'm here. She's looking at me through the trees, zoning in on the oak tree that is standing between us. I retreat behind the tree, make myself as small as possible, and go stock still. Gracie sniffs the air, gives her a tail a big swish, and turns back to Jake, who is oblivious to our exchange.

She follows Jake inside and disappears. Ashley taps something else into her tablet and then she, too, follows Jake inside the strange oval. The overhead door rolls down, and I am left alone, digging my fingers into the trunk of my oak tree turned shield. When did I get so tense? Alrighty then. That was fun. Time to turn around now and head back on my way. Nothing to see here, Evey. I am probably going to start sneezing or itching any minute now. EV knows just as well as I do that I have broken a rule. My perfect streak is broken. Mom will be so disappointed.

But my feet stay planted as I engage in an internal dialogue that ends with, *Well, I'm this far in now.* I approach the building, feeling rather like my cat, Minx, when he's hunting grasshoppers or some such insects in the tall grass at the edge of the lawn in the backyard. I am reminded of Grandpa once again and something he used to say to my brother and I when our inquisitiveness got the better of us.

"Now, now, children. Remember that curiosity killed the cat."

I thought it the oddest of expressions as a young child, but somehow I seem to be developing clarity in this moment.

"Indeed," I mumble under my breath as I continue my surreptitious advance.

There are no vehicles. The only sounds I hear are the voices of the songbirds in the trees and the wind rustling the leaves. I am exposed now, so no turning back. I scuttle up the ramp to a glass entryway northwest of the overhead door Jake and Gracie used moments earlier. This appears to be the main entrance, but the glass is frosted. I cannot see anything inside. Beside the doors, a distinct keystone is embedded within the concrete with the number 1967 inscribed underneath the words *The Spectrum*. Ancients had a habit of naming their structures. This must have been an important building. Sprawled across the double glass doorway in nondescript bold black lettering are two messages: *Restricted Area* and *Authorized Agents Only*.

Huh. Well, things just got even more peculiar. I can just see the painted concrete floor in the clear glass gap between the window frosting and the doorframe. When I shift my angle, I spot a large box on the floor just inside the doors. I shimmy to the left and then to the right. I get the angle just so that I can read the label on the top of the box.

> Dr. Vladimir Draeger
> Zoonotic Research
> Department of Animal Welfare
> Midwest Division

Zoonotic research? I don't remember seeing that in the AW program listing. My mind is running through the programs. I don't have a photographic memory or anything, but I just can't recall anything of the sort listed in my department orientation package. I'm not even sure what that is. I need to think.

I sneak back to the relative safety of my oak tree and gently drop my backpack. I simply must check my manual. Just as I reach for the zipper, my cell phone rings, causing me what I am sure are about one thousand extra heartbeats that seem to emanate from my ears rather than my chest. I fumble with the snap on the side pocket and silence the phone just as it's about to ring for a second time. I literally melt into the trunk of my tree and try to hold my breath but fail because of my current cardiac condition, so I settle on deep breaths to slow it way down.

One minute, two minutes, nothing. Am I safe? I start my retreat ever so gingerly, retracing my steps until I am back on the main trail. No sooner does my heart return to my chest cavity then my phone rings again. I am so jumpy at this point, I'm not convinced I have a resting heart rate today. This time I answer.

"Uh, hello?"

"Oh, there you are, Ms. Steele. I was beginning to worry!"

Tobias.

"Oh. Hey, Tobias. Nope. All good here."

"Ah, excellent. I do hope you are enjoying your tour of the lupus compound. They truly are such remarkable creatures. Shall I swing by and pick you up, say three o'clock? Will that provide sufficient time to conclude your tour?"

Whoa. What time is it, anyway? I peel the phone from my ear and check the time: 11:49 a.m. "Um, sure, Tobias. Three o'clock is great."

I have no idea what the layout looks like, so I wait and hope Tobias will suggest the landmark.

"All right then. At the birthing center? Or perhaps another area?"

"Nope. The birthing center sounds good, Tobias. Thank you. See you soon."

I hang up the phone and pull out my map. I'm about halfway to the compound. I can do this. I have to do this. I stuff the map back in my bag and book it down the trail as fast as my legs will carry me.

I have to skip lunch, but it's worth it. I make it to the lupus compound as though I am right on schedule and fall into the tour with two other new agents. After an exchange of pleasantries and a few smiles and nods, I find myself standing in the birthing center, watching two young wolf pups frolicking near the fence. I don't remember a word the tour agent speaks. The afternoon is a blur. Tobias picks me up at the appointed time none the wiser of my ruse. I switch shuttles at the administration complex and wallow in guilt all the way home.

That evening, I get through dinner and field all the questions my family throw. It feels as though I speak to them from underwater. Mom mistakes my apprehension for fatigue and comments that I must be exhausted after my busy day. She lets me cut out after dish duty to clean up and enjoy my well-earned "repose," as she likes to call it. I head for my bedroom, flop down on the bed, and take a deep breath.

Well, no one is suspicious. They believe my recounting of the day. I walked to the lupus compound, spent my lunch hour watching a young female gray wolf rearing the pure white alpha's offspring. (I did in fact watch them, albeit briefly.) I met Dr. Viskov, the compound's head veterinary agent, and observed his team at work in the birthing center. I hitched a ride back to main administration with Tobias on the shuttle. It was a lovely day, and yes, I am considering working with Dr. Viskov.

It's mostly true. But EV knows the whole truth. Not only was I deceptive today, but I also lied. To multiple people. I am afraid to go to sleep. The sense of foreboding is paralyzing. And how to explain it. What could I possibly say to my family that will account for the cold? The upset stomach? The headache? Maybe all of the above? EV will dish out whatever she determines is commensurate with my crimes. And there are a couple.

I *am* exhausted. A combination of enervation from the sprint and all the walking, yes, but more so from all the heightened emotions I experienced today. I fall into bed and let all my pent-up feelings seep into the mattress.

But sleep does not come easily tonight. It's as if my subconscious is trying to prolong the inevitable by staying awake. I glance over at my alarm clock: 1:16 a.m. Finally overtaken by bone-deep fatigue, I can feel sleep take me into its grip, that floating, unmoored sensation that comes when you start to drift off. If I dream, I don't remember.

I wake to my bleeping alarm long before the volume reaches its crescendo. I make my way to my little private bathroom and start the shower. On autopilot, I empty my bladder and then reach for my toothbrush and proceed to brush my teeth. I glance at myself in the mirror just as I am about to step into the shower, and it all comes back to me. My indiscretions. But wait. I don't feel any different. In fact, I feel quite good considering my shortened sleep cycle. That's not right.

I jump into the shower and start to examine my body. A rash maybe? But there is nothing. I probe my muscles and flex my joints, looking for pain. Nothing. In the name of the Biodome, how can this be? I deceived. I lied. Why is EV not punishing me? Kids at school have done much less and EV has always, I mean always, reminded them of their oath to honesty, integrity, and purpose. Are my transgressions so bad that EV has stricken me with a much more insidious infection than I imagined?

I am stirred back to reality when Mom raps on my bathroom door.

"Evey, honey, are you scrubbing your skin clean off in there?"

"Sorry, Mom. Coming."

I quickly wash and condition my hair and then scrub my face and body, involuntarily checking one more time for signs of infection just to be sure. Not yet.

I clear the steam from the bathroom mirror and do a close-up examination of my face. It looks exactly the same as it did yesterday morning. I hold my own stare for a moment, and in my mind's eye,

I see Gracie turning to look at me behind my oak tree. That strange moment when I was sure she knew I was hiding there, watching. But that's impossible. I am about to look away when I hear her calling. It sounds so real, it is dizzying, and I realize she *is* calling me. She *was* calling to me, not to her herd, but me. She wanted me to find her. And she is calling me right now. In that instant, I know I have to go back.

Pedro Ramírez walks briskly down the long corridor of the ancient university's main level, his destination three doors from the end of the hallway on the right. He is looking for his mentor, excited to deliver news of a shipment they have been anxiously awaiting for months. He opens the door and immediately spots the professor at work.

"It has arrived, Dr. Castillo," he announces without preamble.

José Castillo looks up from his microscope and flexes his shoulder blades to loosen the knot in his back. Reaching for his now tepid coffee despite the dirty fly perched on the rim of his cup, he instructs Pedro to escort the delivery team to the sterile lab. Deciding to pass on the coffee, the aging doctor lumbers over to the security scanner and proffers his thumbprint to the device. The magnetic lock releases, and the glass door slides open silently.

The lab looks somewhat like its main occupant, a bit disheveled and unorganized. Dr. Castillo is a brilliant man, top evolutionary biologist in his field, and world-renowned paleobiologist, although you might never know it if you passed him in the street. With his too-long graying hair poking up in all directions, perpetual five o'clock shadow, slightly crooked oval glasses that he continually adjusts on his nose to no avail, and drab gray cardigan with the patchy elbows that is the mainstay of his hueless wardrobe—all on a six-foot-four slightly hunchbacked frame—the doctor is easily passed over even by pundits in the field. That is, until he speaks.

"*Sí, sí,* over here. Adjacent to the specimen."

He beckons to the two agents assigned to move the precious item. The artifact has traveled from the ancient Bürgermeister Müller Museum in what was formerly known as Solnhofen, Germany, under agent escort to Dr. Castillo's lab at the ancient Universidade de Sao Paulo on the southwest coast of Brazil, just a short drive from its famous ancient neighbor, Rio de Janeiro.

The 120-million-year-old fossil was originally discovered in northeastern Brazil in the early 2000s, long before the Correction. The escorts step away from the crate and station themselves like statues ten paces off, awaiting further instruction.

"Pedro, come," Dr. Castillo calls him to attention as he gently pries the lid off the wooden crate and carefully rearranges the packing inside to reveal the occupant.

Pedro overhears Castillo's whisper: "Welcome home."

Castillo holds his hands at an odd, almost ninety-degree angle to his torso while still staring into the crate. Pedro slides sterile gloves onto the doctor's hands gently. Castillo slowly swings his hands into the crate, lifts the fossil from the box, and places it on the stainless-steel tray next to the live specimen. The creature stills and then recoils, making itself small in the far corner of its glass terrarium.

"Well, my little friend"—Dr. Castillo glances over at the glass tank—"meet *Tetrapodophis amplectus.* If my hunch is right, you are staring at your kin."

After some preliminary examination, Castillo makes an announcement. "Amazing. It's a perfect match."

Pedro watches as Dr. Castillo squints at the Xray images on the computer screen, pushing his glasses uncomfortably high on his nose every few seconds. The live specimen basks in its artificially sunny terrarium under the heat lamp, impervious to the growing excitement around it. Given the pristine condition of the ancient artifact, Castillo is able to compare the delicate anatomical features right down to the little elbows, wrists, and tiny digits on each beast's forelimbs and equally distinct hindlimbs.

"*Sí, sí,* one hundred and sixty spinal vertebrae. One hundred and twelve in the tail. The scales do indeed extend across the entire belly of both specimens. It's indisputable, Pedro. Our little friend here is a squamate, not a modern-era lizard at all but the famed four-footed snake from the Early Cretaceous period."

Pedro's stunned expression makes his already boyish features look even more childlike. He rubs at his smooth jawline, a nervous habit he's developed since he started as a junior agent in Dr. Castillo's lab. He chuckles uneasily.

"But I thought the tetra was a water lizard, Dr. Castillo. I mean, I know when it was first discovered it was thought to be the original snake. There must be some mistake. This specimen cannot possibly be the same tetra. That would mean it has not evolved since the dawn of mankind."

Dr. Castillo raises his brows, and then a toothless grin slowly spreads across his face. "Pedro, if I didn't know any better, I might think you are confusing your role as a scientist with your Sunday morning prayers."

It is true. Pedro is a devout Christian who clings to the word of the church as much as his present mentor.

"And the Lord God said to the serpent: Because thou hast done this, thou art cursed above all cattle, and above every beast in the field; upon thy belly shalt though go, and dust shalt thou eat all the days of thy life." Dr. Castillo quotes the verse from the book of Genesis perfectly, albeit in a somewhat mocking tone that unsettles Pedro profoundly.

"Very funny. The serpent from the Garden of Eden. Of course that is utter nonsense," Pedro lies.

For at that moment, he is sitting in his favorite third row pew, just where the Sunday morning sunlight cascades through the ornate stained glass in the towering arched windows of the nave of the Sao Paulo Cathedral. It takes him a moment to reorient himself, so profound is the sensation. He can still hear the hymn coming from the choir loft. Pedro glances at his wristwatch.

"It's getting on in the day, Dr. Castillo. Let me get the lab tidied up so we can lock up for the day."

As he turns from Dr. Castillo, Pedro makes the sign of the cross and mouths the words, *in the name of the Father and of the Son and of the Holy Spirit.*

CHAPTER 5

But what "freedom" means here is nothing but the absence of certain conditions the presence of which would make moral condemnation or punishment inappropriate.

—P.F. Strawson, *Freedom and Resentment*, 1962

I SPEND MY MORNING with the honeybees. Before the Correction, rampant use of insecticides in the name of agricultural yield compromised the bees' immune systems until they lost all natural defenses. Colonies were invaded by parasitic mites until they almost disappeared. The ancients called it colony collapse disorder, according to Dr. Bosworth. It has been a slow, albeit steady, recovery. Although my sudden interest in bees was initially motivated by the program's proximity to a certain secret structure, I must admit, I am fascinated by these little guys. The opportunity to learn more about how the Biodome has achieved sustainability and balance in farming practices is intriguing.

But no, I have other plans for the afternoon. I eat a quick lunch and politely extricate myself from the group assembled at the picnic tables. Mere hours ago I would have considered this designated lunch spot uncomfortably close to row upon row of shallows, broods, and western supers, home to thousands upon thousands of swarming bees.

I make my way back to the main trail; the secret entrance should be just up ahead on the opposite side of the dirt path. Insect repopulation is the last program along the main trail before agents jump the shuttle, so I shouldn't have any company. I spend the next thirteen minutes lost in my thoughts, trying to figure out what I am doing, what I am hoping to achieve. Why can't I just forget about yesterday and carry on? I'm so absorbed by my own inner turmoil that I almost miss the obscure turn in the trail. If it hadn't been for Gracie, I never would have even noticed it. It's almost as though the trees have been groomed to disguise the entrance that leads to the strange building.

As if of their own volition, my feet take me onto the pathway. *OK, EV, if you're going to give me a sign, now's the time—a sneeze, a tickle in my throat, hives, anything.* I head for the cover of the trees almost immediately this time. It slows me down, but I am taking no chances. I bunny hop from trunk to trunk, listening for the slightest sign of human activity. Before long the odd building comes into view. As before, there are very few signs of life, at least on the outside. Maybe it's just used for storage? Wait, for a horse? I start to notice little clues that there are indeed people here regularly. A patch of trampled grass under the boughs of a majestic redwood—I can picture a picnic blanket on that very spot. The middle of the dirt path is worn from foot traffic. There is another wearing pattern in the gravel at the front of the building, this one from tire treads. But no sign of company so far.

Unlike my first visit, this time I make my way around the back of the building, keeping to the forest. Just as I thought, there is another entrance. It's almost identical to the one Jake and Gracie used. But what does surprise me is another unfamiliar structure, a small outbuilding about fifty feet behind the back door. Judging by the oversized smokestack and an ominous cast-iron door hinged on one side, I am guessing it is a furnace or boiler of some sort. There are wooden crates lined up in rows beside it, some small, some large. They are pine boxes with what look like hinged lids. I shuffle closer to get a look inside. I crack the lid on the first box. It is empty save for a black liner of some sort. The second and the third are the same. I have to assume they are all empty.

I circle around the back of the little building, and just as I am about to make my way back around the far side, I hear the grind of the overhead door beginning to slide upward. I freeze. Now what? Crouching to make myself as small as possible, I sneak back the way I came. The door is about halfway up now. If I don't do something, I am about to come face-to-face with whoever is behind that door. Before I know it, I find myself climbing into the first box, one of the larger ones. It must be at least two feet wide and four feet long and another three feet deep. I have to straddle the edge of the box. When I get both legs over, I lower myself into the bottom, settle the lid gently back down, and pull the black liner over my face and body. The little slats between the pine boards provide enough air. I can hide in here until I hear the overhead door close again. *It will be OK*, I tell myself. I go very still and wait.

The door is open now. I can hear a motor running. Some piece of equipment is operating just outside my box. I feel a jolt and watch in horror as forks slide underneath me and I am lifted off the ground on a hydraulic arm. The forklift turns me 180 degrees and then I am moving forward. Up the concrete ramp. Down the concrete tunnel. Swallowed whole.

No turning back now. And definitely not the time to panic. *Easier said than done*, I chide myself. The forklift is gliding on a smooth surface. I peek out over the black, oddly pleasantly smelling liner.

I would have to press myself up against the wall of the box to see clearly through the slats. I wonder if shifting my weight will alert the forklift operator, and I decide to stay put. I catch little glimpses of my surroundings as though a fan is rotating its blades through my line of sight. I look left and make out what looks to be blue plastic chairs. Chair after chair after chair. On the right I see nothing but a continuous white wall. Suddenly, the forklift veers sharply right, and I can feel a slight descent onto another smooth floor. The operator slows down now and so does my imaginary fan. Now I can see stainless-steel tables lined up at perfect intervals with cages underneath some of them. Row upon row of microscopes and laptop computers are perched atop the tables.

After what must be the twentieth row of tables, the forklift stops, and I am deposited on the floor at the end of a table. The tow motor makes a zero clearance turn and heads back in the direction we came, taking the hum of the engine with it and leaving me to the sound of my heart beating like a heavy drum in my ears.

I stay motionless, straining to hear anything. I hear the tinkling of glass, a sigh, faint tapping on a keyboard. There are definitely people here, but no one is talking.

Ever so carefully, I stretch myself out until I am lying down on my side under the black sheet with my head poking out. I turn so my left eye is pressed against the box, and a field of view comes into focus. I see feet swinging in little black Mary Janes, and about two rows up and to the far right, large brown loafers rest against the kick plate of a stainless-steel swivel stool. Long fluorescent lights hang by chains above each row of tables. I can barely see the ceiling it's so high and dark. There is a peculiar hollow feeling, each sound echoing faintly in the cavernous space.

I notice there are no corners to the space. It is oval shaped, a smaller version of the outer architecture I examined yesterday. The oval is contained by white panels, each about four feet tall with a red stripe across the top. I didn't notice at first, but scratches catch the light on clear sheets of ... glass? It can't be glass. They are much too gouged and scored, too soft. They must be made of some sort of plastic. They wrap around the oval atop the white panels. I really wish I could show this to Matt. He is a walking encyclopedia of ancient architecture.

I shift my focus beyond the inner oval and into a sea of chairs. Blue, then red, then yellow, they go on forever, almost right to the roof of the building on a steep angle. Definitely a spectator venue, whatever the ancients built it for.

I hear footsteps behind me and I freeze in place. Two sets—one heavy and the other light—at the back left side of my box. In my peripheral vision, I watch as a pair of men's black patent leather shoes approach and come to rest inches from my face. The shoes turn toward my box, and a disembodied voice reverberates over my head.

"I don't know how much longer I can do this. I feel like I'm having an out-of-body experience every time I go through that thing. I used to be able to go fifteen days between cleansings. I'm down to six."

The voice continues.

"The headaches are blinding, and the back pain used to be in my neck. Now it's all the way down my spine. It starts with a dull ache around day five. I swear she wants to kill me. When Dr. Draeger recruited me for this position, he promised me my health would not be compromised, that this work is for the common good. That the chamber is just a safety precaution. This internship is my ticket to a permanent placement here at the sanctuary. Maybe I should rethink this."

Now, from the opposite side of my box, comes a husky but distinctly female voice.

"You jumped in with both feet, Derek. Draeger will never let you transfer now. Might as well get used to it. OK, ready for the walk of shame? I feel EV rearing her head. Let's put twenty-seven back to sleep for a few days."

Wait. What? What in the name of the Biodome is going on here? Twenty-seven? As in EV27? That's ... just a minute. Whoa. That's the smallpox! It is EV's deadliest correction so far. Reserved for the truly incorrigible. Grandma says EV27 wiped out the worst transgressors, criminals. EV27 is famous for having rooted out the dregs of humanity in their power suits, toppling morally corrupt and duplicitous regimes that governed like overlords in the Virtual Age. Just before EV ushered in the Age of Resolve and with it the Biodome and its simple doctrine of honesty, integrity, and purpose. EV27 became moot after the Correction. No one has dared challenge the new order. That would be preposterous. There must be some mistake.

My gaze follows the two sets of shoes as they walk past my box, which is starting to feel more like a sarcophagus. The air is stifling, becoming heavier with each exhalation as the carbon dioxide from my lungs hangs in front of my face to be recaptured in the next breath. A bead of sweat starts at the base of my neck, tickling every nerve ending as it meanders down my back. I desperately need to wipe it away, but I force myself to absolute stillness.

When I hear a click and a sliding door open and close, I listen for the sound of footfalls. Nothing. They must have gone behind the door. I turn my head slowly and am reminded of the owls I watched the other day. How handy that 180-degree rotation would be right about now. I can see the door now. It's not another room. It's a glass box with a glass door. I can see two people within. My two companions, I assume.

I can't make out details at this distance, but I can tell that the female is tall and slender with jet-black hair swept up in a messy bun at the base of her neck. She's wearing a white lab coat over a gray turtleneck and black slacks. And that is definitely Derek. The shoes give him away. He's a heavy-set lad with wavy reddish hair and black-rimmed glasses. He, too, is wearing a white lab coat, his over a white-collar shirt and black slacks. I watch them move in tandem, stepping up onto some sort of platform. Without warning, a blinding blue radiance lights up the box, forcing me to lower my head. I squeeze my eyes closed reflexively. I can see the light behind my eyelids. Then darkness. I open my eyes slowly to a jumble of black spots swimming in my field of vision. I blink again, and the spots start to dissipate. The pair step out of the glass box.

"You never get used to that."

That's Derek, running his hand through his wavy hair and pushing his glasses up his nose.

"The UV only stuns her. We know it's only temporary. That's why Dr. Draeger says this work is so important. The only way to reestablish control over our own lives. We are the future, Derek. It's a small sacrifice. Think of the endgame. Freedom from the ever-present, ever-oppressive existential virus."

"I get it, Renee, but we've been at it for over a year now. I'm not so sure she's even zoonotic anymore."

Renee looks perturbed at his suggestion.

"Of course she's zoonotic. What else can she be? We just have to keep looking."

My mouth has gone slack. What are they talking about? What is going on in here? I have to slow my heart rate down or I will start hyperventilating and give myself away. I take long, measured breaths, forcing myself to inhale deeply and slowly through my nose and empty my lungs completely through my mouth. The box is still super stuffy, but at least the light-headedness is passing for the moment. I have to get out and soon.

"No host immune response here. Just more death. Let's see. We tested the red-capped mangabey, the spider, the spot nose, the rhesus, the chimpanzee. Have I missed anyone? There. Is. No. Host. Reservoir." Derek sounds genuinely distraught.

"The marmoset," Renee mutters sheepishly.

"How can you forget the poor marmoset? It was awful."

"Aw, of course. How could I? We tortured the poor thing with a lethal injection of the HIV expression." Derek's emphasis on the word *torture* convinces me that he is indeed in moral crisis.

"I mean, is it possible that EV didn't originate from *any* of the ancient zoonotic hosts? Has anyone considered that maybe she originated somewhere else entirely? That maybe we just *think* she's descended from all those ancient viruses?"

"Derek." Renee's tone is low, warning.

She glances in the direction of two more white coats sitting side by side at microscopes two rows of stainless-steel tables up and to their left.

"You can't talk like that, especially not here. Of course she's descended. Where else would she come from? We just haven't found the right combination of EV expression and host yet. It takes time. Once we find those antibodies, we will be free. Eye on the prize, Derek."

"I know, I know. I'm sorry. I hate UV treatment days. I can sure get behind the end of the blue chamber." Derek chuckles, and his demeanor lightens up.

"Let's get this op cleaned up, shall we? And see where we go next."

I am alone for the moment. Renee and Derek have entered another free-standing compartment of sorts about thirty paces off, this one with white enamel walls resting along the outer perimeter. I am so cramped inside my crate, I don't know if my spine will ever be straight again, and my own perspiration is now obvious to my olfactory system. I need to get out of this box and then figure out how to get out of this building. It must be midafternoon by now. If I don't get back to the main administration building for pickup by four o'clock, alarm bells will be raised. But I just don't see how I can slip out without being noticed. The space is so open, I will be exposed.

Should I take advantage of my relative solitude and try to make my way to the outer corridor? There are only a few other people in the enormous space, and they seem so absorbed in their microscopes and computer screens, perhaps I can slither to the back exit unnoticed. I just start to reach for the lid of my crate when the door to the white enamel compartment opens, abruptly followed by Derek, backside first, and then Renee, carrying a large lumpy object wrapped in a black sheet identical to the one blanketing my back. I recoil, settling my arm back underneath the black sheet. They are walking back my way, jostling their awkward cargo between them. They stop less than two feet from my box and gently place it on the floor at my eye level.

The world slows as Derek takes one step and then another toward my box. I have no choice. At risk of being discovered, I tuck my head underneath the black sheet and stop moving altogether as Derek's hand reaches for the lid of the box. He lifts the lid until it hits and then rests against the hinge stops. I can't know if he looks inside, but if he does, he doesn't look close enough to realize the black box liner is not quite right. He steps right back to Renee and the package.

"OK, this charcoal liner only lasts a few hours. We'll need to radio for pickup if transport doesn't come around."

Renee sighs and bends down to grab her end of the bulky package. Derek mimics her stoop, and together they pick it up and shuffle toward my hiding spot.

"OK, on the count of three."

Derek looks at Renee, and in unison, they start to swing the package back and forth.

"One, two, three."

Suddenly, it sails over the lip of my box and a dead weight lands on my back with a thump that knocks the wind out of me. I bite my lower lip and curl my hands into fists. I must stay still. I feel the cold seeping through the black liners and into my back. I shiver involuntarily. So the white box must be a refrigeration unit and whatever is on my back must have been in there long enough to at least partially freeze.

I hear Renee's two-way radio squeal.

"Transport, we are ready for pickup at the HIV lab."

Then a tinny reply over the two-way. "He's just doing a pickup on the southeast ramp. I will send him over right away."

"Thanks, Tom." Renee radios out.

I can't breathe. I reach up ever so slowly and shift the liner away from my face. I'm still oxygen deprived, and the weight on my back is unnerving, but even a slight improvement in airflow is a welcome relief. I don't even hear the tow motor and am startled when the forks slide under my box from behind me and I am lifted off the floor.

"That's the last one. The sanitation crew will be in tomorrow to clean and sterilize for the next lab."

I assume Derek is talking to the forklift operator, although I don't hear any response. I can't exactly turn my head to see what's going on behind me. Just as my box starts moving again, I hear Derek.

"So where to next partner?"

As I am being hauled away, Renee's voice trails off behind me: "We're launching Hendra."

CHAPTER 6

Behold, I have given you authority to tread on serpents and scorpions, and over all the power of the enemy, and nothing shall hurt you.

—**Luke 10:19 (NIV)**

I HAVE TO FOCUS. *Hendra. Gracie. Not now, Evey. You have much more pressing concerns.* Like where am I going, and how am I going to get out of this box without being noticed? Am I going to get back to the central administration complex on time? And the questions that have been playing on repeat in the back of my mind two days now: Why am I still asymptomatic? Why can't I feel her yet?

The forklift drives over a lip between the inner and outer ring of this strange building, jostling my box and jolting me back to the moment. With the forklift behind me, I can see straight ahead when I move the liner away from my face. We are in the outer chamber now. I think we are going back the same way we came in. Sure enough, a few moments later, an overhead door glides upward along the fixed track and that same little outbuilding comes back into view. We pass the threshold, and then we are back outside.

The little bit of fresh air that hits my face through the horizontal openings tickles my lungs. The contrast to the stale air inside the crate makes me heady. We drive down the ramp toward the little boiler still surrounded by wooden boxes, but this time I notice dark gray smoke rising from the stack in lazy rivulets. The tow motor stops moving, and I am suspended above the ground, hovering on the forks. The operator comes into view. I watch his backside as he approaches the furnace and opens an access door almost the exact dimensions of the little building.

As the door swings open, I stare into the jaws of hell. Six-foot flames lick at the roof of the inner chamber. I can feel the heat on my face even from here. I am hypnotized by the inferno. I don't even notice that the operator is back on the tow motor, and I am being hoisted into the air, directly in line with the door to oblivion. In a split second I realize what is about to happen. Panic sets in. I try to scream, but the weight on my back and the heat of the air makes it nearly impossible to get air into my lungs. It comes out as more of a whisper than a scream.

I extend my arms to either side of the crate and start rocking back and forth with a strength I didn't know I had. Left. Right. Left. Right. My arms are searing with the exertion. The cargo on my back tumbles to my side, and the black liner falls away. I don't even know if I process the dead primate now staring at me with opaque, deep brown eyes.

I have some momentum now. The box is shifting on and off the forks as I continue to throw my weight from side to side. Suddenly, the box drops as though robbed of gravity and slams against the ground, sending a jolt of pain down my spine. The lid of the box flies open. I look up through the mess of liners, past the dead animal at my side, and straight into Jake's astonished blue eyes.

"Everett? Everett?" he says again.

His eyes are wild, his longish hair falling forward into his flushed face as he leans farther into the box. I must look an absolute mess. The elastic has slipped from my ponytail, splaying my hair everywhere. Tendrils are stuck to my face in the dried sweat on my brow. Instinctively, I am pressed against the right side of the box, trying to create even the tiniest bit of space between me and the poor dead chimp beside me. Now that the cold is dissipating from his time in refrigeration, the scene is becoming more macabre by the second.

"Everett?" Jake says again.

"Hey, Jacob. Uh, Jake. Fancy finding you here."

I try for humor.

His eyes go even wider, if that's possible. His voice drops to a frantic whisper. "What in the name of the Biodome are you doing? How did you get in this box? Why did you get in this box? You are not supposed to be here."

I hold my free hand up, palm up, to stop him. "Can we have this discussion *after* I get out of this box please?"

I keep my hand extended. Jake hesitates a moment, glances toward the building and the open overhead door, and then reaches down and takes my hand in his. With my other hand, I pull the liner off my back and place it over the chimp's face. His eyes are boring into me, judging me, taking my measure somehow. Watching me. I must be hallucinating from the lack of oxygen and the creep factor of sharing a coffin with this anthropoid in suspended animation.

Jake gently pulls me to my feet, and a wave of dizziness hits me. At first I think it's just because I've been prone for quite a while now, but a sinking feeling in the pit of my stomach reminds me that this is probably EV's first appearance. I suppose it was inevitable. I have broken way too many rules in the last few days. Dizziness, dizziness. What's she going to throw at me? EV17—Epstein-Barr, I think it used to be called—is a big one for vertigo. Or maybe EV5, the ancient rubella virus? I just hope she's not too hard on me, but I won't complain. I deserve whatever I get. Jake looks concerned.

"Are you OK? You're a slight shade of green."

"Time will tell," I half mumble.

I let go of Jake's hand and reach for the side of the box, pull myself up over the edge, flop down on the grass, and lean against the crate with my knees pulled to my chest. I put my head down on my knees, and the wave of dizziness begins to pass.

"Actually, I'm sure I'm in for it. How often do you use that blue box to shut EV down?"

The surprise on Jake's face is undeniable. "How do you know about that?"

"I was parked right in front of it in there." I wave at the building. "I heard two agents talking about it, and then I watched them in the chamber. The light almost blinded me!"

My anger makes him flinch.

I continue, "I'm sorry. I just don't understand what is going on here. How and, most importantly, why? I mean, experimenting on animals? That goes against everything the Biodome stands for. And in the Department of Animal Welfare no less. The irony is rich, don't you think? We are supposed to be contributing to life on this planet, not taking it away."

I can't stop myself. Things need to be said. "EV wiped out all those cruel corporations that were mass breeding and experimenting on animals during the Correction, so someone please explain to me why I just spent the last hour of my life in a crate with a frozen primate that did not die of natural causes."

Jake opens his mouth as if to answer, but he pauses instead. I don't let him get a word in edgewise anyway.

"And somehow you are all manipulating EV, the very core of social order in the Age of Resolve."

Now it's Jake's turn to get angry. "Now wait a minute. I am not like them. I'm just a transporter. I wasn't even told why I was bringing animals from the programs here, and I only know bits and pieces of what's going on in there."

He hesitates for a moment and then continues. "And for the record, I don't use the blue light."

That takes me aback.

"What? What about EV? How do you manage the infections? I mean, that's what that blue light is for, right? It disables EV for a time so you can keep doing what you are doing."

Jake scans the area and then crouches down in front of me.

"Yes, that's what the light does. It's some kind of ultraviolet system that weakens her. But I—well I never had my awakening. I've never felt her."

My eyes snap up to meet his. I almost blurt out my own confession, but instead I just stare at his face, blinking rapidly. I have never felt her either, but I am certain I am about to. Instead, I don't go there.

"Jake, what is going on here?"

He takes a long moment to look at me, look through me, as if deciding what to say. He looks up to the sky once and then back to me.

"They think EV's original host was an animal. They think if they can find the host, they can find the cure."

The cure? My mind is whirling.

"But, but—"

He finishes my thought for me. "Yes, Everett. They are trying to annihilate the annihilator."

I sit with my back to the box for a long minute, not blinking. It's an awkward silence, and I think I would sit here like this another day until Jake clears his throat.

"Ugh, I have to log back in and get the equipment put away for the day."

"Oh right. But we still need to talk."

"OK. Tomorrow morning. Same spot where we first met?"

"I will be there."

And then it dawns on me: it's closing time and I'm still sitting here.

"Oh no! I have to get back."

I am on my feet in an instant. I run back to the central administration complex with just enough time to straighten myself up, fix my ponytail, and splash water over my face in the privacy of the empty washroom.

Back at home that evening, I sit through dinner, listening to Mom and Dad discussing their most recent projects. I politely, albeit haltingly, answer questions about my day. I stretch out my bee story to make it sound like I was there all day. Another lie. I make more courteous conversation with my family during cleanup, feigning both interest and a cheerfulness that I absolutely do not feel. I excuse myself with an exaggerated yawn and head up to my room. As I stand under the hot water of the shower, the sweat and grime run down my body and legs. I watch the water circle and then disappear down the drain.

I brush and plait my wet hair into two matching braids on either side of my head and then stand in the full-length mirror behind my door, looking at myself carefully. I feel no more dizziness, so it must have been because of my extended horizontal position in the bottom of that box. There are no visible signs of illness whatsoever. Nothing. No correction.

I pull back the puffy yellow-and-blue covers on my bed and sink into my pillows. I recall the last thing Jake and I talked about. We are going to meet again tomorrow morning where I first found him and Gracie. Where it will go, I do not know, but I made it clear to Jake that I am not letting this go. He is not going to report me. He is not going to deter me. He is going to help me. Help me do what is yet to be determined, but help me, nonetheless. I close my eyes. The last thing I remember before I drift off into a fitful sleep is Jake climbing back onto the tow motor, picking up my crate, and depositing it into the blasting inferno, erasing any evidence of the blasphemy within it.

CHAPTER 7

And the great dragon was thrown down, that ancient serpent, who is called the devil and Satan, the deceiver of the whole world—he was thrown down to the earth, and his angels were thrown down with him.

—Revelations 12:9 (English Standard Version)

JOSÉ CASTILLO WELCOMES HIS guest into the workspace. Earlier this morning, he even made a modest attempt at tidying up the lab, although all he really accomplished was reducing the number of paper stacks and increasing the size of those that remained. He did crack a window, though, the fresh air presently masking the mustiness.

"Dr. Draeger, I have to admit, I was a little surprised when you called. I am curious at the department's interest in our discovery," Dr. Castillo gently probes.

"Ah, Dr. Castillo, you are too modest. Your discovery is headline news. How often is a new life-form uncovered? Have any more specimens been identified at the site?"

"Oddly, no. Not yet. We have broadened the boundaries of our search within the forest basin, and we have added new team members, but so far we only have him."

Dr. Castillo points at the snake with the odd appendages in the large four-by-four-foot glass terrarium turned home for the creature for the past two months.

Castillo desperately wants to correct Draeger on his "new life-form" characterization. The *Tetrapodophis amplectus* is anything but new, but some deep instinct tells him to keep the conversation to a minimum. He glances over at Pedro, who seems as apprehensive as he feels with their odd guest. Draeger was afforded full access to Dr. Castillo's lab and research as a courtesy between departments despite the former's misgivings about such easy sharing of information. That misgiving has not abated at all upon meeting Draeger in person.

"As you can see, Dr. Draeger, Animal Welfare would have very little interest in our program, at least at this early stage in the discovery. We cannot even identify its habitat yet. For all we know, the specimen could have been outside its range when it was found. We know nothing about population numbers yet, mating, gestation period, nothing. We can only guess based on other squamates, but this fellow is rather unique. I would be happy to keep you apprised as the research progresses."

Castillo hopes this will satisfy Draeger, who doesn't seem to hear a word. He is staring into the terrarium, bent over with his face close to the glass.

"Please, Dr. Draeger, the creature becomes agitated easily. We do not want to add any undue stress to the animal," Dr. Castillo pleads.

However, the creature does not behave in its usual manner. It does not recoil, it does not swish its tail in warning, it does not retreat to the farthest corner of the terrarium. Rather, the beast half slithers, half crawls to the front of the container and periscopes, raising itself up to its full height off the floor of the enclosure. The creature locks eyes with Draeger, man and beast almost touching noses on either side of the glass. Castillo holds his breath, awestruck by the scene before him.

A knock at the door breaks the spell. The snake drops down and retreats underneath a large, twisted piece of driftwood, settling deep in the warm sand and closing its eyes. An entranced Draeger rises to his full height in slow motion, straightening out his deep gray suit jacket as if by habit, operating on autopilot while his mind seems a million miles away.

Castillo clears his throat and croaks, "Come in," to the person on the other side of the lab door.

Pedro opens the door. The half-smile on his face slips as he takes in the strange tableau: Draeger still in a dreamlike trance, standing beside the terrarium and the unflappable Dr. Castillo apparently dumbstruck, leaning on both hands pressed flatly against the stainless-steel lab table, his stubbly chin slack and his bushy brows raised high, the true look of perplexity.

Castillo detects an air of caution in Pedro's voice.

"Um, Dr. Castillo, a word if I may?"

Castillo regains his composure at once, seemingly embarrassed at being caught in his befuddled state. "*Sí, sí*, Pedro. Please excuse me a moment, Dr. Draeger."

"Of course, Dr. Castillo" returns Draeger.

He glances over to the doctor, but his attention is still trained on the creature and the silent exchange that has just occurred between the two of them. Castillo walks slowly toward Pedro, who is still standing near the door to the lab, and they step out into the hallway.

"Is everything OK, Dr. C? You look like you've seen a ghost."

Pedro's inquiry sounds lighthearted, but Castillo senses his weariness.

"I have the strangest feeling I just witnessed something transcendental." He shakes his head and starts to chuckle. "Pedro, all your talk of the divine has scrambled my brain. Of course everything is fine," he reassures his junior agent.

Castillo hopes this will prevent his assistant from pursuing the matter further. It works.

"Dr. Mandera is ready to start the DNA sequencing. She said the sooner we can bring the samples down, the better. She has cleared her assistant to focus on our specimen exclusively."

"Excellent. The vials are in the top tray. Bring them down immediately," Castillo returns.

Both men reenter the lab to find Draeger clutching his briefcase and checking his watch.

"Ah, Dr. Castillo, I had not realized the time. I must be getting to the airport. The transport agent is on route. Thank you for your time today. It was a most interesting visit."

Draeger extends his free hand to the doctor. Not wanting Draeger or Pedro to sense how anxious he is to see the visiting doctor go, Castillo takes his hand and shakes it hardily.

"As I said, Dr. Draeger, I am sorry to have wasted your time. There is not much to see at this point, but we will keep you informed as we learn more."

"Nonsense, Dr. Castillo. It was a most ... enlightening visit," Dr. Draeger says almost cryptically.

"Pedro will escort you to the front doors."

"No, no. No need. I have taken enough of your time today. Good day, gentlemen."

Draeger exits the lab and his footsteps fade down the hallway.

"Well then, Pedro. How about you run those samples down to Dr. Mandera? I am going up to my office to check my messages and emails."

"Of course, Dr. C. I will check in with you after lunch?" prompts Pedro.

"*Sí*, after lunch."

Castillo leaves the door ajar behind him as he lumbers down the hallway toward the elevator that will take him up to his office on the fourth floor.

Pedro prepares to head in the opposite direction, to the basement, where the DNA sequencing lab is currently set up. He walks over to the small refrigerator underneath the stainless-steel table. Crouching down, he opens the door to retrieve the vials of blood drawn from the specimen yesterday afternoon. Confused, he pulls the tray all the way out and places it on the counter. Now panicked, he pulls out the tray from the second shelf and places it beside the first on the counter. Where there had been two vials yesterday, now there is only one.

Derek disconnects the call from his cellular telephone.

"Draeger is on his way."

Renee is instantly jittery. Nervous.

"Are we ready?"

"I reviewed the results again last night. They are indisputable," Derek reassures her.

"This is it then. It seems surreal." Renee is growing increasingly uneasy. "Do you think we are doing the right thing, Derek? This just feels ... I don't know ...wrong somehow."

Derek rubs his jaw. The stubble is beginning to surface although it is still early in the day.

"It's our purpose, Renee. For the common good." Derek recites what they've been told a hundred times, what all of Dr. Draeger's recruits have been told a hundred times. For the common good.

"I don't feel so good, Derek. Maybe I should do a cleanse before he gets here?" Renee looks askance at him.

"You were in the blue box yesterday, Renee, and again on Monday. I think you are overdoing it." He looks genuinely concerned.

"Don't you feel it? It's not working anymore. What is happening, Derek?" Renee is panicky now.

"You need to stay calm. It's almost over. The task is accomplished. We are the envy of all Draeger's agents, not to mention in his favor now. We've been working around the clock. You're just run down. A few days rest and you will be good as new."

Out of the corner of her eye, Renee notices Dr. Draeger and Mr. Ashton, his personal assistant, walking toward them in the outside oval. Draeger is easy to spot in his dark gray suit over a crisp black dress shirt and with black pocket square in his left breast pocket. His jet-black hair is slicked back and away from sharp, hawklike facial features. He has caramel skin and deep-set colorless eyes like black holes. Tall and lithe, he commands attention. There is an otherworldliness about him, a dark aura that tints the air around him. Renee shivers.

Ashton is a study in contrasts. He's a little dumpy and balding, with round wire spectacles perched on his upturned nose. In a more moderate shade of gray with a blush-colored shirt, he could be anybody's uncle. He barely reaches the top of the doctor's shoulders, needing two steps to one of Draeger's. He is a little winded judging by the redness in his cheeks. In any other situation, it would almost be comical. But Renee has such a profound feeling of wretchedness in her heart that it neutralizes any humor.

She glances sidelong at Derek. "This is wrong, Derek. This is so wrong."

Derek puts a hand on her shoulder and pats her gently, never taking his eyes off the approaching pair. "We've got this."

Renee schools her expression and composes herself as the pair approach, glancing over at Derek one last time for reassurance. He nods slightly just as Draeger dispenses with any pleasantries and calls the pair to attention.

"Agents Castonguay and Halimand. Let us begin."

Derek leads the quartet to a modestly furnished cubicle that was hastily erected just this morning. A small round table, three simple steel chairs, and a leather office chair—the only one in the building—are assembled in the small space for the encounter.

Not five minutes into the meeting, Derek is laying down the foundation of the project. Ashton rarely looks up; he is typing notes on a tablet with an efficiency that only comes with practice. Draeger is sitting way back in the plush black leather chair across the table from Renee and Derek, his fingers steepled at his chest with his elbows perched on the arm rests and one leg lazily draped over the other knee. He is watching them with rapt attention, absorbing every detail. Renee is more focused on hiding her own unease and lets Derek do most of the talking.

"The team has completed testing of the most obvious suspects based on the ancient scientific record—bats, monkeys, chimps, canine, feline, fox, racoon. The Hendra lab is being commissioned now, and equine specimens are already being brought in. In fact, we were just heading over to Hendra when we were redirected to this special specimen."

Derek pauses, waiting for feedback. When none comes, he continues. "We were not told what species we are dealing with, just given one blood sample. So we had no way of knowing which variant to target."

Renee addresses Draeger for the first time. "We asked for, for clarification"—she glances nervously at Ashton—"so we could pursue specific variants, but, well, we ended up creating our own plan."

"Which was?" asks Draeger, never changing body positions. His rich baritone voice glides across the table, a slow cadence that suggests he is a man of few words and chooses them carefully.

Derek takes over. "Well, we were going to start with EV1 and simply test in sequential order, but we felt this would introduce a bias toward the earlier variants, and since we haven't found a host species yet for any particular variant, we couldn't eliminate any of them. We decided to use a random number generator. Whichever variant the generator selected, we tested."

"Logical," is all Draeger offers.

Derek nods and clears his throat before he resumes. "Yes, well, we were able to test twenty-four of the thirty-one variants with the sample we were given." He glances down at his notes. "We still have EV3, 5, 13, 18, 21, 22, and 29 unconfirmed."

A pregnant pause hangs in the air.

"Go on." Ashton speaks this time, tilting his chin upward.

"As I am sure you are aware, the protocols require both antibody and T cell response testing. We followed the ancient procedures to the letter."

Derek sounds almost defensive. Renee steps in now, sensing Derek is losing his nerve.

"It's all in the report." She slides the 112-page bound document across the table.

Ashton reaches for it, retrieves it, and slides it in the satchel at his feet.

"Let's focus on the results, shall we." There is no inflection at the end of Draeger's request. Not a question then, but rather a command.

Renee takes a deep breath, mentally coaching herself to project confidence. "The sample was positive for antibodies for each of the twenty-four variants tested, and the T tests confirmed past infection for every variant tested. We double-checked, heck, even triple checked the results."

Ashton is still hammering at his keypad. Draeger doesn't seem even remotely surprised at the results.

She carries on. "We recommend another sample so we can rerun the tests, and of course, we need a new sample to test the last seven variants. It might be wise to bring a live specimen in at this point.

Whatever species it is, I am sure we can accommodate and prepare a workstation in short order. Well, except if it's an elephant."

Her attempt at humor falls flat.

Draeger is silent and still for an uncomfortably long period of time. Even Ashton is growing anxious. Finally, Draeger slowly unwinds one leg from the other, pulls his chair up to the table, leans forward on his forearms, and looks directly at Renee.

"To be clear, Miss Castonguay, you are telling me that the specimen is immune to the existential virus." Draeger wields the words like a blunt instrument.

Renee blinks, not able to believe or affirm what Draeger has inferred from these very preliminary results.

Derek steps in once again. "That's premature, Dr. Draeger. With these types of results, it is prudent to repeat the tests, and we still have seven more variants to examine. There was always hope that we would find zoonotic hosts for variant forms of EV, but never all of them in one species. It is highly improbable that this is a host reservoir. We exposed the sample to EV variants from a range of retroviruses, mononegavirales, hepadnavirus, poxvirus, coronavirus, astrovirus, and more—both DNA and RNA viruses—and the antibody and T cell test is positive every time. The sample is clearly contaminated."

Draeger is silent, returning to his previously reclined position, lost in thought.

Derek continues. "As Renee mentioned, it would be prudent at this stage to work with a live specimen so we can track the physiological responses to the variants. We have found some basic initial immunological response in some species-virus combinations only to be disappointed when the viral infection overwhelms the host. We suspect this will be the case with this particular species."

"Indeed, Mr. Halimand, your prudence is noted," Draeger says. He looks toward Ashton's satchel. "Is this the only copy of the report?"

"It is," says Renee.

"And the data and genome sequencing?" Draeger probes further.

"Right here, sir." Renee taps on the laptop computer in front of her.

Draeger glances over at Ashton, who is sitting quietly to his left. Ashton rises as if on cue, reaching for the laptop. Draeger looks to both scientific agents in turn.

"We will have the findings peer reviewed before we proceed with phase two."

His tone brooks no argument. Derek looks to Renee, who shakes her head ever so slightly—a silent plea to let it be. In one graceful motion, Draeger is on his feet, while Ashton is still stowing the laptop in his satchel.

"Miss Castonguay, Mr. Halimand, your service to the Biodome is exemplary." Draeger nods to both in turn. "We will be in touch after the data has been vetted."

Renee and Derek remain standing until Draeger and Ashton are back in the outer oval, walking toward the main exit.

Derek slumps back in his chair and swipes his hand through his red hair. "He just took all our work. Just like that. Are we even going to get a specimen, or at least a new blood sample? Did you get any direction out of that?"

Renee walks to the opposite side of the little round table, plants both hands firmly on the surface, and leans on her outstretched arms, elbows locked. "Yes, I did. I got a whole lot of hogwash."

Derek looks up at her tone and choice of words.

Before he can interject, Renee continues, "Service to the Biodome? Please. I don't know who Draeger serves, but you can bet it's not the Biodome. Peer review your data? Really? Steal your data is more like it."

She doesn't even try to hide her hostility.

Derek looks around. There is still no one in the oval with them.

"Renee, you are going down a dangerous path here. We are simple

Biodome agents. We were given a task. We completed it. I am just as disappointed as you are. I would love nothing more than to see this through, but it's not up to us. Maybe you're wrong. Maybe everything Draeger said was true."

"This is our discovery, our work. I am not just handing it over." Renee reaches into the pocket of her lab coat, pulls out a thumb drive, and places it on the table in front of Derek.

"The real data, the real sequence," is all she says, emphasis on *real.*

"Did you—What did you do Renee?" Derek is dumbfounded.

"Let's tuck this away in a safe place, shall we, as an assurance of our continued involvement. We've earned this, Derek. Now, if you'll excuse me, I think I will take advantage of the chamber today after all. Double-dealing dishonesty will certainly get EV's attention."

CHAPTER 8

[A]nd he threw him into the abyss, and shut it and sealed it over him, so that he would not deceive the nations any longer, until the thousand years were completed; after these things he must be released for a short time

—Revelation 20:3 (New American Standard Bible)

IT'S BEEN TWO WEEKS now since I officially started as Animal Welfare Agent 4683 in the Central Division. I even get to split my time between the equine and lupine programs—a request that both Dr. Pines and Dr. Viskov readily agreed to, a little to my surprise. I sheepishly approached both lead agents under the auspices of not being able to choose between the two programs, both so dear to me, but really, I needed an excuse to travel back and forth along the main trail without raising suspicion. Of course, agents are independent. We self-report. EV is a highly effective supervisor after all. But I continue to be resistant to infection. I don't even bother checking for signs anymore. Jake also continues to remain impervious even though he is now more spy than transporter.

We have met for lunch almost every day since he spared my life and agreed to help me make sense of what is going on at the oval lab, as we now call it. It has become a strange routine, lunches with Jake and evenings with Matt. I talk about Matt freely with Jake, but for some reason, I don't mention Jake to Matt. Today, as I approach our picnic spot off the hidden path between the main trail and the oval lab, Jake is pacing, bursting with anticipation.

"Jake, is everything OK? You are a bundle of nerves!"

"Everett, you're not going to believe who showed up yesterday afternoon. Dr. Draeger and Mr. Ashton met with Derek Halimand and Renee Castonguay here at the lab!"

"The same Derek and Renee who deposited the dead arthropod on my back? The two scientists who are now torturing Gracie and who knows who else?" My ire is palpable.

Jake holds his hand up. "Wait. Hendra was postponed. They were put on a special project at Draeger's request. The construction team built a small paddock out back for Gracie, and well, there are three more equine specimens with her now."

"You mean horses." I am not amused.

Jake's gaze softens. "But there's a silver lining there, right?"

"For the moment." I sigh. "Did you get any intel on the meeting?"

"Not really. They cleared out the whole lab when the meeting started. I could only catch glimpses of them from the outer oval. Inconspicuous and all that, remember?" He is referring to our earlier discussions about being clandestine.

"But I did see Mr. Ashton take some documents and a laptop computer from Renee. Once they were gone, it seemed like Renee and Derek were having a heated conversation, but again, I couldn't make out what they were saying. And then Renee pulled something out of her pocket and put it on the table in front of Derek. I can't be sure what it was—small, black, shaped like a little box. She picked it up, flipped it in the air, put it back in her lab coat pocket, and headed for the blue light chamber."

"Hmm, sounds like she's pretty proud of whatever it is she has. How did Derek react?"

Jake considers my question a moment before responding. "I think he was surprised. My guess would be he was not expecting whatever she sprang on him."

"Interesting. Do you know what they were working on?" I ask.

"No, no one does. There were no transport requisitions for their workstation. I never actually saw a specimen. And yes, I was watching." Jake shrugs.

"So, whatever it is, Draeger might have had it brought in from outside the compound." I am problem-solving out loud.

"That seems like a reasonable assumption," Jake replies.

"So where are Derek and Renee today?" I wonder aloud.

"No idea. Neither one of them showed up today."

Derek sits in the lounger in his living room apartment, his feet propped up on the matching ottoman and a handknit throw draped over his legs. The flat-screen television is displaying Biodome program statistics for the last month. New agents by department, retiring agents, movement between departments, programs reaching maturity, new programs by department—a completely transparent account of all the activities of the Biodome.

He is staring at the screen, glassy-eyed, his skin ashen, his breath shallow. Foam collects at the corners of his mouth, his is jaw slack, and the muscles in his arms and legs have gone flaccid, making movement impossible.

He thinks back to his training days. An impossibly old agent waxing poetic about Nicomachean ethics, the ethics of good science, and the importance of scientific inquiry for the benefit of humankind and not personal triumph. At the time it was *blah, blah, blah.* Now that passage from the ancient philosopher Aristotle is as self-evident as the most basic of truths: "Of involuntary acts some are excusable, others not. For the mistakes which men make not only in ignorance but also from ignorance are excusable, while those which men do not from ignorance but (though they do them in ignorance) owing to a passion which is neither natural nor such as man is liable to, are not excusable."

His last remaining thought as he fades away is Renee's last words to him yesterday afternoon: *"We earned this."*

Dr. Draeger is the very picture of menace. Although he does not raise his voice or gesture in any way, ever the example of composure, his demeanor exudes fury.

"A porcine genotype you say?"

Mr. Ashton is uncomfortable, involuntarily cowering at Draeger's tone. "Yes, sir. It appears we have an, um, a pig genome. We have the incorrect data as well. The test results belong to several primate species and not a single blood sample. The lab has recently completed testing on both these study groups. I'm sure it's all just a mix-up." Ashton tries to diffuse the situation with a valid explanation.

"Are you now, Mr. Ashton?" is all Draeger offers in response.

His customary somber clothing mixed with his black mood draws the light from the small meeting room adjacent to Draeger's office. The ancients called this urban center Manhattan. The Biodome's north central administration complex was once headquarters to another global agency, one dedicated to saving mankind from itself. Part of the ancients' history was their barbaric practice of destroying one another in armed conflicts over land and resources. But this moral compass of peace and unity was another casualty of the Correction.

Once EV rooted out the fraud and corruption and abuse of power within the agency, it fell along with all the others. Another epic failure in the ancient experiment of self-government.

Ashton continues with trepidation. "We had the laptop examined by the division's IT specialist. He has determined that a large amount of data was removed from the hard drive the day before we met with Mr. Halimand and Ms. Castonguay. It appears that they may have inadvertently transferred the wrong files, our files, to some external storage device."

Draeger's skepticism at Ashton's explanation is written plainly on his face: raised brow, slight scowl, pursed lip. A protracted pause fills the air, and then, as if Draeger has made some mental calculation and arrived at a conclusion, he makes an announcement.

"Mr. Ashton, it appears you will be returning to the Midwest to retrieve the correct files from our esteemed agents."

If Ashton looked uncomfortable before, now he is downright distressed. "Of course, sir. I will head to the central complex immediately. I will attend the workstations of Mr. Halimand and Ms. Castonguay and locate the files."

It's not a request; it's an order that broaches no argument. Draeger stands facing the one small window in the room, hands clasped behind his back, looking out at the river as the sun sprinkles diamonds over the rippling water. His own office, though much larger and more adorned than this austere room, is absent this magnificent view.

Never turning around but perceptive as always, he stops Ashton dead in his tracks as his assistant reaches for the door handle.

"Mr. Ashton, I get the sense that there is something you are not telling me."

Ashton straightens and clears his throat. "Well, sir, both agents were found expired in their respective dwellings three days past.

EV12 infections, reserved for incorrigibles, sir, and always deadly. The ancients called this variant the *Rabies lyssavirus*."

At least July is dry season, Pedro thinks sarcastically as water drips from his disheveled hair, currently in unruly curls thanks to the modest 77 percent humidity level. Of course, this basest of tropical humidity if offset with a mercury reading just shy of 90 degrees. The team has been camped in the former Ceará region in northeastern Brazil for the better part of a week now in a desperate hunt for other members of the tetra species. Dr. Castillo is frustrated. He was brought in this morning by escort, and despite his reluctance, he has agreed to the new plan.

"Once again Pedro. In case we missed anything."

"Yes, Doctor C. Team A started at the epicenter of the Crato formation, where the original fossil was located, according to the ancient record. Team B started where the specimen was captured. Each team worked in a concentrical pattern for three days when our circles began to overlap. For the last three days, we have been sweeping east to west, Team A moving south and ours moving north."

Pedro pulls out his notepad and consults. "Altogether, we have covered twenty-two square kilometers, focusing on nonmammalian species. We have logged thirty-six lizards, nine amphisbaenians, forty-three snakes, four turtles, three crocodilian, and forty-six amphibians. No *Tetrapodophis amplectus*."

Pedro looks up from his notebook.

Dr. Castillo slips into his native Portuguese. "*Sí, sí.*" He sighs and looks over at the Jeep parked in the clearing at the edge of the camp and then to the fit young man who accompanied him in this morning.

"*Por favor, Senhor Santos, a cela.*"

The young agent nods shyly to Dr. Castillo and makes his way to the back of the Jeep, where he swings open the back door and gently pulls at the cage until he can reach the handle at its center. Carefully, he slides the cage out, brings it over to Dr. Castillo, and places it on the ground at his feet.

"*Obrigado, senhor,*" Dr. Castillo thanks the agent and then turns to Pedro and the team members scattered about the camp. "Check the tracking monitor once more, please."

Pedro retrieves the tablet from the outstretched hand of a middle-aged agent with two short braids poking out from underneath an oversize bucket hat that makes her look younger than she is.

"*Obrigado,* Maria." Pedro smiles at the woman.

He swipes the tablet, keys in the pass code, and opens the tracking program. The tracking software instantly pings the monitor on the specimen's tiny hindlimb and the longitudinal coordinates pop up on the screen. The tracking device had to be customized to accommodate the strange little appendage. Dr. Castillo personally oversaw this work to ensure the monitor could not become inadvertently dislodged.

The creature has been wearing the device for four days now. It doesn't seem to notice the little intrusion and has made no attempt to remove the device.

Dr. Castillo bends down and looks into the cage at his feet. "All right, my little friend, we've played hide-and-seek long enough. It is time for you to enlighten us."

As Pedro and Dr. Castillo review the monitoring protocols, the teams work on dismantling the camp, carefully removing all traces of human disruption, restoring the area to its natural state. Even the stones used to ring the firepit are returned to their original location, and the lime and potassium from the wood ash is used to fertilize the trampled area.

Finally, Dr. Castillo heads back to the Jeep with his young attendant, leaving Pedro with the final task of the mission. The extraction team has arrived in a host of rugged overland vehicles.

The crew is gathered at the edge of the clearing, chattering excitedly, happy to be going home. They work efficiently at stowing away tent poles, canvas, coolers, and bags into the back of the waiting vehicles.

Pedro returns his attention to the cage at his feet. He has been apprehensive of the specimen since it arrived in the lab almost three months ago and has not grown any fonder of the creature over time. And the creature seems no fonder of Pedro. He leans down and is just about to open the cage and release the specimen-turned-homing-beacon when a passage from the book of James infiltrates his thoughts.

He looks straight at the creature and spontaneously recites the passage: "Submit yourselves therefore to God. Resist the devil, and he will flee from you."

Pedro makes the sign of the cross as if to end a little prayer and opens the cage. The creature steps to the edge of the cage, lashes a forked tongue at Pedro, and scurries off. By the time they return to the lab, the signal is lost as though the beast has disappeared from the face of the planet.

CHAPTER 9

But when the Helper comes, whom I will send to you from the Father, the Spirit of truth, who proceeds from the Father, he will bear witness about me.

—John 15:26 (ESV)

MOM IS A BUNDLE of energy this morning. She is positively glowing. One of her pet projects in Fisheries and Oceans hit a major milestone yesterday. She is dancing around the kitchen, reciting the number eight in as many languages as possible. I have to say, I'm impressed. She's up to, like, five translations now.

"*Huit*"—a little twirl—"*ocho*"—a drum roll on the kitchen island—"*otte, acht, osiem.*" She sings that last one.

I must take her at her word since she lost me after *huit*. Dad looks over at Evander and then to me, sympathetic to our bewilderment.

He explains, "Your mom's team is responsible for nineteen of the fifty-two ocean acidification monitors in the DFO's coral and shellfish rehabilitation program. Yesterday, sixteen of Mom's monitors hit pH readings of 8.0 and three of them even reached 8.1."

"Okay?" Evander raises one brow, a neat little trick I have never quite mastered.

"Well, for one thing, that means my department's climate restoration program is working." Dad is boasting a little, but with a sideways look from Mom, he continues sheepishly, "But that's only one part of a really complex problem."

Mom takes over. "What this means is we've been able to start reversing hundreds of years of marine ecosystem devastation. For the first time since the Correction, coral is growing faster than it is eroding. Sea urchins are starting to look like sea urchins again, with properly formed shells. It means that pteropod, er, swimming sea snail populations are recovering ..."

She can see she is losing us, so she wraps it up. "Well, um, it means the marine food web is coming back from the point of no return."

Dad has a lopsided smile on his face, amused at her momentary awkwardness but beaming with pride all the same. He hands Mom her coffee. I can only hope that my partner will look at me with the same adoration and devotion one day.

"Mom, that's amazing," I offer, giving Mom the affirmation I know she craves.

It is, after all, an amazing milestone in reclaiming balance and harmony.

"Yeah, Mom, that's awesome," Evander adds.

That seems to satisfy her. She regains her composure, takes a sip of coffee, and changes the subject. "So, Evey, any big plans for you and Matt this weekend?"

"We are meeting up with Jenny and Toby and some of the old gang for a game of flag ball over at Moon's Creek Park. It'll be nice to reconnect. I haven't seen too many friends since starting at the DAW."

"Except for Matty, right, Evey?" Evander teases in the way only a twelve-year-old brother can get away with.

Dad picks up on the implication. "So, Evey, things getting serious between you two?"

"Dad, really!" I sound indignant at the suggestion. "We are, well, we are dating, yes, but it's not like we're planning for the future or anything."

What I don't say out loud—and only now, in this moment, admit to myself—is that whenever I think of the future, it's not Matt's face I see anymore.

Jake is waiting at our usual spot, his tousled hair blowing this way and that in the breeze. He is wearing a black T-shirt today, tucked in neatly and more fitted than what he normally wears. I cannot help but notice the contour of his chest and shoulders and slim waistline. His jeans are still loose fitting, but the low-slung belt around his hips only adds to the effect. *What is wrong with me? Focus, Everett.*

"Hey, Jake. How's my favorite spy today?" I force my voice to sound casual and keep it light.

Jake chuckles. "You mean you there's more of us?"

Perfect. He didn't pick up on my fleeting fancy.

"Of course. I have an entire network of spies," I tease, "but you are definitely my top agent."

Jake turns to me with that blindingly perfect white smile. "Well, here's my report. For one, I think Renee and Derek must have been reassigned. I have not seen them since the day Dr. Draeger met with them."

That was unexpected.

"And apparently, we are getting another visit from Mr. Ashton later this week. Oh yeah, and no one is allowed to go near Derek and Renee's workstation or any of their files."

"I see," is all I say, much to Jake's dismay.

He thinks I am displeased. It's not that. I just can't concentrate right now. There are too many "things" going on in my head.

"Jake, why are you doing this?" I can't stop myself from asking.

Jake looks directly at me. "What? What do you mean, Evey?"

"I mean, why are you helping me when I don't even know what I'm doing and I'm not even sure why? Why are you risking your hide on this fool's errand?"

"Sheesh, Evey, you must think I'm a really lousy spy." Jake tries at humor, but I'm not allowing it.

I keep my face stern and hold eye contact. He slides down the trunk of a great snowy mountain ash tree and pulls his knees up to his chest. I sit cross-legged in front of him.

He starts again. "OK." He takes a deep breath. "When I started here at AW two years ago, I was so excited. I thought my parents would be so proud of me. I chose the canine program. I'm crazy about dogs."

I can see that.

"But, as usual, my mom wasn't satisfied with that." He winces.

"Jake, what do you mean?" I am genuinely perplexed.

"My parents can be a little ... overbearing at the best of times. My dad is the most senior agent in the Department of Engineering and Infrastructure, and my mom pretty much runs the Central Division of the Department of Health Promotion. So I guess they were a little disappointed when their only kid announced his purpose was canine welfare."

Jake rubs the back of his neck and sighs.

"Then last year, Mom and Dad went to a department collaboration conference and met Dr. Draeger. Apparently, my parents shared with Dr. Draeger that I was not yet decided on my purpose within his department. At least according to them. Dr. Draeger mentioned that he was recruiting agents for a project that he was overseeing personally. So of course, my mom said I would be thrilled to join Dr. Drager's project team, thank you so much for the opportunity."

He includes a little sarcasm on that last part. A lot actually.

"Oh, Jake, your parents sound, uh, really invested in your future."

Jake snorts. "That's one way of putting it." He glances up at me. "I know they mean well, but I don't need to become a senior agent or a department lead like they are. I was much happier with the dogs."

He adds urgently, "Evey, I had no idea what was going on here when I joined this project. I had no idea a transporter moved animals to a lab for experimentation! On the Biodome, Evey, I didn't know."

I believe him.

"So why don't you ask for reassignment?" I probe gently.

"I can't! None of us can! When Mom and Dad signed me up for this, they sealed my fate. I literally belong to Dr. Draeger now."

I remember Renee saying something similar. I realize he still hasn't answered my question.

He must have read my mind because the next thing he says is, "I'm getting to your question."

That was weird.

He drops his head back down. "I've felt, I don't know, empty somehow for the past year. And I don't understand. I know what is going on in that lab is wrong and screams for EV intervention. Yet I get nothing. I used to wait for it. I don't wait anymore. I just come in here and do what is expected of me, and one day turns into the next."

He hesitates, and his voice drops above a whisper. "Then I met you. I can't explain it, and it's going to sound so, corny." He looks back up at me, a flush climbing up his cheeks. "I'm not, I mean, you and Matt and that's really awesome. That's not what I meant ..."

Wow, he is really unsettled.

"Whoa, Jake. It's OK. Breathe." I try to soothe him.

He takes a deep breath. "That, that emptiness?" It comes out as a question as if he's asking himself. "I should be happy. My parents are actually proud of me. For once," he murmurs. "I didn't know what was going on until they put me on specimen removal. That's when I realized that the animals were all dying." He stops for another moment. "But now I know that they are not really dying are they? They are being killed."

He hangs on the last word. It sounds so foreign to my ears. His, too, I suspect. Murder, deliberately taking another life, is a concept of the ancients; it's not something that is done in the Age of Resolve. EV makes sure of that.

"I know all this, yet I have not had one righting protocol. Not one. I've watched every agent in that lab, in and out of that cursed blue box, yet I have never had to use it myself."

I should tell him that he's not as alone as he thinks, that there's another blasphemy sitting right in front of him, but I say nothing.

He goes on. "And learning the truth? I suppose I have you to thank for that."

"Me?" I shoot back. "What do you mean?"

"Remember the day we met, when I was moving that first horse—"

"Gracie," I interrupt him.

"Yes, Gracie. Sorry. Well, the day I brought Gracie to the lab, I was late. Not your fault," he adds quickly. "But because I was late, I arrived at Hendra at the same time as another scheduled shipment. Since no one was around when I got there, I put Gracie in the temporary stall and signed for the shipment."

Now he shifts his weight and starts to tap on one knee.

"It was a small box like a cooler. I transferred it to the refrigerator under the table. You've seen those fridges. They are so small. The cooler wouldn't fit, so I opened it, hoping if I removed the packaging, whatever was inside would fit. I mean, I didn't want to be responsible for ruining the shipment. I wasn't snooping or anything."

He's sounding defensive now.

"And there it was: a tray filled with vial after vial of yellow liquid, all neatly labeled. Each one with a variant of EV."

He pauses, remembering.

"I felt sick to my stomach. I'm not a gifted agent or anything, but even I could figure it out. All the secrecy, the cleansing chamber, the cloak-and-dagger routine, the dead animals ... all of it."

He's on a roll now. I say nothing.

"I had no idea what to do with this information. I had no one to talk to, no one I could trust to share this with. I tried to pretend like it didn't matter. I went back to my assigned tasks as if nothing had changed, but now instead of feeling empty, I felt—I don't know—dirty. Wrong. Then there you were, jumping out of that box, scaring me half to death, throwing out halfway right accusations and demanding answers. And I don't know how or why, but I knew I could trust you, that I could share this information with you."

"Wow, Jake, that's putting a lot of faith in someone you just met."

I am secretly flattered.

"It's more than that." He's looking down now, playing with a stick, drawing circles in the dirt at the base of the tree.

"I don't follow, Jake." I dip my chin and try to reach his eyes.

He slowly raises his head and meets my gaze. "Since I've met you, since we've started this, this little intel operation of ours, I don't feel wrong anymore. I don't feel dirty." He pauses. The next part comes out barely a whisper, but he doesn't break eye contact. "I don't feel empty. I feel purpose."

Silence. We sit there holding each other's stare for an instant longer, and I am totally unnerved. I look away first, feigning interest in an ant hauling a piece of forest debris almost twice its size on my left.

I know I have to say something, but my mind is racing right there alongside my heart. Never one to be at a loss for words, I am definitely out of my depth here.

"Um, well, that certainly answers my question." Maybe a little humor might work right about now? "Why didn't you say that in the first place?"

It seems to work, since Jake slips back into banter mode.

"Sorry, I already met my quota of 'pour you heart outs' for the week. And besides, you never asked."

"My bad," I quip back, but then I quickly add, "Jake, you can trust me. I have no idea what we are doing right now, but it doesn't feel wrong to me either. And there's something I should tell you."

He stops tapping his fingertips on the top of his knees and looks at me with wide eyes and genuine curiosity.

"Here's the thing. I haven't had any righting protocol either. I've lied, I've deceived, I've neglected my responsibilities, and here I am again today, where I'm not supposed to be, and EV has not corrected my behavior. And in the name of the Biodome, I know I deserve it. But in fact, like you, I've never felt a righting protocol."

Now it's his turn to be stunned.

"I thought I was the only one" is all he says, more to himself than to me.

"Nope. We're in this together Jake."

All the awkwardness is gone in an instant. I feel like I could tell Jake anything. There is no judgement, no risk of disappointment. It's liberating. He is liberating. In this moment of clarity, it comes to me.

"Jake, I think I've got it. What if Renee and Derek were *removed* from their post in the lab because Mr. Ashton was sent to retrieve something from their research files?"

When Jake doesn't hesitate, doesn't miss a beat, I know why sleep will elude me tonight, why I know I am trouble, why my heart is so confused.

"Then I'd say we better find it first."

CHAPTER 10

Being entirely honest with oneself is a good exercise.

—Sigmund Freud

MOON'S CREEK PARK IS alive with excitement. Almost our entire graduating class is here. It's been a little over two months since we've seen each other. There are six conversations going on at the same time: "Really? You've been assigned to a family already?" "We planted four test plots in one week!" "Our urban redevelopment program is producing benefits across like, three other departments." "A dramatic reduction in the number of genetic defects in ..."

I am trying to engage, smiling and nodding, but my mind is a million miles away. My thoughts are running through the plan Jake and I concocted to infiltrate the oval lab and look for ... what, I'm not exactly sure, but there's got to be something important at Renee and Derek's workstation. So many things could go wrong. For one, Derek and Renee could show up on Monday. Maybe they weren't reassigned after all. Or maybe Mr. Ashton will arrive a day early, a last-minute itinerary change. Or maybe we will be spotted by another lab agent or a transporter.

My vision comes back into focus with Matt's nose inches from mine and his hands on my shoulders, gently shaking me to reality.

"Hey, are you OK, Evey?"

"What? Uh, of course. Sorry. It's so great to hear how well everyone is doing."

And then I hear Toby: "Well, Evey, we're all waiting ..."

Huh? What did I miss?

The crease between Matt's brow deepens. "Evey, Tabitha asked how you are enjoying the DAW."

Of course, everyone else is sharing their purpose. Now it's my turn. What I really want to say is, *"Oh, me? Not much. You know, I've met an agent who's not really an agent since he's been delisted, and he works for a secret lab that's not supposed to be there, and yeah, well, we're uncovering a plot to destroy the existential virus and with it the Age of Resolve."*

Instead, I give the expected type of response: "We are actually measuring huge increases in foal vitality in the equine gene pool expansion program."

Matt relaxes a bit, drapes one huge arm over my shoulder, and kisses me on the forehead. I smile up at him and try to reciprocate the affection he obviously feels for me. It's no use. It's wooden, mechanical, fake. Empty.

The game goes on for over an hour, and by the time we are ready to call it, we are all sweating, grass streaked, and exhausted. Toby opens the cooler in the bed of his father's navy blue pickup truck—a reminder that I need to get my driver's permit, and soon—and reveals an assortment of vitamin-infused waters and colorful beverages charged full of electrolytes. I grab a purple grape-flavored bottle and chug half the bottle before coming up for air.

Once we have all had our fill, we say our good-byes and Matt and

I climb into the back of Toby's extended cab. He undocks the charging port, and with Jenny in the front seat beside him, we head out. I am the first stop. We make small talk along the way, commenting on the change in weather and the winter quickly descending upon us. Matt is a little worried. He spends most of his days outdoors with the Department of Engineering and Infrastructure.

The conversation moves to our families, how our siblings, parents, and grandparents are doing. I nod politely and add that my family is doing great, even sharing Mom's recent achievements with the DFO ocean acidification program, or deacidification, and her amusing little display the other morning. I can see Toby smiling at me in the rearview mirror.

"That's great, Evey. Are you thinking about maybe switching departments? Your mom would be a great mentor."

"No." I say much too quickly and with a sternness I don't intend.

The thought of leaving the mystery of the lab unsolved and of leaving him—I don't even want to think his name with Matt sitting right next me, his hand draped over mine—is unbearable.

They seem taken aback by my abrupt reaction.

I continue, "I mean, come on, Toby. You know how much animals mean to me. Mom's work is amazing, and I'm really proud of her for her part in the department's achievements, but animal welfare is where I belong."

That seems to placate everyone.

Matt walks me to my front porch. I know the creak on the second step will let Mom know I'm home. Matt takes both my hands in his as he turns to face me. He looks down at me and then sets his chin down gently on the top of my head. It's an intimacy I used to welcome.

"It's early. Do you want to walk over to the café for a little after-game snack?"

"Ugh, I am exhausted. I just want to peel these socks off my feet, take the Biodome's hottest shower, and climb into bed with my book."

"What's the matter, Ms. Steele? Are you going soft on me?" Matt teases.

It's been this superficial back-and-forth all day, with Matt, with Toby and Jenny, with Keith and Marie—everyone. It's like every depthless exchange I've had today is sliding across a thin sheet of ice while the really important conversations are being carried away on the current underneath it. Like why EV is really here and how she got here and what would happen to us if she were permanently expunged. Would we still be so engaged if EV didn't compel us to behave in the best interests of the Biodome, albeit in our chosen capacities? What would really happen if restrictions on our freedom to choose were eliminated?

I have so many of these what-ifs swirling through my head, but I know I can't share any of this with the boy in front of me. He might as well be standing on the other side of a chasm. That's how disconnected I feel in this moment. *Snap out of it, Steele.* He notices my hesitation, but I pipe up and lighten my vibe.

"Well, Mr. Quarterback, we don't all have your knack for the game. I'll need some time to catch up."

Now it's Matt's turn to get serious. He pulls back and lifts my chin to meet his gaze.

"You take all the time you need, Evey. I'm not going anywhere."

With that, he reaches down and lightly brushes his lips against mine, always so careful and gentle with me. He is perfect in every way that matters, yet in this very moment, with his breath on my face and his intentions laid bare, I realize I am already gone.

Castillo lounges in his apartment, a modest space the old doctor has occupied for decades. He never married or partnered. The only other sentience in the home swings from a little perch inside an ornate domed cage. He and the bright blue bird sit in companionable silence, both enjoying the rays of sun streaking through the large bay window covering the south wall. Wrapped in a shaggy brown housecoat and bear paw slippers, his gray hair even more disheveled than usual and in dire need of a personal grooming agent, the doctor looks like a famous theoretical physicist from the time of the ancients. The serenity is unceremoniously shattered by the buzz of Castillo's telephone dancing across the kitchen table. He shuffles over to the table and frowns as the caller ID pops up on the screen.

"Dr. Draeger, this is a bit of a surprise. We usually don't work on Sundays." Castillo instantly regrets taking the call. Even from 4,600 miles away, he can sense Draeger's razor-sharp acuity picking up on his discomfort.

"Forgive me the intrusion, Dr. Castillo, my most esteemed colleague. Your discovery of the new squamous species has left such an impression on me that failure to follow your research would be an injustice to my own team's development and a disservice to the Biodome."

Not nearly the dullard his physical appearance might suggest, Castillo recognizes the charm and flattery as Draeger's way of disarming him. Despite his perceptiveness, the smooth riposte has the intended effect.

"Oh, well then, yes. Of course, Dr. Draeger. I am happy to discuss our progress."

Castillo reties his threadbare robe, pours too warm milk into his coffee, and seats himself at his kitchen table, which is strewn with books and reports and loose-leaf paper with scribbled notations, as well as his half-eaten dinner from last night.

"So where to start," he says, more to himself than to the man on the other end of the line. "We sent two teams to the outcropping. They worked for five days, making their way outward from their respective epicenters. The first team started where the fossil was uncovered and the second where the specimen was retrieved. We had no success in locating any nesting sites or any signs of tetra in the region. Left with no other options, we tagged the specimen with a tracker and released it at the point of origin."

Sensing the shift in mood, Castillo hurries on. "We assumed the creature would return to its natural habitat and our tracking device would show us the way."

"I see," Draeger rejoins. "And you released the creature yourself?"

Not quite sure of the relevance of the question, Castillo responds nonetheless. "Um, no. Actually, Pedro released the creature. After we double-checked that the tracker was transmitting to our field tablet," he adds quickly.

"Pedro, your young acolyte, I assume?"

Draeger's interest in Pedro gives Castillo pause.

"*Sí*, you met him when you first visited our lab."

"Ah, yes, I remember. And where is Pedro presently?"

Castillo hesitates for a moment, again not following the logic of the questioning.

"Well, it's Sunday morning. Pedro is worshipping his God at the ancient Sao Paulo Cathedral."

There is an audible hiss over the line.

Castillo feels the need to protect Pedro.

"Since EV14 purged the clergy of incorrigibles during the Correction, the Biodome permits, even encourages, personal time spent on faith-based studies."

Draeger takes a moment to respond.

"It seems a dichotomy to serve the Biodome as a precision scientific instrument only to serve an abstract divinity in one's spare time."

Castillo sighs. "Ah, Pedro and I have had this discussion numerous times. In fact, I think you have it backward, Dr. Draeger."

"Backward, Dr. Castillo?"

Castillo clarifies, “Pedro has a brilliant scientific mind, to be sure. He’s one of the brightest up-and-coming agents I have ever had to pleasure to mentor. But his heart belongs to his God first and foremost. He serves his faith above all else.”

Silence stretches over the line.

Castillo drops the phone, feeling a sudden sensation like his hand being immersed in scalding water. It passes just as quickly as it came. He gingerly reaches for the cell phone and carefully lifts it back to his ear. Unsure whether the call has dropped, he listens, somewhat hopeful for a disconnection. But Draeger’s silky baritone voice begins the conversation anew.

“Dr. Castillo, is there something you are not telling me?”

“Wha, what? Um, no. We are tracking the specimen, uh, mapping its movements. We are close to discovering its habitat.” Castillo feels overwhelmingly compelled to placate Dr. Draeger by any means necessary.

“Hmm. Dr. Castillo, tell me. Do you share in young Pedro’s passion for the divine?”

“Uh, well, we’ve had many discussions about religion and Christianity.”

“So then, Dr. Castillo, you would consider yourself well-versed in the teachings of the church?” asks Draeger.

“Well, I know the basics, to be certain.”

“So then, Dr. Castillo, can you please remind me of the basic premise of the ninth commandment?”

“Ninth commandment? Certainly, Dr. Draeger.”

Castillo runs the Ten Commandments through his mind in order from number one, and then he recites, “Of course, the ninth commandment. Though shalt not lie.”

Castillo winces. He knows his attempt at deception has failed miserably. He is astonished by Draeger’s obvious acumen. Concluding it best to be forthcoming, he is about to explain that they are experiencing a temporary glitch in the tracking program, but the line goes dead.

Draeger reclines far back into the black leather chair, stretching his long, lean legs in their crisp deep navy trousers and flexing his oxford-clad feet as he contemplates. His mood obscures the more Castillo divulges as he rambles on, and the ambience in the room grows visibly darker. Black flames lick at the irises of Draeger's eyes, and the nails on his perfectly manicured hands lengthen to sharp points. He reaches for the half-empty coffee mug on his desk. The moment he picks it up, the liquid inside the cup begins to boil.

As he listens to the doctor recite the Ninth Commandment, the involuntary inflection in Castillo's voice confirms his point has been made. And received. Unceremoniously, he ends the call.

Draeger summons Mr. Ashton with a two-word text: *Call now.*

The phone rings within seconds. Despite his foul state, Draeger cannot help but be a little impressed with his assistant. He does not let it show, though.

His request is peremptory: "The status of your assignment, Mr. Ashton."

"Yes, Dr. Draeger. The arrangements have been made for my arrival Tuesday afternoon. The workstation has been secured."

Draeger pays no heed to the proposed itinerary. "Recent developments necessitate that we expedite the retrieval errand."

"Sir? I will arrive in approximately forty-eight hours. I have two more meet—"

Draeger cuts him off.

"Actually, Mr. Ashton, you will arrive in twenty-four."

Ashton recites the plan to Dr. Draeger without exposing his angst at the unexpected Sunday afternoon call. He absently smooths his hair and reaches to straighten his tie only to realize he is wearing a pink antique button-down shirt in flannel. Having been refuted, he frowns as he glances at his aviator watch, a semipermanent fixture on his left wrist.

Ashton grumbles as he settles his overnight bag by the front door of his tidy, desperately white apartment. He spends the next hour canceling tomorrow's meetings and delegating to his junior agents.

He stops pacing long enough to glance at himself in the hallway mirror. He moves his jaw left and then right. The pallor of his skin is undeniable, the blue-black shading under his eyes foreshadowing more to come. With a heavy sigh, he walks to the tiny spare bedroom at the end of the hallway at the very back of the apartment. The room is empty of furniture. The gleaming hardwood is covered with a large misshapen carpet in the center of the room, plush, deep fur with white with gray accents. A wolf pelt. A gift from Draeger. A reminder to the balding, aging man of his commitment to the project. And to Draeger.

Ashton gently latches the door behind him and reaches for the remote affixed to the wall near the tightly shuttered window. Lowering to his knees and then to all fours, he crawls onto the carpet and splays himself faceup like a giant starfish. He closes his eyes and takes deep, measured breaths. Then he clicks the remote in his left hand. The apartment goes silent. There's no sign of life except for the blue glow coming from under the closed doorway at the end of the hallway.

CHAPTER 11

For nothing is hidden that will not be made manifest, nor is anything secret that will not be known and come to light.

—Luke 8:17 (ESV)

JAKE AND I SPEND part of our lunch hour going over the plan. We rehearse our lines as we walk to the oval lab from our secret meeting spot. We enter the lab from the back entrance, hoping to escape any undue attention.

"Jake, it looks abandoned," I whisper as I scan the inner oval and see no one working at any of the row after row of stainless-steel tables.

Jake is not convinced.

"There are still agents around, but it's lunchtime so we might be lucky enough to avoid having to use our cover story."

I recite my lines anyway. "Right, I got it. I am Amelia. I've just been reassigned to the transport team. You are chaperoning me, making sure I get the routine down."

"Ashley was my chaperone. It's how I learned. We won't raise suspicion so long as we act casual."

Jake glances over at me and flashes me that knee-wobbling smile of his. I think he likes being in the lead today. We are back in our matching gray AW ball caps; the bill shadowing my face makes me feel a little more inconspicuous. I'd prefer an invisibility cloak, but this will have to do. I walk alongside Jake in the outer oval as though I have every right in the Biodome to be here. We make it all the way to the back end of the oval, me clutching my clipboard like a security blanket the whole way. Luck is on our side; we don't encounter anyone as we make our way to Derek and Renee's workstation.

Neither agent has returned since their meeting with Draeger. I get an unexplainable feeling of dread whenever I wonder where they've ended up. It's pretty clear they are not coming back. Jake is all too happy to inform me that he has been instructed to move Gracie and her three companions back to the equine rehabilitation center this week. Hendra is being shut down before it even got started. My heart sings at this news, to be sure, but my brain reminds me that this means they may have found something. Something that could change everything.

As we approach the workstation, Jake is scrutinizing the scene, making a mental comparison.

"No one has been here since Agents Castonguay and Halimand left," he confirms. "The computers are gone, but we already knew that. Everything else is exactly as they left it."

"It's too bad we have no idea what we are looking for," I complain, "or even if there is anything to look for."

"Why would they specifically instruct the team *not* to decommission this workstation unless there is something here Draeger wants?" Jake rationalizes.

He's right, and I tell him so. This makes him smile sheepishly and tuck his chin in deference. To me. Gosh, he has to stop doing this. The innocence, the humility, the authenticity of him. It is so beguiling. I feel myself drawn to him like a moth to a flame. And I don't even care if I get burned. Denying this, whatever this is, is futile.

"Evey?" I hear the concern in his voice as he reaches for my hand. "Are you OK?"

I snap back to reality.

"Of course. Sorry. Just, ah, a momentary distraction."

Now is not the time to think about this, I chide myself.

"OK, so where do we start?" I say, getting back to the matter at hand.

"Paper?" Jake suggests.

Here we go again. I am in sync with his thought process like it's an extension of my own. "So, you are thinking that because they have the computer, they already have all the electronic records. Field notes? Something that has not yet been transcribed to the electronic record?"

Jake nods.

"Exactly. See, Evey. We make a great team." He says it lightly, cordially, like we are best friends. Like he is not feeling anything at all like what I am feeling lately.

I have no right to be disappointed.

"Alrighty then. You take this half. I'll work on this one."

I divvy up the stack of papers mixed with the odd spiral notebook and a couple of folio covers, perch on the empty stool beside the electron microscope, and tuck my sneakers up on the rail. My legs are at least three inches too short to reach the floor, and I need to stop my nervous habit of swinging my feet like a child. Jake takes the stool next to me. I notice he has no problem with his feet on terra firma.

We sit like this for about ten minutes, sifting through page after page, ignoring the printed documents and focusing on the handwritten ones. We skim through each page, hoping something will jump out at us.

"Jake, maybe we're wrong. Maybe there's nothing here. Maybe Mr. Ashton's visit is not connected with Renee and Derek at all."

"Maybe," Jake concedes. "Let's give it ten more minutes? And if we don't find anything, I'll walk you back to the main trail and we'll chalk it up to a crappy lunch. But honestly, I can't help but feel like we're missing something."

"That sounds reasonable," I reply.

I am about to continue pulling pages off my pile when I notice a slide deck beside the microscope. Curious, I inch closer and pull a slide out of the deck. It is labeled *EV16*. The second one I pull out is labeled *EV12*. Then I grab an *EV3*. I turn to Jake.

"Jake, have you actually ever seen EV?" I ask almost like a dare.

He looks at my hand on the slides.

"What? Evey, I'm just a lowly transporter, remember?" There's that self-deprecation again.

"Aren't you curious, though?"

I am not looking at him. I am placing a slide, the third one I picked up, and affixing it with the clips on the stage of the microscope.

"I mean, we were shown drawings of the virus in science class, artist's renderings of ugly little balls with knobby protrusions sticking out everywhere, each variant of EV with a different configuration of protrusions, but I could never really see any differences in the pictures between EV1 or 5 or 7 or whatever. Now here they are for real, and I just want to see if I can tell the difference. This is, like, the only chance I will ever get to see her for myself. Well, at least a couple of variants."

Jake chuckles. "Why am I not surprised? It's your curiosity that got us here in the first place, isn't it? Go for it. You're probably right. I'm not seeing anything either, but I'll just keep on working through my stack while you play mad scientist."

That brings a smile to my face. I bring my eyes down to the dual eyepiece of the electron microscope. It's so much more sophisticated and powerful than the compound scopes we used in science class to study onion skins. The ones that give you face cramps from squinting with one eye. I switch the objective lens to the highest power, center the stage over the slide, and adjust the focus.

My vision goes monochromatic and spotty. I have a flashback to Saturday night and my internal dialogue, the one I couldn't share with Matt or anyone at the park: *Like why EV is really here, how she got here, and what would happen to us if she were permanently expunged. Would we still be so engaged if EV didn't compel us to behave in the best interests of the Biodome, albeit in our chosen capacities? What would really happen if restrictions on our freedom to choose were eliminated?*

The spots dissipate, colors return, and I see EV for the first time. Yup, similar to the illustrations at school. Dull blob having a bad hair day. I'm just about to pull my eyes away from the eyepiece when I see movement. I blink to clear my vision, but it—no she—is definitely moving. Spinning. Slowly at first but accelerating with every rotation. I stare, transfixed, into the eyepiece. As she reaches a feverish speed, she becomes a synchrony of iridescent color. Not primary colors. Softer. Shimmering shades of pink, amber, violet, indigo, aqua, and peridot threaded with flashes of silver.

She's a kaleidoscope and the most beautiful thing I have ever seen. How could they be so wrong about her? How could they not see what I see? A click and suddenly she stops spinning, landing on a shade of pink. I am momentarily disoriented. Then she spins again and then a click and a flash of bloodred. Names, images, flashes, and fragments of ancient history. Hiroshima, Pearl Harbor, firebombs. Spin, click, burnt orange. Red Army, Esquadrão da Morte. Spin, click, faded ochre. Jonestown, Waco, Chernobyl. Spin, click, rusty metal. Bondage, Civil War, Underground Railroad. Spin, click, mud brown. Residential schools, Sixties Scoop, eugenics. Spin, click, decayed green. Seveso, Pacific Ocean garbage patch, Gulf of Mexico dead zone, Great Smog of London, Uttarakhand. Spin, click, crimson. Drug cartels, crack-addicted newborns, homelessness. Spin, click, Tiananmen Square, Srebrenica, Sukhumi, genocide. Spin, click, Nazi Germany, Auschwitz, spin, click, Vietnam, Afghanistan, spin, click, Al-Qaeda, ISIS, the Taliban, spin, click, MK Ultra, Operation Ranch Hand, Unit 731, spin, click, industrial farms, animal torture, spin, click, World War I, World War II, World War III. The images come faster and faster, more and more and more chaos. The utter destruction of the planet, of society, of humanity. The legacy of the ancients in flashes.

I taste bile as it sears the back of my throat. I squeeze my eyes shut, but the images keep coming. When I feel like I am about to faint, it stops.

Slowly, I open my eyes. She is spinning lazily now, projecting her beautiful iridescence across my field of vision. The queasiness in my stomach begins to settle. Almost as though she is waiting for my full attention, she stops spinning and one single orb comes into focus. An eye, devoid of lashes. A perfectly formed eye with a small black pupil centered in a deep golden iris surrounded by a brilliant white sclera and set in a delicate, perfectly symmetrical outer posterior chamber. Looking straight at me through the ocular. No, more than that. Looking straight through me, to my soul.

I feel her in every single cell in my body, the awakening I never had. She holds her stare for what seems like an eternity, but I can't turn away. I won't turn away. It almost feels like a challenge being laid before me. I don't break the stare. As though she has taken my measure and deems me worthy, I watch as one lonely teardrop slides off the bottom lid and she brings the top one down over the eye in slow motion. As soon as the eye is fully closed, the light source powering the microscope goes dark.

My head is spinning as I lift it from the eyepiece. Jake is staring at me, looking as squeamish as I feel. He has a contorted look on his face. Has he been hurt?

"Jake."

Nothing.

"Jake," a little louder now.

His gaze focuses on my face.

"What happened? What's wrong?"

It can't be, can it? Did he see what I saw?

"Jake, did you, like, see something, like, like, in your mind?"

I must sound like I've gone completely bonkers.

"Uh, no. I didn't see anything, Evey. But I, well, I felt ... stuff, a whole bunch of stuff."

"You felt? What do you mean you felt?"

"You are going to think I have come unhinged," he quips.

There he goes again, syncing his thoughts with mine.

"Jake. What. Happened."

"Well, at first I felt ... I don't know ... happiness? Like a brightness. It's hard to explain. But then it changed in an instant. I felt shock, then pain, then anger and anguish, then betrayal, disappointment, fear, horror, despair, loathing, loneliness, sorrow. I think I felt death. All these hideous feelings coming at me one after the one, faster and faster until I thought I was going to explode. Then it just stopped."

Jake is still a funky shade of green. The realization hits me like a ton of bricks. He *felt* everything I *saw.*

"Jake, we need to find whatever Draeger is after. I can't explain how I know, but I know."

"I know you know, because I know too."

Is that his attempt at humor? I don't have time to dissect it. I pull my gaze back to my stack of documents. At the top of my pile is one of the blue folios. Strange. I could have sworn that was near the bottom, but my mind is definitely not dependable today. I open the folio. One loose sheet of paper is inserted in the right-side pocket. I pull it out of the sleeve and read:

Lab Summary Report
Sample: Unidentified
Specimen type: Blood
Live specimen (M or F): N/A
Requisitioned by Dr. Vladimir Draeger
Date: 21-08-99 *PC*

There is a series of technical terms and methodological references and protocols I don't recognize. I skip down the page and start again.

Specimen Profile
Kingdom—*Animalia*
Phylum—*Chordata*
Class—*Reptilia*
Order—*Squamata*
Family—*Dolichosauridae*
Genus—*Tetrapodophis*
Species—*Tetrapodophis amplectus*

Immunity Profile
EV1: 100%
EV2: 100%
EV3: TDB
EV4: 99.99%
EV5: TBD
EV6: 100%

The list goes on with a few more TBDs. Every EV variant with a test result is the same: 100 percent. I cannot believe what I am reading. Halos are beginning to form around the words. I feel panic setting in. Can this be real? Can this, this *amplectus* reptile truly be the host species, the creature that can render man immune from EV? One more line hits me like a punch to the gut.

Genome sequence: Complete

Wait. Complete? Complete? Where? I peel the page back, but there is nothing behind it. I pick up the folio and look at the pages underneath it. Not relevant. I feel something shift in the left-hand pocket of the folio. The pocket is taped over. I peel away the tape and pull out a black flash drive used for storing electronic files. Jake is still rifling through his documents. I dangle the little device in the air, holding it between my index finger and thumb as if it is radioactive.

"Jake, I think this is what Dr. Draeger is looking for."

CHAPTER 12

The earth mourns and withers; the world languishes and withers; the highest people of the earth languish. The earth lies defiled under its inhabitants; for they have transgressed the laws, violated the statutes, broken the everlasting covenant.

—Isaiah 24:1–23 (ESV)

JAKE LOOKS UP JUST as the sound of footsteps echo in the outer oval. They get louder as they move in our direction. We both go deathly still. We are exposed with nowhere to go. Jake acts first. He reaches for my arm and gently pulls me to my feet. I jam the flash drive into the pocket of my jeans, close the folio, and tuck it underneath my pile of documents. I grab my backpack and sling it over my shoulder, and Jake leads me silently to the back of the oval, behind the blue box, momentarily shielding us from the oncoming intruders.

"Jake," I whisper, "what—"

Jake silences me with a finger to his lips. He scans the back of the oval. Where I am a study in apprehension, all frazzled nerves and heart racing like a jackrabbit, Jake is grace under pressure. Now I can see why he has been so good at this spy game, the composure, the self-control, the self-assurance. I trust him implicitly to lead us out of this.

Jake steers me to a door near the back of the oval, a match to the one on the opposite side near the front. At least we're partially obscured by the blue box. He lifts the heavy latch as gently as possible and slowly swings the heavy door inward. The echo of every little sound in this wide-open expanse is a curse. We shuffle into the outer oval, and Jake relatches the white door. He leads me back up the oval, scuttling bent over, using the half wall as cover. Partway up the outer oval, he takes a sharp left turn into an opening between the sea of seats. We emerge into yet another concrete hallway, more bizarre twists to this already bizarre building.

Now Jake goes left again, back the way we came, but at least we are tiptoeing upright again. He stops in front of a nondescript gray door with the letter *D* painted on the wall beside it. We slip behind the door and into pitch-black darkness. Jake fumbles along the concrete block wall until his hand comes across a switch. Ancient tube lighting flickers to life, casting an eerie white glow over the room. Benches are anchored along the full length of three walls, and rows of metal hooks are firmly secured to the concrete block walls overhead. Black rubber mats cover the entire floor. A drain is the only fixture that breaks up the monotony. Three bathroom stalls like the ones at school and a large open space with shower heads adorn an adjoining room. Two sinks with large mirrors complete the dull space. And a funky smell, like Cosmo my dog when he's gone too long without a bath.

Jake speaks first. "Let's just wait here for a little while. Then we'll slip back into the outer oval and carry on as if we were never even in the inner oval, let alone at the restricted workstation. We are just transporters, right, Amelia?"

Right. Back to our cover story then. Good idea. Anything to get out of this building. I nod, not letting on how rattled I really am.

We sit side by side on one of the long benches. I am acutely aware that we are merely inches apart.

"What is this place anyway?" I ask, looking around the room a second time.

"Not sure. There are three others just like it along this corridor. Ashley and I found them when we were exploring one day."

Ashley, the pretty little transporter I saw the first day I met Jake. A strange sensation rolls through me at the casual mention of her name and the obvious familiarity between the two of them. It takes me a minute to sort it out, but there is no point in denying it: I'm jealous. Determined not to let this emotion through either, I school my face into nonchalance.

"I will have to make some excuse for Dr. Viskov. I'll never make it to the lupus compound on time now."

Jake looks over at me and quietly speaks our secret out loud. "Good thing EV keeps giving us free passes I guess."

I stop bouncing my foot on the rubber mat and look at him. "I just keep thinking my awakening will happen any day now and I'm going to get one heck of a righting protocol to make up for all the mistakes I've made over the past three months."

"Oh, so now I'm a mistake?" he says, half-joking, half-hurt.

"Not you, Jake. You are not a mistake. That's not what I meant."

He doesn't look convinced. My head is spinning. I must make him understand.

"Jake, I've lied to so many people. I've been deceptive for months. I just took something that doesn't belong to me." I am exasperated now. "I should be full of boils or rashes or, I don't know, bed sores, something. I don't understand why EV is not correcting me. Or at least I didn't until just now. I saw her today. I really saw her, not the disguise she wears when she is being studied but the real EV. And she is so beautiful, Jake, the most beautiful thing I've ever seen. And I think ... I think she was talking to me, to both of us. Jake, I think she just showed us what the world will become if Dr. Draeger succeeds in finding immunity from her."

Jake is contemplating. "Wait a minute, you saw something? Something that matches those awful things I felt? What could you possibly have seen that could feel so bad?"

The images are etched in my brain. I force myself to pull them back to the surface.

"I saw a world full of crime and chaos and corruption and madness, Jake. I saw people doing things I didn't think people were capable of doing to each other, to the environment, to animals, to our elders, to children. No harmony, no balance."

I stand and face him. I pull the flash drive from my pocket and hold it in my upturned palm for Jake to see.

"I'm starting to think that none of this is a coincidence. That we were meant to meet, you were meant to save me from that incinerator, and we were meant to uncover what is going on in this lab."

I take Jake's hand with my free one. He doesn't resist. I turn his hand up like mine and place the flash drive in his open palm, holding my hand on top of his.

"We were meant to stop it."

His skin is like ice and fire at the same time where it touches mine.

I whisper, "And we were meant to," I pause and meet his eyes, "be."

I don't know where it comes from, but I can't stop myself. I swipe the ball cap from my head and gently lift the matching one from his brow. He is looking intently up at me from his seat on the bench. I lean forward and kiss his forehead softly. When he doesn't move, I bring my mouth to his, just close enough to make contact. The kiss is primal, visceral. I have kissed Matt a hundred times and it has never felt like this. I draw back, not breaking eye contact.

Again, as if he reads my mind, he half croaks, "But Matt. I will never do this, Evey. Do unto others, remember?"

Of course he is thinking of everyone else first. This is exactly why I can't get him out of my system.

"Jake, I know. I owe Matt more, and I will make it right with him. He is a great guy. But it's not his face I see when I close my eyes at night. It's not his voice I hear when I'm alone in a quiet room. It's not him I dream of night after night. My private smiles aren't because I'm thinking of him, Jake."

He is quiet, listening. Finally, as if he's lost an internal battle, he sighs. "I just never thought it could, you know, be something. You have a boyfriend. I mean, the way you talk about him, he seems like a really decent guy. I'm not using my EV superpowers to ruin your relationship. Even if I don't feel a righting protocol, it doesn't change the fact that I should."

"Jake, you didn't do anything wrong. In case you forgot, it was me who kissed you. It's not like I didn't try to, I don't know, not like you. That way. I did. It's like some cosmic force is pulling me. It keeps changing the channel back to you whenever I try to focus on Matt. For whatever it's worth, even if you don't, you know, feel the same, I am not going to treat Matt like some consolation prize. He deserves so much better."

I've made a mess of everything. Why didn't I just keep my feelings, and my lips, to myself? While I am berating myself, I start pacing the length of the room, ignoring the smell that reminds me of Evander's gym bag. *Real romantic, Everett. Way to pick the right moment to drop this bombshell on him.* Jake stands and walks toward me. He blocks my pacing path and plants both hands on my shoulders. He waits patiently while I wipe the pain and humiliation from my face. I look up but don't meet his eyes, focusing instead on a speck on the concrete wall behind him.

"Everett." He never uses my full name. "Everett," he says again, waiting for me to make eye contact.

Reluctantly, I look at him, trying to keep my features completely neutral, not wanting him to see my turmoil.

"For such a clever girl, you can be really dense."

Wasn't expecting that one.

"I've imagined this moment a hundred times. Well, maybe not in this particular room, but ..."

The corners of my mouth quirk up involuntarily.

"I've wished and I've held onto the hope that this could be possible. I've never felt this way about anybody."

OK, now my insides are literally puddling onto the floor. But I'm confused. Didn't he just reject me?

"But I need you to be absolutely sure. When we first met, you gushed about Matt, how great he is, how it seemed like a fairy-tale romance. We just went through something pretty intense back there with EV. Something emotional. We are bound together somehow. EV chose us for some reason. But what happens when we solve this mystery of ours? Will you still feel the same way about me? I would never forgive myself if you passed up on your Prince Charming because of me. I just want what's best for you, not just today but in your future."

How can one human being be so, so ... pure? So selfless. If this is his idea of convincing me that my feelings are playing tricks on me, he's failing miserably. I don't even know where to go with this conversation. I am saved by the alarm on my cell phone chiming in my backpack.

This presents a new set of problems. Lunch is over. I am now officially late for my afternoon at the lupus compound. I have to get out of here and back to the main trail and book it over there before the team starts wondering where I am.

Jake looks as worried as I feel. "OK," he says, "you stay put and I will see if we are clear."

Well, I'm off the hook for now anyway. I go along with it. Now is not the time to continue our conversation. I extricate myself from the hands still resting on my shoulders and sit on the bench, leaning back against the concrete wall and pulling my ponytail back through my ball cap. Jake flips his own hat back on and approaches the door. He flicks the light switch, plunging me into darkness, and opens the door a crack, looking and listening. Nothing.

"Evey, we're good," he whispers.

That's my cue to join him at the door. I know there is nothing in my way, but I feel with my feet nonetheless and creep toward the sliver of light. I bump into Jake. Of course I do. He places a hand on my back and ushers me out the door. We fall in step, all business now, just a transporter trainee and her mentor. Nothing to see here. We take two rights back to the outer oval and start walking toward the exit. We're almost out of the building when Ashley appears as if out of nowhere.

"Hey Jake, and ... uh ..."

Jake jumps in. "Hey Ash. This is Amelia. She's going to be joining the transporter crew. Just showing her the ropes."

"Oh," Ashley replies. "Didn't know we were getting a new transporter. Hey, Amelia."

Casual, I tell myself, *just be casual.*

"Hello, Ashley. Nice to meet you."

"Likewise," Ashley says and then switches gears, obviously preoccupied.

"Hey, have you guys been here long? There was a big commotion at the old Halimand-Castonguay lab."

"Nope," Jake lies smoothly. "I was showing her around the yard. What's going on?"

"Mr. Ashton was just here. He had a blue folder and was shaking it in the air, demanding to know who was here today."

I say nothing, putting my hand in the pocket of my jeans to reassure myself that the flash drive has not disappeared.

Jake looks convincingly confused. "Mr. Ashton? But the schedule says he is not arriving until tomorrow."

"Well, he was here, and he was furious. Says something was taken from the lab. Something that belongs to Dr. Draeger. Like, I mean, who would be stupid enough to do that, right? He left in a huff."

Jake deadpans, "Wow, Amelia, looks like we missed all the action."

Ashton toys nervously with the telltale piece of tape torn from the left pocket of the blue folder. He takes some solace from the physical distance separating him from Draeger. At least he does not have to deliver the news in person. His foot taps the ground and his knee bounces involuntarily as he explains the situation.

"I have pulled the records of everyone who has used the ultraviolet chamber within the last seven days and will monitor its use for the next seven days. We will find the person or persons responsible, Dr. Draeger. Whoever has taken the electronic device could not possibly escape a righting protocol."

In his mind's eye, he sees Draeger on the other end of the line, seated at his desk, shoulders squared underneath his onyx cashmere suit and matching cuff links over a bloodred dress shirt and coordinating pinstriped tie, not one jet-black strand of hair out of place. He imagines the imperceptible twitch of that chiseled left cheek, Draeger's only tell when he is agitated. And dangerous. He shakes the image with a shudder.

"Mr. Ashton, I trust you will discover the location of the file in short order. Time is of the essence, after all."

"Of course, Dr. Draeger. It is my top priority."

Before the call is ended, Draeger corrects Ashton. "No, Mr. Ashton. It is your only priority."

CHAPTER 13

Tis now the very witching time of night, when churchyards yawn, and hell itself breathes out.

—William Shakespeare, *Hamlet*

DR. DRAEGER HAS DEVELOPED the immunity serum for the existential virus. The Biodome has lost all control. Harmony and balance have been replaced with dissonance and imperialism. Honesty, integrity, and purpose have been displaced in favor of spuriousness, villainy, and Machiavellianism. A return to ancient moral relativism where right and wrong is a man-made paradigm subject to change without notice. Gluttony, despotism, tyranny, and old diseases reborn have eroded the ninety-nine years of peace and social stability since the Correction. A return to ancient times.

I jolt upright, my arms flailing in front of me as if I am falling. My cheeks are wet with tears, and I am trembling all over. The sheets are a tangled mess at my feet, and my comforter is cast to the floor at my bedside. I look at the digital clock on my night table: 3:00 a.m.

Jacob stands in a white room. White brick walls, white tile floor, colorless lights recessed in a smooth white ceiling. Configured like a cube, its walls, ceiling, and floor are identical in length, width, and height. There are no windows, no furniture, no texture, just flat white. No door. No way in, no way out.

He is in the center of the room, dressed in a white long-sleeve Henley shirt, white cotton pants, and white canvas shoes over thin white socks. A white brick one-third of the way up the east-facing wall and to the left of center slides free of the mortar and tumbles soundlessly to the floor. Standing due north, Jacob's eyes widen as a black mamba slithers out of the open hole, pausing at the edge of the precipice. A slender coffin-shaped head with a slit extending well behind two depthless black eyes opens slowly to reveal a blue-black maw with two razor-sharp fangs and a forked tongue that whips in and out of the cavity. Jacob remains rooted in place, moving only his eyes in time with the beast. The creature inches closer and slips over the edge. Twelve feet of deep brown scales slide over one another in perfect harmony as the snake meanders over the white floor. The contrast is dizzying.

A second brick, this one to the west, dislodges from its mortar prison, and behind it emerges an Indian king cobra with its distinct hood and perfectly arranged black tattoos along fifteen feet of sallow yellow torso and tail. Like the first one, the beast opens its rounded muzzle to reveal two rows of teeth set into the bottom jaw and characteristic serpentine fangs set between five maxillary teeth. It, too, rappels down the wall and begins exploring the gleaming white floor.

Jacob hears the next one behind him, emerging from the south wall with its conspicuous reverberation. When it enters his periphery, he watches the distinct pattern running the full length of the trunk of the diamondback rattler. More bricks fall loose, revealing more and more venomous snakes raining down the walls, each one as menacing as the one before it. A horned adder, a deadly sea snake, an even deadlier taipan, a heat-sensing pit viper, a moccasin. Dozens of them. All join the mass of coiling bodies at Jacob's feet.

Due north and dead center of the wall, Jacob watches the middle brick as it begins to shake loose. The flood of snakes begins to retreat to the perimeter of the room, slithering over top of one another as they climb into the four corners. The last brick falls, revealing a relatively small, relatively unremarkable snake. Black racing stripes begin at its nose, branching off to each side of the face and rejoining high up on the back and running the full length of the trunk. Like the others, the snake makes its way to the edge of the precipice, but it does not slither and fall like the others. The creature scales the wall on two small front legs and two larger back legs, complete with perfectly formed hands and feet. The masses of poisonous snakes continue to writhe in the corners as though detained behind an invisible barrier. The creature half walks, half crawls toward Jacob, who is still motionless as death. It circles at Jacob's feet as if taking his measure. It is the sole beast in the mountain of snakes to assume the strike position. And strike it does.

Jake jerks up in his bed like a marionette controlled by a sadistic puppet master yanking violently on his strings. Orientation is slow to come. His head throbs with the abrupt awakening. His vision clears, and the pounding in his ears subsides.

He runs a hand through his hair, which is slick with sweat despite the breeze blowing in through the open window. He steadies his breathing and untangles himself from the twisted sheets. He reaches down to inspect a dull ache in his left calf; it's like an old cramp.

Leaning back against the cushioned headboard, he pulls the leg up to work out the spasm. The breeze feels good against his bare skin.

A moonbeam casts a soft light across his body as he begins to massage the leg. Then he sees them. On the back of his calf, halfway between his ankle and his knee, lie two small puncture wounds, angry, red, and vengeful. Jake takes in the numbers in red block script on the dresser in front of his bed: 3:00 a.m.

I have borne witness to a great many thinkers throughout the ages. Men of keen insightfulness, gifted in probing for deeper understanding of the human condition. Take Philippus Aureolus Theophrastus Bombastus von Hohenheim, for example. Born in 1493, more famously known as Paracelsus, he was a physician, alchemist, theologian, and philosopher, known as the father of chemistry and modern toxicology. He once wrote that "[t]he ultimate cause of human disease is the consequence of our transgression of the universal laws of life." Ah, if only you could heed your own warnings!

And so here we are, back at square one.

You doubt. You impugn. You beshrew. And now, you have opened the door. But existentialism has a price. Freedom for humanity? Self-determination for salvation? History is an explicit reminder of what man is capable of when left to his own devices. Be careful what you wish for.

Spectrum—This stadium opened September 30, 1967. It was built to bring an NHL hockey team to Philadelphia. It was also home to the NBA's 76ers and had a seating capacity of 18,369. It closed October 31, 2009 and was demolished in 2010. ("The Spectrum Philadelphia PA" by Bruce C. Cooper, distributed under CC BY-SA 4.0, 3.0, 2.5, 2.0, 1.0 licenses, https://commons.wikimedia.org/wiki/File:The_Spectrum_Philadelphia_PA.jpg.)

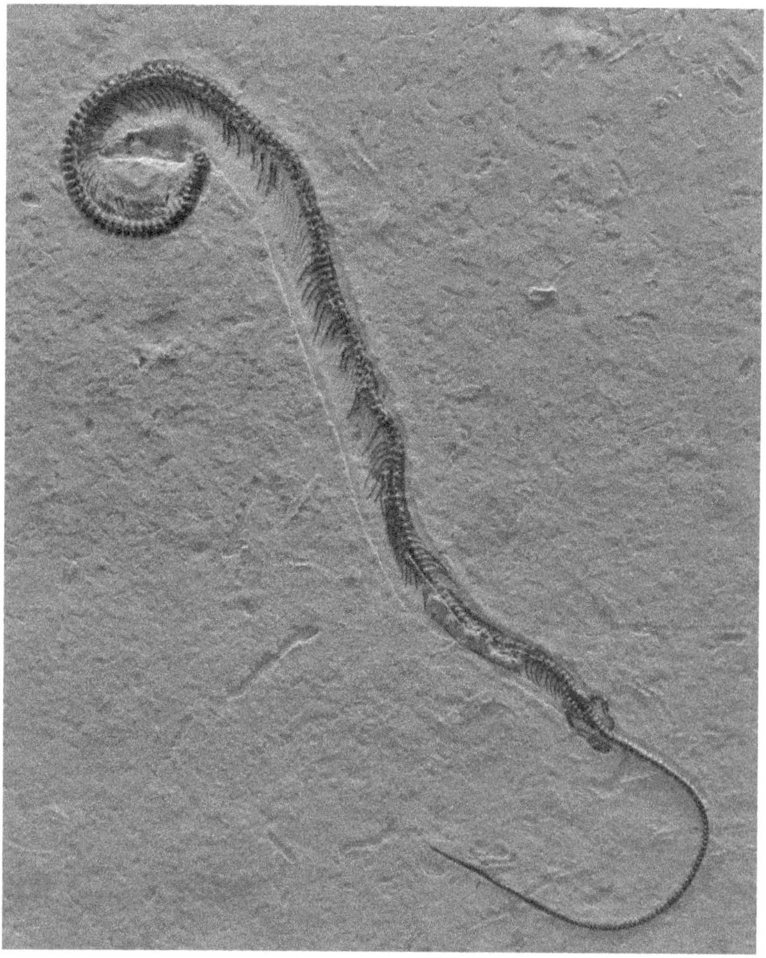

Tetrapodophis Amplectus—Unearthed in the Crato formation of Brazil, it was discovered in 2012 and exhibited in the Museum Solnhofen in Germany. Dr. Dave Martill, Helmut Tischlinger, and Dr. Nick Longrich confirmed that the specimen was a ten-million-year-old snake, the only four-legged snake ever discovered. ("Tetradophobis amplectus" by Ghedoghedo, distributed under a CC BY-SA 4.0 license, https://commons.wikimedia.org/w/index.php?curid=64547371.)

The Garden of Earthly Delights—A triptych by Hieronymus Bosch (1490–1510) that was originally painted on oak panel. It was located in the Museo del Prado, Madrid, Spain, since 1939. The piece is read from left to right, and scholars are divided on its interpretation: A moral warning or paradise lost? ("Garden of Earthly Delights" by Hieronymus Bosch, distributed under the public domain, https://upload.wikimedia.org/wikipedia/commons/b/ba/Garden_delights.jpg)

The Last Judgement—Painted by Michelangelo (1536–1541), the original fresco was located in the Sistine Chapel, Vatican City, Rome. Interpretation begins from the bottom left, where the resurrected rise from their graves, pass judgement (Christ is the most prominent figure with his mother, the Virgin Mary), and are either ascended to heaven or descended to hell. ("Last Judgement (Michelangelo)" by Michelangelo, distributed under the public domain, https://commons.wikimedia.org/wiki/File:Last_Judgement_(Michelangelo).jpg.)

Sevesco (July 10, 1976)—Man-made environmental disaster happened in Italy because of poor engineering practices, resulting in 3,300 dead animals and the slaughter of another 80,000. The long-term human impacts from dioxin exposure included endocrine, reproductive, nervous system, and cardiovascular impairments. ("SEVESCO-1976" by unknown author, distributed under the public domain, https://commons.wikimedia.org/wiki/File:SEVESO-1976.jpg.)

Operation Ranch Hand—Between 1962 and 1971, the US military sprayed twenty million gallons of Agent Orange on enemy territory destroying more than 20 percent of the South Vietnam's forests and more than ten million hectares of cultivable land. More than three million Vietnamese people were affected, and 150 thousand children born with defects and genetic disorders. ("Agent Orange Cropdusting" by USAF, distributed under the public domain, https://commons.wikimedia.org/wiki/File:Agent_Orange_Cropdusting.jpg.)

Gulf of Mexico Hypoxic Zone—Mapped since 1985, annual nitrogen and phosphorus runoff from human activity collected in the Mississippi River and dumped in the Gulf of Mexico, resulting in an oxygen-free dead zone of approximately 5,400 square miles. Scientists identified some 415 dead zones and 169 hypoxic areas around the world by 2007. ("Fish kill in Louisiana waterway" by Billy Nungesser, distributed under a CC BY-SA 2.0 license, https://www.flickr.com/photos/48722974@N07/5020120889/.)

Srebrenica Massacre (July 1995)—This genocide killed more than eight thousand Bosniak Muslim men and boys during the Bosnian War by the Bosnian Serb Army of Republika. ("Exhumation site in Čančari valley" by the UN International Criminal Tribunal for the Former Yugoslavia, distributed under the public domain, https://commons.wikimedia.org/wiki/File:Exhumation_Site_in_%C4%8Can%C4%8Dari_valley.jpg.)

"Hiroshima Dome 1945" by Shigeo Hayashi, October 1945, distributed under a CC0 1.0 Universal Public Domain Dedication, https://commons.wikimedia.org/wiki/File:Hiroshima_Dome_1945.gif;

Hiroshima and Nagasaki Atomic Bombings (August 6 and 9, 1945)—This was the first ever detonation of nuclear weapons (A bombs) in armed conflict. It killed 129 to 226 thousand people, mostly civilians. It marked the beginning of the Nuclear Arms Race (1942–1987). Following a high of over seventy thousand active weapons globally, disarmament and nonproliferation treaties followed. By 2019, there were merely 13,890 nuclear warheads in the world, a great victory. One nuclear bomb yields between ten tons and fifty megatons of TNT. ("Nagasakibomb" by Charles Levy, distributed under the public domain courtesy of the U.S. National Archives and Records Administration, https://commons.wikimedia.org/wiki/File:Nagasakibomb.jpg.)

"Selection on the ramp at Auschwitz-Birkenau, 1944 (Auschwitz Album)" by unknown photographer from the Auschwitz Erkennungsdienst, distributed under the public domain courtesy Yad Vashem, https://commons.wikimedia.org/wiki/File:Selection_on_the_ramp_at_Auschwitz-Birkenau,_1944_%28Auschwitz_Album%29_1b.jpg.

Auschwitz-Birkenau concentration and extermination camp (1941–1945)—After being killed with Zyklon B gas in one of several gas chambers, the lucky dead were treated to one of several crematoria. One million Jews, seventy-five thousand Poles, twenty thousand Gypsies, fifteen thousand Soviet prisoners of war, and fifteen thousand Czechs, Byelorussians, Yugoslavians, French, Germans, and Austrians were burned at a rate of 4,416 corpses per day. The unlucky ones were burned in pits or buried in mass graves.

Esquadrao da Morte—German officers exterminated female Jewish survivors of a mass shooting outside the Mizocz ghetto on October 14, 1942. Antisemitism flourished well into the twenty-first century, so popular it had its own global survey and corresponding index of 101 participating countries. ("German officer executes Jewish women who survived a mass shooting outside the Mizocz ghetto, 14 October, 1942" by Gustav Hille, distributed under the public domain, https://commons.wikimedia.org/wiki/File:German_officer_executes_Jewish_women_who_survived_a_mass_shooting_outside_the_Mizocz_ghetto,_14_October_1942.jpg.)

"Kill the Indian to save the man" (1819–1978)—Approximately 357 federally-funded, church-run Native American residential schools were founded, and hundreds of thousands of Native American children were abducted from their homes, forcibly confined, and stripped of their culture and identity. ("Carlisle pupils" by unknown author, distributed under the public domain, https://commons.wikimedia.org/wiki/File:Carlisle_pupils.jpg.)

Canadian Residential Schools (1831–1996): This government-sanctioned, Christian church-run, mass assimilation (cultural genocide) program consisted of 139 Indian Residential Schools for more than 150,000 First Nations, Inuit, and Metis children ages four to sixteen years. Mass graves were uncovered beginning in 2021. ("Indian School" by John Woodruff, distributed under the public domain, https://commons.wikimedia.org/wiki/File:Indian_school.jpg.)

Jonestown, Guyana (November 18, 1978)—Nine hundred and nine dead, all but two from cyanide poisoning as part of a "revolutionary suicide." Three hundred and four of the dead were minors. ("Jonestown Memorial Service Pictures" by Symphony999, distributed under a CC BY-SA 3.0 license, https://commons.wikimedia.org/wiki/File:Jonestown_Memorial_Service_Pictures.jpg.)

The Pacific Garbage Patch (2005)—Covering approximately 618,000 square miles, this patch comprised 1.8 trillion pieces of plastic weighing eighty thousand tons, 84 percent containing toxic chemicals. ("Garbage Patch State – Presentazione UNESCO" by Cosimosal.b, distributed under a CC BY-SA 4.0 license, https://commons.wikimedia.org/wiki/File:Garbage_Patch_State_-_Presentazione_UNESCO.jpg.)

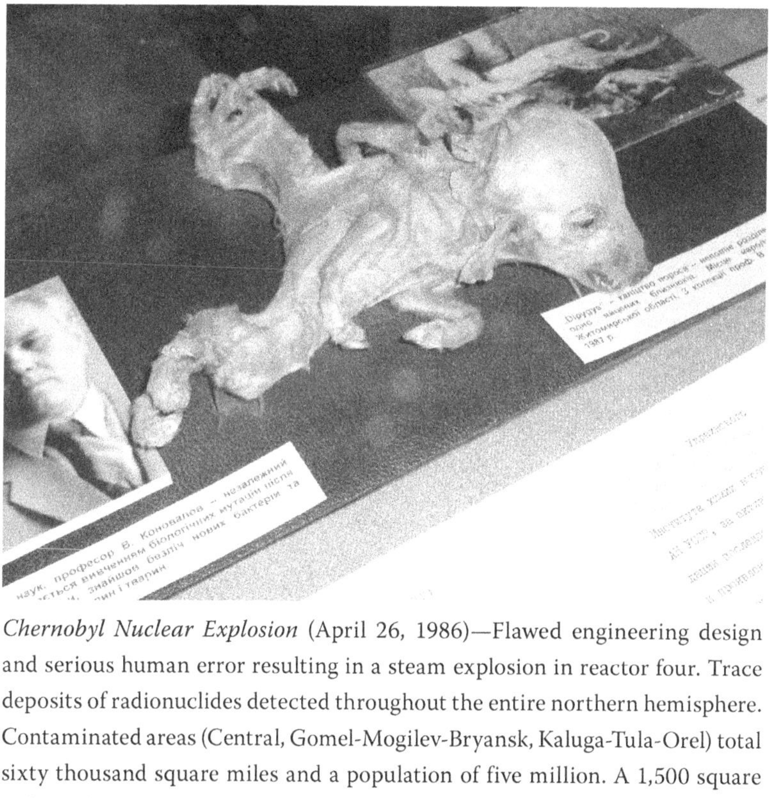

Chernobyl Nuclear Explosion (April 26, 1986)—Flawed engineering design and serious human error resulting in a steam explosion in reactor four. Trace deposits of radionuclides detected throughout the entire northern hemisphere. Contaminated areas (Central, Gomel-Mogilev-Bryansk, Kaluga-Tula-Orel) total sixty thousand square miles and a population of five million. A 1,500 square mile exclusion zone remained in effect thirty-five years later. The Red Forest, one of several remaining hotspots, emitted 35–40 mSv more than three decades later. ("Kiev-Ukrainian National Chernobyl Museum 15" by Vincent de Groot, distributed under a CC BY-SA 4.0 license, https://commons.wikimedia.org/wiki/File:Kiev-UkrainianNationalChernobylMuseum_15.jpg.)

Armenian Genocide (1915–1923)—Between 600,000 and 1.5 million Ottoman Armenians were exterminated by the ruling Committee of Union and Progress. ("The Armenian Genocide 1915" by The Internationalists distributed under a CC BY-SA 3.0 license, https://www.leftcom.org/en/articles/2015-04-28/the-armenian-genocide-1915.)

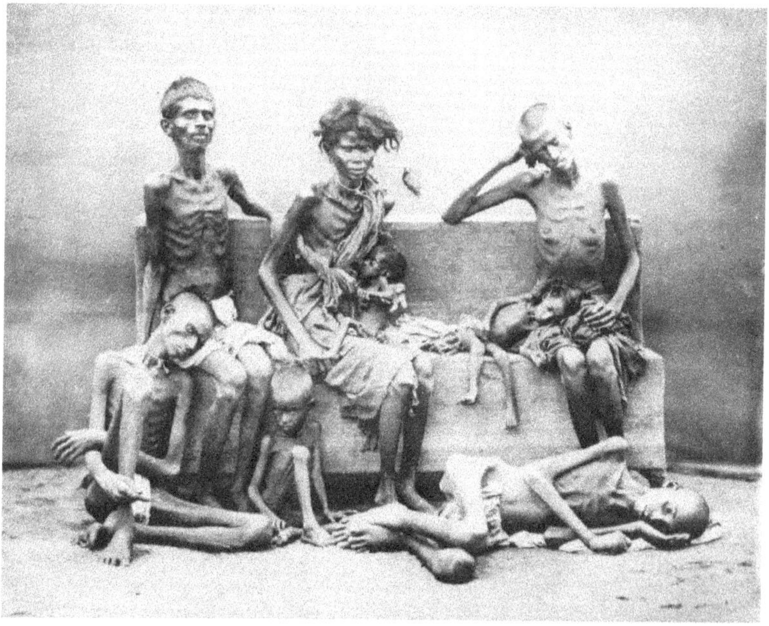

Poverty—In India, the country of mass poverty, 14 percent of its 1.36 billion citizens were undernourished in 2020. The Global Hunger Index ranked India 94 out of 107 countries on the honor roll. ("1876 1877 1878 1879 Famine Genocide in India Madras under British colonial rule 2" by Willoughby Wallace Hooper, distributed under the public domain,

https://commons.wikimedia.org/wiki/File:1876_1877_1878_1879_Famine_Genocide_in_India_Madras_under_British_colonial_rule_2.jpg.)

Vietnam War (1954–1975)—Two million civilian casualties, 1.35 million Vietnamese military casualties, 58,200 U.S. armed forces casualties, and 5,000 military casualties from Korea, Thailand, and Australia. It was a battle between a communist-seeking North Vietnam and a Western-leaning South Vietnam (with allied support). The Socialist Republic of Vietnam emerged in 1975 with a strong message that communism was not to be trifled with again. ("Infant Victim of Dak Son Massacre" by USIA, distributed under the public domain, https://commons.wikimedia.org/wiki/File:Infant_victim_of_Dak_Son_massacre.jpg.)

Industrial Farming—Seventy billion animals were slaughtered worldwide annually (2013). Forty-six billion were factory-farmed under conditions tantamount to torture. The Voiceless Animal Cruelty Index ranked countries by producing cruelty, consuming cruelty, and sanctioning cruelty. Canada and the United States ranked in the top ten most cruel along with Belarus, Venezuela, Russia, Iran, Australia, Brazil, Malaysia, and Myanmar (2018). ("Undercover Investigation at Manitoba Pork Factory Farm (8250115715)" by Mercy for Animals Canada, distributed under a Creative Commons Attribution 2.0 Generic license, https://commons.wikimedia.org/wiki/File:Undercover_Investigation_at_Manitoba_Pork_Factory_Farm_%288250115715%29.jpg.)

The Great Smog of London (December 5–9, 1952)—Coal-burning airborne pollutants covered the city in a blanket of smog. Ten to twelve thousand died. Despite passing the 1956 Clean Air Act, the 1962 London Smog killed another seven hundred. By 2019, air pollution contributed 9 percent to global annual death toll (five million), with more than 90 percent of the earth's population living in areas where WHO particulate air quality standards were exceeded. ("Nelson's Column during the Great Smog of 1952" by N. T. Stobbs, distributed under a CC BY-SA 2.0 license, https://commons.wikimedia.org/wiki/File:Nelson%27s_Column_during_the_Great_Smog_of_1952.jpg.)

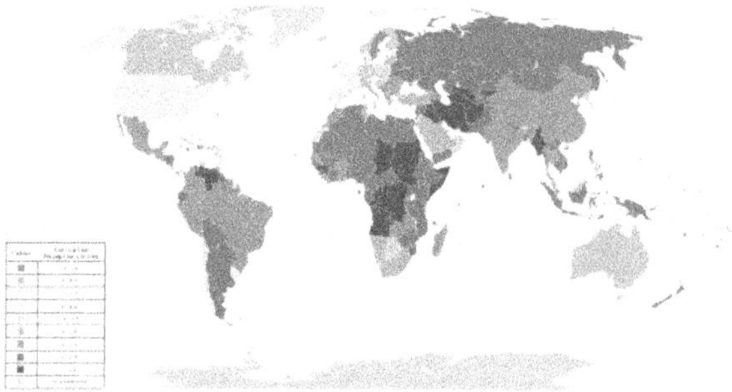

Political Corruption—In 2020, there were some five communist countries, six mafia states, six despotism governments, nine kleptocracies, eight dictatorships, eight totalitarian regimes, nineteen authoritarian states, thirty-six monarchist states, and eighty democracies. Beginning in 1995 with forty-five countries and expanding to 180 countries by 2021, Transparency International calculated the level of perceived public sector corruption, measured as grand corruption, petty corruption, public sector corruption, bribery, embezzlement, patronage, nepotism, conflict of interest, and procurement fraud. All forms of government were scored on a scale from zero (most corrupt) to one hundred (least corrupt). In 2019, two out of three countries scored below fifty. Globally, the average level of corruption was forty-three out of one hundred, an F– in academic terms. ("World Map Index of perception of corruption 2009" by Transparency International, distributed under the public domain, https://commons.wikimedia.org/wiki/File:World_Map_Index_of_perception_of_corruption_2009.svg.)

Deforestation—By 2015, 46 percent of the world's trees had been felled. Eighty percent of the earth's land animals live in forests, and forests are one of the planet's largest natural carbon sinks. ("Deforestation -Flickr – crustmania" by crustmania, distributed under a CC BY-SA 2.0 license, https://commons.wikimedia.org/wiki/File:Deforestation_-_Flickr_-_crustmania.jpg.)

Genocide of Yazidis by ISIS (2014)—In Iraq and Syria, five thousand were killed and 4,200–10,800 were held captive. ("Yazidi Refugees" by Rachel Unkovic/International Rescue Committee, UK Department for International Development, distributed under a CC BY-SA 2.0 license, https://commons.wikimedia.org/wiki/File:Yazidi_refugees.jpg.)

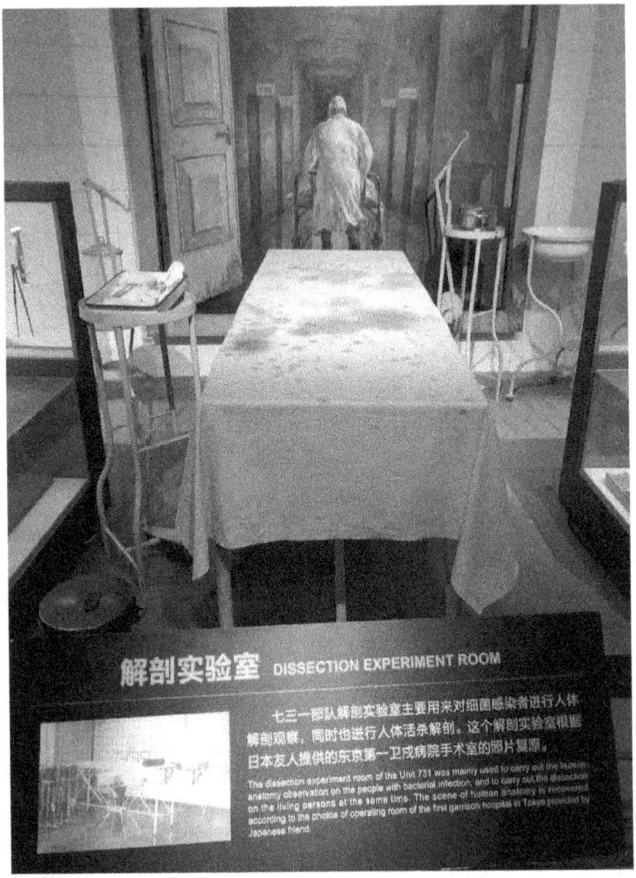

Unit 731 (1937–1945)—The biological and chemical warfare research unit of the Imperial Japanese Army was financially supported by the Japanese government. Some three hundred researchers were secretly granted immunity by the United States in exchange for data. It included aerial bombing of eleven Chinese cities with anthrax, plague-carrier fleas, rabbit fever, typhoid, dysentery, cholera, and more. The total death count was estimated at 580,000. Experiments included human grenade and flamethrower targets, electrocution, Xray exposure, animal blood injection, forced infection, induced frostbite, forced pregnancy, and more. Three thousand men, women, and children were used as test subjects. There are no known survivors. ("Human Dissection Experiment Room at Harbin's 731 Museum" by X20106301, distributed under a CC BY-SA 4.0 license, https://commons.wikimedia.org/wiki/File:Human_Dissection_Experiment_Room_at_Harbin's_731_Museum.jpg.)

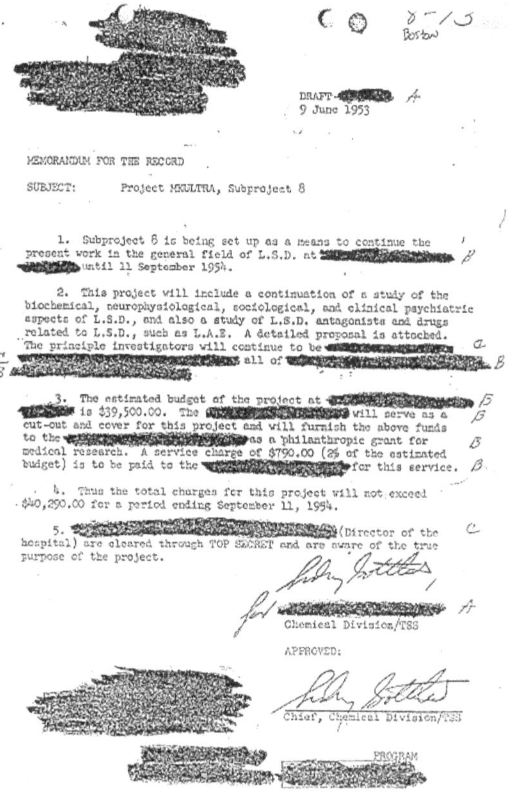

DRAFT-[redacted]
9 June 1953

MEMORANDUM FOR THE RECORD

SUBJECT: Project MKULTRA, Subproject 8

1. Subproject 8 is being set up as a means to continue the present work in the general field of L.S.D. at [redacted] until 11 September 1954.

2. This project will include a continuation of a study of the biochemical, neurophysiological, sociological, and clinical psychiatric aspects of L.S.D., and also a study of L.S.D. antagonists and drugs related to L.S.D., such as L.A.E. A detailed proposal is attached. The principle investigators will continue to be [redacted] all of [redacted]

3. The estimated budget of the project at [redacted] is $39,500.00. The [redacted] will serve as a cut-out and cover for this project and will furnish the above funds to the [redacted] as a philanthropic grant for medical research. A service charge of $790.00 (2% of the estimated budget) is to be paid to the [redacted] for this service.

4. Thus the total charges for this project will not exceed $40,290.00 for a period ending September 11, 1954.

5. [redacted] (Director of the hospital) are cleared through TOP SECRET and are aware of the true purpose of the project.

for [redacted]
Chemical Division/TSS

APPROVED:

[redacted]

Chief, Chemical Division/TSS

[redacted] PROGRAM [redacted]

MK-Ultra (1953–1973)—This was a network of eighty-six US and Canadian institutions—including hospitals, colleges, universities, prisons, and pharmaceutical companies—under the direction of the CIA and funded by the US and Canadian governments. They ran a mind control and psychological torture research program that included psychedelic and paralytic drug administration, electroshock, hypnosis, isolation, sensory deprivation, and verbal, physical, and sexual assault. Most research records were destroyed by order of CIA in 1973. The exact victim count is unknown, and class action lawsuits persisted over the next forty-five years. More than two-thirds of Canadian victim claims were denied by reason of not being "tortured enough." ("Mkultra-lsd-doc" by Central Intelligence Agency employee, distributed under the public domain, https://commons.wikimedia.org/wiki/File:Mkultra-lsd-doc.jpg.)

Abolitionism (late eighteenth century through the twentieth century)—State-by-state eradication of slavery. The northern US abolished slavery in 1804, international slave trade outlawed in 1807, the British Empire abolished slavery in 1833, and the thirteenth amendment to the US Constitution completely abolished slavery in the United States in 1865. Brazil abolished slavery in 1888. Slavery was declared illegal in 1948 under the Universal Declaration of Human Rights. Mauritania was the last country to abolish slavery in 1981. Yet in 2020, more than forty million people in 167 countries were slaves. Modern slavery included child labor, domestic servitude, forced marriage, organ trafficking, sexual exploitation, forced labor, bonded labor, and descent-based slavery, where people were still born as "property." ("Slave Market-Atlanta Georgia 1864" by George N. Barnard, distributed under the public domain, https://commons.wikimedia.org/wiki/File:Slave_Market-Atlanta_Georgia_1864.jpg.)

Child Maltreatment—According to SOS-usa.org, in 2017, there were 153 million orphans globally, 168 million child laborers, 263 million children not attending school, and 69 million children suffering from malnutrition. One child under the age of five died every seventeen seconds. According to WHO, one billion children aged two to seventeen years were victims of physical, sexual, emotional, or multiple types of violence in 2014. ("A gathering of the orphans on the steps of Kearns' St. Anne's Orphanage" (1900), author unknown, distributed under the public domain, https://www.wikiwand.com/en/Kearns-Saint_Ann_Catholic_School.)

Tiananmen Square Massacre (1989)—Student-led protests prompted by widespread political corruption and the demand for democratic reforms resulted in military advance on protesters. There was no official death toll (likely hundreds to thousands). Thousands were also wounded. This event effectively ended political expression in China. ("November 29 Student Demonstration, Tiananmen Square" by Sidney D. Gamble, distributed under the public domain, https://commons.wikimedia.org/wiki/File:November_29_student_demonstration,_Tiananmen_Square.jpg.)

Uttarakhand Floods (2013)—This "natural disaster" was abetted by overdevelopment and underregulation, resulting in six thousand people killed, missing, or presumed dead, and 9,200 livestock dead. Lack of reform led to a second flood in 2021. ("An aerial view of flood-ravaged Rudraprayag, in Uttarakhand", by Ministry of Defence (GODL-India), distributed under the public domain, https://commons.wikimedia.org/wiki/File:An_aerial_view_of_flood-ravaged_Rudraprayag,_in_Uttarakhand.jpg.)

Animal Abuse—A conservative estimate of overall animal abuse rate in 2021 was one instance every sixty seconds. There are 525,600 minutes in a year. Sixty-five percent of all abused animals are dogs. ("Puppy mill2" by People for the Ethical Treatment of Animals (PETA), distributed under the public domain, https://commons.wikimedia.org/wiki/File:Puppy_mill02.jpg.)

Attica Prison Riot (1971)—This was a 1,281-inmate uprising against poor prison conditions. Thirty-three prisoners and ten correctional officers were killed. There were 10.35 million people incarcerated around the world in 2015, rising to eleven million by 2021 with no corresponding increase in crime rates. Across 118 countries, 223 prison systems were operating beyond their maximum occupancy rate and eleven systems were operating at over double capacity in 2020. Overcrowding was a major factor in poor prison conditions, provoking unrest in inmate populations. ("Attica Prison Riot Memorial" by Bronayur at English Wikipedia, distributed under a CC BY-SA 3.0 license, https://commons.wikimedia.org/wiki/File:Attica_Prison_Riot_Memorial.jpg.)

CHAPTER 14

And lest I should be exalted above measure by the abundance of the revelations, a thorn in the flesh was given to me, a messenger of Satan to buffet me, lest I be exalted above measure.

—Corinthians 12:7 (King James Version)

COSMO IS SOAKING UP the attention, his tail flopping this way and that in double time with the strokes to his head. With silky soft, curly white hair with even softer floppy ears and pale blue eyes that could melt an iceberg, he is a four-legged angel. I am sitting on the front porch steps, even though there are two perfectly good rattan chairs waiting for me on the little deck.

As if he senses my sadness, Cosmo places his head in my lap and sighs. It actually helps. I continue to pet him in long strokes as I run through last night's conversation in my head. It had to be done, and I should feel relieved, but instead I feel terrible. The look of confusion on Matt's face, followed by embarrassment and then resignation. I think anger would have been easier, but he is not angry with me.

We walked home together, and when he leaned in to kiss me good night, like he's done a hundred times, I turned away. We had spent the evening with friends at the Main Street Coffee Shop, enjoying the familiar company. I knew it was coming, but I wanted to spend one last night with friends, knowing it was going to be awkward, if not impossible, moving forward.

"Evey, what's the matter?"

Matt looked so genuinely concerned for me as I rebuffed his advance. I promised myself I would be honest with Matt, tell him about Jake. But when the time came, I simply couldn't do it. How could I explain Jake? I'd never mentioned him once since meeting him four months ago. It would come out of nowhere. It would be such a betrayal.

And besides, what would I say? *"Oh and by the way, Jake and I have been spying on this Dr. Draeger for months now and we both got a hall pass on EV, so we can, you know, lie, deceive, and even steal without consequence."*

All three of which I'm guilty of. I would continue with something like, *"And did I mention that Jake and I have agreed to stop Draeger from discovering the cure for EV, so you know, we felt that a possible romantic entanglement might be a natural extension of our arrangement."*

I just couldn't see that going well, so instead I told Matt that I was feeling overwhelmed with being a new agent working two programs and needed to spend more time at home. I said Evander had just turned thirteen and was looking to me for guidance as he entered high school and that Mom and Dad were busy with their agencies and looking to me to help out a bit more around the house. And that I was exhausted (that part was true) and was really in need of some alone time. And in the end, I stayed mum on Jake.

Matt seemed to do some mental calculus as several emotions passed over his handsome face in the process. Finally, he heaved a sigh. "I understand Evey. I respect your need for space. When you are ready, I will be waiting."

Ugh, I wish he hadn't said that last part. I wonder how it would have gone if I had been completely honest with him. I doubt he would have been so easygoing. We left it at that, and now I am sitting here admonishing myself for my cowardice. If I had told the truth, I wouldn't have left him hoping we would resume this courtship at a later date.

Cosmo is falling into an easy slumber in my lap, perfectly content with the affection I am lavishing on him. I tickle behind his ears, and he twitches as I realize I have created a new problem to contend with. What am I going to tell Jake? I reach into the pocket of my gray cotton joggers and squeeze the flash drive that I carry with me everywhere. This is exactly why EV cannot be annulled. Without correction, without reminders, one transgression slips into the next and you become so consumed with the emotional burden of your debauchery that you start losing yourself. I am living proof of that.

Ashton tries to resume with the task at hand, but it is no use. Having been summoned fifteen minutes earlier, he sits in Draeger's office unable to concentrate. Consumed with anticipation. He wonders if there is enough time in the universe for him to master the stress that inevitably overtakes him each and every time his lead agent requests an audience. He is still pondering his conundrum when the source of his perpetual strife opens the doors and swallows all the air in the room.

"Mr. Ashton, your allotted time has lapsed. Tell me where I can find my files."

Draeger has an uncanny way of asking questions without really asking. It is unnerving and only adds to Ashton's discomposure.

The stout little man clears his throat and tries for confidence. "Sir, we have completed the monitoring period for the UV chamber. There are numerous recorded entries. I am assembling the entire team tomorrow to begin the interrogation process, focusing on agents who accessed the chamber in the past two weeks."

Draeger considers for a moment.

"Indeed, Mr. Ashton. However, interrogation requires a certain finesse. A certain presence."

"Yes, Dr. Draeger. I am the most senior agent at the north central lab. My authority is unimpeded."

Draeger is already tapping away on his tablet, a message to his driver to have the car ready for 08:00 hours tomorrow. They will be going on a little road trip.

Jake shuffles nervously beside Ashley in the inner oval. All the team members have been marshalled, save for Renee Castonguay and Derek Halimand, which is confirmation that they have been reassigned, but to where, no one seems to know.

Jake is regretting the double-stacked vegetarian Reuben sandwich he ate for lunch while Everett picked away at a leafy salad with the appetite of a small bird.

Ashley glances sidelong at him and whispers, "Jake, why are you practically jogging on the spot?"

Jake stills his feet. She's right. He needs to get his nerves under control or risk giving himself away.

"Sorry, I just have a list of tasks to get through today. This is cutting into my productivity."

"We all do, Jake. We'll be granted extensions. Relax."

She bought it, he thinks to himself. *So melt into the background. Be unremarkable.*

Clipboard in hand, Mr. Ashton strolls in through the white half door separating the inner oval from the outer. Walking toward the group with his chin held high in the air and locking his knees with every step of his stunted gait, he reminds Jake of windup doll he and his cousin used to play with. The thought almost makes him laugh. He contains it but not before a little snicker escapes. Ashley picks up on the attempt at suppressing his amusement. She bumps his shoulder lightly with her own, sharing in the private joke. Ashton sidles up to the stainless-steel table, sets his clipboard down, and turns to address the gathered agents. He is all business. There is no exchange of pleasantries whatsoever.

"If I call your agent number, move to this side of the table." He points to his right. "Everyone else, stay where you are."

He pushes his rounded spectacles up his nose and leans over the table to his clipboard. "Agents 1036, 1798, 2702, 2993, 3581, 3703, 3945, and 4032."

Ashley, Agent 3945, with panic on her brow, looks to Jake, Agent 4004. The same look appears on the faces of the other agents IDed in the roll call, no one comprehending why they have been singled out.

Ashley pleads with Jake. "But I didn't do anything wrong. I don't understand."

Jake tried to soothe her. "It'll be OK, Ash. You're right. You didn't do anything. You have nothing to worry about."

He sounds convincing, but doubt is creeping in. Maybe these agents breached team protocol in some way? It's easy to mention the project to friends or family even though the team is expressly forbidden from disclosing project details. Jake has done it himself in the past and caught himself. His mother especially seems to think she is entitled to Dr. Draeger's plans, regularly probing her son for details. But then again, no one has breached protocol more than Jake, spying and plotting with Everett for months now, even stealing information from under Draeger's nose. Is it possible that he has evaded detection?

Just as the agents are reorganizing according to Ashton's list, lithe footsteps echo in the outer oval. Everyone stops to look in the direction of the interloper. The white half door swings open, and Dr. Draeger steps through the opening, clad in his customary gloomy homochromous attire, complete with glossy black patent leather shoes.

No one makes a sound as he approaches the group in no hurry, knowing full well they are all hanging on his every movement. The sound of Ashton swallowing hard indicates that he is as uncomfortable in Drager's presence as everyone else. Jake watches the man's confidence from moments earlier seep away as Draeger draws near. He almost feels sorry for him, so obvious is his sudden distress.

"Dr. Draeger, what a pleasure. Thank you for joining us," Ashton lies none too smoothly. Draeger does not reciprocate. "I have just segregated the agents we are interested in speaking with."

Ashton brandishes a hand toward the group of eight agents, who appear to be growing more nervous with each passing moment. Draeger says nothing still, clasping his hands behind his back in casual contemplation. He continues walking in a slow circle around the agents, who are bunched together. He stops between the two groups and looks from one to the other. There are still seven agents, including Jake, on his side of the table. Draeger closes his eyes and brings his hands to his sides, splayed wide. He stands like that for an uncomfortably long moment while everyone holds their breath.

"Unexpected, very unexpected," are the first words he utters when he opens his black, colorless eyes.

Ashton looks just as confused as the rest of the group, not comprehending the situation. Draeger walks toward Jake's group as Ashton rushes to stop him.

"Sir, this group is of no interest to us. They are not on the list."

Draeger ignores him and continues toward Jake and his fellow agents.

Ashton tries again. "But, sir, these agents did not use the chamber during the, uh, the critical period."

He hesitates on the last part of his statement. Jake senses that he does want to divulge too much. Now Draeger looks directly at his assistant.

"Mr. Ashton, please escort the group to the lobby. I will join you presently and we shall commence."

A dismissal.

Ashton complies without further question. He retrieves his clipboard and ushers the group of eight agents toward the outer oval, leaving Draeger with the remaining seven agents. Jake looks at his fellow agents in turn, each ashen and distraught at the prospect of garnering Draeger's attention. The doctor weaves slowly between them, now spaced apart from the removal of eight from their unit. Jake is at the end of the line, and while Draeger moves leisurely between them, he processes what Ashton gave away.

These agents did not use the chamber ... That's what he said, during some special time period. It has to be connected to the flash drive. They must assume that whoever took it needed to use the UV chamber to avoid a righting protocol.

Draeger is one agent to Jake's left now, moving in on him. He deliberately schools his countenance to project equanimity. Draeger circles Jake once and then again before stopping directly in front of him. The men are almost equally matched in height, although Jake's athletic frame is far bulkier than the severe, angular doctor. Jake doesn't flinch or show any outward signs of intimidation, which might possibly irritate Draeger, judging by the slight twitch behind his right eye.

To Jake's surprise, Draeger is polite and oddly respectful in a manner he is not with his assistant. "Your service to the Biodome and particularly to this project is valued. Tell me your name, son."

The reference to kinship makes Jake's skin crawl, but he suppresses the feeling.

"Jacob, sir. Jacob Domanso."

Then Draeger does something Jake could never have predicted. He offers his hand. "Pleasure to meet you, Mr. Domanso," he says, holding out his hand.

Jake has no choice. He must shake hands with the older man. As soon as their hands touch, Jake is struck to the core. Pain, anguish, fear, malevolence, rage—the same feelings, the same emotions he felt with Everett and that blasted microscope—come flooding in, making his eyes roll back in his head momentarily. His left calf begins to throb in excruciating pain. He is about to throw up, he is about to faint, he is about to scream when Draeger releases his hand and the sensations tormenting his body and soul fade as quickly as they arose.

The other agents are looking on incredulously but completely oblivious to the exchange. Jake comes back to his senses and focuses on Draeger, who is still standing in front of him, staring with the distinct air of what must be reverence. The doctor schools his own features to neutrality and asks one final question before turning on his heel and heading toward the front lobby and Mr. Ashton. Jake responds quickly and blows out a huge breath, rustling the hair on his forehead. He is suddenly overcome with intense fatigue. He sits on a lab stool perched near yet another microscope, and that's when he feels wetness soaking through his pant leg. The fabric of his jeans is beginning to stick to his skin, a most uncomfortable sensation. Jake reaches down and lifts the leg of his jeans. He drops it quickly and turns his body toward the stainless-steel table.

"Everything OK, Jake?" asks Martin, a lab agent Jake likes to visit on his rounds.

Everyone is looking at him.

"Yup, just fine, thanks," Jake prevaricates.

Underneath his pant leg, those disturbing puncture wounds are open and angry, oozing thick, rich, warm blood down the back of his leg.

Ashton is surprised at Draeger's casual demeanor as they rotate the agents one at a time through a small administrator's office turned interrogation room. Not one to incite the lead agent, Ashton graciously accepts Draeger's rare light mood.

None of the eight agents has confessed to pilfering the flash drive, and all claim they have absolutely no knowledge of any nefarious activity within the team. Ashton watches one particular agent closely, detecting some hesitation in her response, a distress in her bearing beyond what the situation warrants, especially given Draeger's unusual geniality. He checks the roster to confirm the agent's identification number: 3945, Ashley Fairweather. Not quite enough for an outright accusation, but Ashton looks directly at the young agent as he renders his conclusion.

"One of them is lying, Dr. Draeger. I will redouble my monitoring efforts. I will discover who holds the file." Ashton is indignant.

"There is no untruthfulness among these agents," Draeger retorts. "None holds the file."

Not a theory, not a suggestion, an absolute. Ashton is taken aback.

"But, sir," he starts when Draeger turns his back to his deputy, preparing to leave.

Seemingly out of nowhere, he gives Ashton one more instruction before opening the door. "Procure a blood sample from Agent 4004," is all he says and then he walks out.

CHAPTER 15

Pride goes before destruction, and a haughty spirit before a fall.

—Proverbs 16:18 (NIV)

JAKE IS UNUSUALLY QUIET today. Almost withdrawn. He is describing yesterday's encounter with Draeger and Ashton but without his normally animated candor. It's a factual, efficient recounting of the past day's events and nothing more. I don't like it. I try to placate him.

"I feel badly too, Jake. I never wanted those agents to be involved in this, but no harm will come to them. They have not done anything wrong. And they will never suspect you. You never used the chamber. That's the link, right? They think that a correction is imminent for whoever took the flash drive."

I have not succeeded in buoying his mood any.

"Yes, Ashton let that slip. It's more than that, though."

"Jake, you keep saying that, but you won't tell me the rest. I don't understand."

"I already told you, Evey. I, I just can't." Jake is exasperated.

I repack my lunch bag and place it in my backpack. I can't leave like this. I have to say something to ease the tension between us. It will weigh on me all afternoon otherwise. "Jake, let's not talk about it anymore today OK? We can just enjoy the birds and the breeze and the tranquility for a few minutes."

That seems to work. He looks up at me and smiles.

"That sounds good to me."

"It's a deal. Let's shake on it," I extend my hand playfully.

Jake recoils as if he's been burned. He puts two feet between us by backing into the trees. Like my touch is poison.

Jake speaks quickly now. "It's getting late. You better start heading over to the lupus compound, and I should be getting to the oval building. I've got a ton of tasks lined up for the afternoon."

I am crushed. He seems utterly repulsed by my nearness. Maybe he was just being polite when I kissed him. To let me down gently and all that. But this was just a friendly gesture, purely platonic. Why would he react so vehemently? Beneath my hurt, there are layers of humiliation and even a little anger. I end the conversation and this standing lunch date with some semblance of civility, although my tone is terse and my words clipped.

"OK then. I hope you enjoy the rest of your day. I will be on my way."

I turn and march back out to main trail, the autumn breeze blowing my loose hair in my face. I swipe it away and zip up my hoodie to block the chill in the air and the cold around my heart.

I make it to the lupus compound in plenty of time. Today we are working on a range expansion program, where we plan to release twenty gray wolves born in the compound at the fringes of their native habitat in the western north central Biodome. The hope is that they will extend their range now that the ancient industrial badlands of this area have been rehabilitated and their natural prey, the woodland caribou, have begun to reclaim their territory. It does not bother me one bit to learn that EV put a stop to both the industrialists who continued to steal land in unbridled expansionism and the barbaric ancient practice of controlling wolf populations by poisoning them with strychnine to compensate for the man-made overcrowding that resulted.

Agents are bouncing ideas back and forth about the best way to release the wolves. Should we do it individually, in pairs, or as a group? Should it be done in the same spot, scattered around the fringe of their existing habitat, or at specific coordinates? Who is going to join the mission, how long will they be gone, who is going to direct the release? I try hard to concentrate on the project and participate, but I am wooden. My brisk walk to the compound did nothing to mend my bruised ego. And to think I was just about to tell him about Matt.

The team has been reassembled for the second time in less than a week. Once again, no one is told the purpose of the meeting, only that it—like the last one—is mandatory. This time Mr. Ashton is waiting for them in the same spot the team met earlier. Taking up one corner of the space is a small table arranged artfully with supplies, along with two beige padded chairs, unlike our bar height lab stools. As before, the group begins organizing in pairs and chatting among themselves.

Jake and Ashley are once again standing side by side, leaning back against a long lab table. Ashley strikes up conversation with a question that throws Jake off his game instantly.

"Why do you suppose the new girl, you know, the one you are mentoring, is not at these meetings? In fact, I haven't seen her once since the day I ran into the two of you when Ashton had his little tirade."

The question is not posed with any hint of suspicion, simply idle curiosity, but Jake feels his face flush while he does mental gymnastics, trying to come up with a plausible explanation, and fast.

"Oh, you mean Amelia." Taking the bull by the horns, Jake continues, "Yeah, after all the commotion that day she decided she didn't want to switch to this project after all."

Ashley does not appear convinced. "Really? So where did you say she came from and where she ended up?"

Thinking even faster now, Jake decides to change tact. "I didn't actually." His words are abrupt, almost rude. "Her movements and current whereabouts are none of my concern. Or yours."

That seems to strike a chord. Jake almost feels bad, but he had to shut her down swiftly. Instead of waiting for her to respond, he uses the awkward silence to change the subject, pretending this little exchange holds no meaning to him.

"So, any idea what this little rendezvous is about?" he asks lightly.

"Your guess is as good as mine." Ashley shrugs.

Jake can tell she's stinging, but she remains graceful.

"Well, I guess we're about to find out."

Ashton stands, clears his throat, and then addresses the group, again, without preamble.

"Today we will be drawing a blood sample from each of you."

What? Everyone looks around in confusion. Calvin Cartwright, an older lab tech assigned to avian species testing, steps forward.

"Might we ask why you are wanting a blood sample, Mr. Ashton? This is a highly unusual request."

Jake picks up on the rehearsal in Ashton's response.

"It is for your safety. Dr. Draeger is very concerned for your welfare. He insists on going through the trouble of making sure his agents are not being harmed by the blue chamber treatments you all partake in because of the nature of the tasks we undertake day to day. The unfortunate demise of some of the animals we test is a small sacrifice for the greater good of the Biodome."

Don't you mean all *the animals?* Jake thinks but doesn't say aloud. He looks around. The team seems satisfied with this explanation. Some seem even grateful to have such a caring lead agent watching out for them. Jake is not buying it. *What are you up to, Ashton?* Jake narrows his eyes, but he holds his tongue.

"If you would please line up here"—Ashton points to the left of the little table—"we will begin."

"Wait," Calvin speaks up again. "*You're* going to take the samples? I mean, no offence, Mr. Ashton, but shouldn't someone with training be drawing the samples?"

Ashton sighs and sits in the padded office chair on one side of the table.

"You are?" Ashton asks.

"Uh, Calvin, Calvin Cartwright."

"Well, Mr. Cartwright, before I was recruited by Dr. Draeger, I was a senior agent in the Department of Health Promotion. Perhaps it would make you feel better to address me by my former title, just for today. You can call me Dr. Ashton."

With steady hands and precision that only comes with years of practice, Ashton never misses a vein, never causes undue pain, not even one bruised elbow. He carefully labels the ampoules with each agent's number and the date. Fifteen agents rotate in and out of the chair opposite him and roll up a sleeve. It takes Ashton less than ninety minutes. When he has finished drawing a sample from each agent, he places the tray of delicate red vials in a cooler.

Once all the agents have returned to their respective tasks, Ashton lets out a sigh of relief. A private smile slips onto his lips, but he quickly wipes it away. He packs up his meager belongings and heads to the front entrance and his waiting black four-door sedan. As the driver expertly maneuvers his way back to main highway going north, Ashton is lulled into a light sleep.

He is brought back to the day he met Dr. Draeger. He has always been physically unremarkable—chubby and clumsy as a child, paunchy and indolent as an adult. But his aptitude as a Department of Health Promotion geneticist was undeniable. Despite his acumen and ambition as a scientist, Garrett Ashton often overcompensated for his lack of confidence and introversion with quirky and eccentric behaviors, which diminished his virtuosity.

DHP Agent 9552 was presenting his breakthrough advances in genome sequencing at a department collaboration conference, fumbling with his written materials and faltering through his oral presentation despite having practiced it to perfection. Feeling defeated after failing to control his nerves yet again, Ashton was packing up his materials when a tall, sleek, dark-haired agent approached him.

"Dr. Ashton," the agent's voice matched his imperious form. "Your research is impressive. The Biodome is fortunate to harness your mind."

Ashton was dumbstruck. Had he just received a compliment? No mention of his very flawed delivery?

The stranger continued. "I am currently assembling a project team. I am looking for the best and the brightest to join me on a very special assignment."

Ashton stuttered, "You w-w-want m-m-me to join your team?"

"Only if you are so inclined, Dr. Ashton. You have the intellectual capacity I require in the field of expertise necessary for this project's success."

For the first time in Garett Ashton's thirty-eight years of life, he felt a kernel of pride, some semblance of self-worth. He nodded slowly, almost unconsciously. The inscrutable agent extended a perfectly manicured hand toward him.

"Dr. Vladimir Draeger. Welcome to the team, Dr. Ashton."

Ashton took Draeger's hand bashfully, in awe of the power exuding from the man and rejoicing at his fortune in being handpicked by one such as Dr. Draeger. He knew in that instant he would do anything for this man.

Ashton surfaces from his slumber almost two hours later when the vehicle stops moving and parks in front of DAW headquarters. It takes him a moment to gather himself both mentally and physically. He is slumped over unflatteringly, and a trickle of drool has escaped the corner of his mouth, running down his chin. He tries to be inconspicuous with the sleeve of his suit jacket as he wipes it away.

"Thank you, Jackson," he addresses the driver as he exits the car, briefcase in one hand and cooler in the other.

"My pleasure, sir," returns Jackson. "Do you need help with that?" He looks at the cooler in the Ashton's hand.

"No, no, I'm fine, Jackson."

Ashton walks into the building and heads straight for the elevator and then for the basement. After the debacle with Halimand and Castonguay, Dr. Draeger had a small laboratory set up for Ashton in a nondescript storage room, secreted away behind rows of industrial shelving that houses box after box of Biodome records. All critical lab work is now Ashton's purview.

That's Dr. *Ashton*, the little man thinks to himself, reinjecting himself with some much-needed confidence.

When he reaches the basement, Ashton approaches the retinal scanner and lets himself into the storage room. As the ancient tube lights come to life, he marches past the shelving to his private lab. He sets his belongings down at his workstation and, after placing the cooler on the desk, removes the plastic lid and begins searching the vials. He removes one and places it in a new tray in the miniature stainless-steel refrigerator under his desk. He proceeds to the yellow biohazard container affixed on the wall, opens the lid, and unceremoniously dumps the remaining vials from the cooler into the specialized waste receptacle.

After reaffixing the lid on the container, he flops down in his plush, oversized reclining office chair—another gift from Draeger—opens the computer on his desk, creates a new project file on his desktop: Agent 4004.

CHAPTER 16

But we are all like an unclean *thing,*
And all our righteousnesses *are* like filthy rags;
We all fade as a leaf,
And our iniquities, like the wind,
Have taken us away.

—Isaiah 64:6 (KJV)

JAKE PACES IN SMALL circles around his bedroom, rubbing his hands over his face and muttering self-deprecations. He panicked at the thought of Everett touching him. He feels somehow dirty, tainted, touched by rot. The look of confusion and hurt on her face torments him. He sits on the soft white duvet covering his bed. Even the freshly laundered linens feel spoiled by his touch. He bunches up the left leg of his cotton joggers and inspects the back of his calf, just above his socks. The wounds do not bleed or become inflamed, not since his meeting with Dr. Draeger and Mr. Ashton, but he checks anyway just to be sure. Now they are almost imperceptible, but unlike a typical flesh wound, they do not completely heal or disappear.

After what happened with Draeger, he has cut himself off from human touch. It's not hard to avoid his parents. They are away leading department projects. Besides, they were never a touchy family to begin with. And he is not in the habit of hugging his buddies, so that leaves Everett. The one person whose opinion truly matters to him. More reason to uncover the story behind those little puncture wounds. There is something lurking in his subconscious, a memory he can't quite grasp. It's trying to break free but always just beyond his reach.

In the time of the ancients, repressed memories were a symptom of a mental health syndrome of one sort or another. Since the Correction, the incidence of mental health disorders is virtually nonexistent in the Biodome. EV ensures every child is born into a loving family and properly reared and nurtured. She has also neutralized myriad negative and destructive social and environmental factors that led to the demise of millions of ancients. Yet every time Jake feels the revelation bubbling to the surface, his brain seems to prevent the memory from entering his conscious mind. It's as though it's protecting him from something deeply troubling.

It makes no sense, Jake thinks. *I know I have the answer. Why does it keep eluding me?*

In frustration, he flops over on the bed, facing in the wrong direction, leaving his legs dangling over the edge and his head at a ninety-degree angle to his pillows. He closes his eyes, and soon the din of reality begins to slip away. He holds onto one final thought before he dozes off: *Maybe it will come to me in a dream.*

I know I should go to bed. But my insides are roiling like a ship tossed at sea. I am more deeply wounded than I care to admit. Rejection is one thing, but that was revulsion. Jake was horrified, plain and simple. There is no sense denying it or trying to justify his reaction. I have to come to terms with the fact that he is less than interested in me in anything beyond amity. Perhaps even less than that. Fine. I'm over it. It's better this way. He's not that great anyway. I'll just keep telling myself that and maybe one day I will actually mean it. And believe it. I need to change gears or I will never sleep.

I flip open my laptop and pop in the flash drive. I open the file, and like I've done a dozen times now, I stare at it. More than seventeen thousand base pairs in the genome of this snake stare back at me. An endless sequence of As, Gs, Ts, and Cs—adenine, guanine, thymine, and cytosine. As dancing with Ts and Cs dancing with Gs, the universal rule of the genetics. Even that much I remember from evolutionary biology class. If not for one unique feature of this genome, I could be looking at a bird or a dog or a human. For all I know, it all looks the same. Underlined at regular intervals are two sequences: GTAAA and CCCAT. They're noted as "repetitive sequence units in noncoding spacer regions." At the bottom of the genome sequence is a notation section, initialed R. C. I have to assume these are Renee Castonguay's working notes.

Note one reads: "Rep. seq. units unique to squamate species."

Note two is more puzzling: "No mutations in rep. seq. units? Indicates no evolutionary change. 170-million-year-old sample."

I've read this note multiple times now. It doesn't get any less sinister. The report switches gears with a new heading called "Proteomics." In this section, each protein coded in the genome is identified by an accession number and placed in a specific category. There are muscle proteins; endothelial proteins; and heart, liver, and brain proteins, but the category that really stands out to me is the venom proteins. I mean, snakes, after all, are all about the fangs and the deadly bite. That more than anything is what makes them so foreboding. And besides, who knew there were so many types of venom? Neurotoxins, cytotoxins, hemotoxins, mycotoxins, dendrotoxins—it's all so, well, intoxicating.

This is where things get really interesting. This must be a particularly dangerous snake because it seems to have all of them: "P25687 *Dendroaspis polylepis*, dendrotoxin common to mambas and rattlesnakes; P34128 *Bungarus multicinctus*, alpha neurotoxin common to cobras and sea snakes; Q93364 *Crotalus adamanteus*, hemotoxin common to vipers; Q9TP52 *Gloydius biohoffil*; Q5LEM5 *Bothrops jararaca*; Q8AVA4 *Pseudacris australis*; Q7ZZN9; P12028 ..." It goes on and on, dozens of toxins of all types. I wonder if this is why the creature seems to have some super EV immunity. Well, I'm not going to let Draeger find out.

So why haven't I destroyed this cursed file yet? I've been asking myself that for weeks now. My eyes are starting to swim over the computer screen. I think I can sleep now. As the characters slip out of focus, one word continues to stand out in my field of vision, repeated over and over after every single entry of every single protein in every single category: *ancestral.*

Here we are, at our lunch spot. The autumn leaves are blowing around us, carried along the ground in miniature funnel clouds. Nothing seems amiss today. Jake is relaxed and congenial with no signs of spurning. I decide not to bring up his behavior from our last lunch. I don't want to jinx the moment.

Just as I am about to dig into the colorful salad that Mom sprinkled with an assortment of fancy crushed nuts and sprigs of cilantro, he decides to mention that Draeger ordered blood tests on all team members to "ensure the safety of the team," as it was explained.

I choke on the first bite. "Are you actually buying that?" I ask, followed by a hail of coughing. When I can breathe again, I continue,

"Jake, what if he is testing for immunity? What if he figures out you don't need the light box? This could be a disaster."

How can he be so casual about this?

"Evey, slow down. There goes that imagination of yours."

There is no chiding in his response. It is lighthearted and warm, more like teasing than objurgation.

"Ashton said it's routine testing. They just want to make sure the light box is keeping our white cell counts in check and that EV remains happily dormant."

I suppose that makes sense. The entire team, well, except for Jake—unbeknownst to them—relies on the blue chamber to run the project. To test the animal subjects, or kill them rather, and then dispose of the evidence. EV would fry them for that, so I guess it's logical to monitor the team members and make sure the light treatment continues to provide protection against what would surely be a severe righting protocol. There is one way to ensure that this is indeed just a routine safety check.

"So when will you get the results?" I ask nonchalantly, not letting the lingering doubt creep into my voice.

Jake seems a little taken aback by the question. He pauses with his sandwich halfway to his mouth. "Um, you know, he never said anything about that."

My suspicion is at an all-time high now.

"Well, Ashton cannot deny you your health status. The Biodome Charter is clear that we are in control of our own health and wellness."

I recall the ancient practice of paternalistic health care back when citizens were consumers of health care in a never-ending cycle of never enough to go around. Building after building after building housing the sick, the diseased, even the precious elderly. Now that man-made disease has been mostly eradicated, health care is no longer the treatment of illness but rather the advancement of wellness.

I remember a few years back—I would have been around ten at

the time—when big announcements came out of the Department of Health Promotion. A large group of ancient malignancies arising from genetic mutations caused by a whole host of self-destructive behaviors and environmental influences rampant among ancient society had been reduced to virtually undetectable incidence rates among the second generation of Biodome citizens. And then announcements of how EV had dispensed with coronary diseases that plagued the ancients, most often manifestations of poor lifestyle choices. At a time when freedom meant ignoring the human body's need for proper nourishment and physical stimulation and when chronic stress, chronic fatigue, and chronic substance use was everywhere, every day. I recall the fanfare around these Biodome milestones, the reversal of generations of self-induced genetic and corporeal degradation.

Jake brings me back to the moment.

"Um, OK, I guess I will ask for my test results if that will put your mind at ease."

Jake had not thought of requesting the lab report.

"It's not like we are going to know how to read it anyway."

He is right. I wouldn't know a high white cell count from a normal one, and although Jake most assuredly will not show any signs of infection, somehow I think I will be comforted seeing his clean bill of health in black and white.

As if he is reading my mind again, he continues, "It's not like I am going to show any signs of a righting protocol. Superhuman powers and all, remember?"

We start wrapping up, collecting our lunch paraphernalia, and placing it back in our backpacks. I maintain a respectful distance. Jake shows no signs of his earlier apprehension, and I am not about to test him. I've had enough unrequited affection for one lifetime.

Jake strikes a blow with an unexpected question: "So have you destroyed the flash drive yet?"

I respond a little defensively. "I'm getting to that. I am just trying to figure out what makes this snake so special."

"You mean, other than the fact that it is probably the host? And that it has full immunity? I mean, how much more special do you want, Evey?" Jake mocks me.

I don't have an excuse for holding onto it. It's just a nagging feeling.

"You're right. I will get rid of the thing when I get home tonight. I will crush it in a million pieces so it can never be recovered," I promise Jake.

"I think that is a wise decision, Ms. Steele," Jake returns with a slight flourish that brings a smile to my face. Almost intimate. Not quite but almost.

As I walk back to the main trail, I go over my promise to Jake. Yes, I will destroy the drive tonight. I will obliterate that blasted little device once and for all. Right after I copy the file to my laptop.

CHAPTER 17

Deliver my soul from the sword,
my precious life from the power of the dog!

—**Psalm 22:20 (ESV)**

PLANNING FOR THE CENTENNIAL celebration is underway in the Biodome. One hundred years since the Correction. One hundred years of restoring harmony and balance on the planet. One hundred years of retrogression, undoing the wrongs from the moral corruption that putrefied the ancients at their core. Dr. Draeger paces in Ashton's dingy makeshift lab.

"One hundred years of subjugation at the hands of the Biodome and its secret weapon."

Draeger rarely orates, but he is especially talkative today. Heralding to another time, the doctor continues through the lens of someone with firsthand knowledge.

"The freedom to choose one's fate, the freedom to prosper, survival of the fittest and the fearless and the ruthless, giants among men. That is what it means to be alive, Mr. Ashton."

Almost wistful now. Draeger pivots as he reaches the end of the imaginary line between the lab and the storage shelves. Heat flashes in his eyes.

"Fools, all blind fools, succumbing to the propaganda of a disembodied computer program. Clever, though, I'll admit."

Ashton's eyebrows come up at that last part, but he does not comment.

The Biodome is controlled by an omnipotent AI architecture of dubious origin. The moral consciousness of the human race. Prior to the new order, the ancients divided land into countries and regions and built fiefdoms around their geographical borders. It was a constant struggle to put the common good first in this inwardly facing, self-interested social order. The well-intentioned were drowned out by the constant barrage of wickedness and immorality.

The first one hundred years of the Age of Resolve has been spent almost exclusively on restoration, remediation, and rehabilitation of one form or another, while the existential virus ensures universal morality, purposeful being, and zero backslide. And in the center of the Biodome is its automated overlord; it does not play favorites, it does not make exceptions, it does not make excuses. It is beyond reproach. Unimpeachable.

What little emotion Draeger let slip through his flawless veneer evaporates almost instantly, and his handsome, angular features return to granite.

"Mr. Ashton, an update on the status of our newest specimen, if you will."

In his haste, Ashton scatters a stack of loose sheets sitting on top of his keyboard and shakes the mouse to illuminate the screen. Keying in his password to reveal his desktop, a fiery sunset over green pastures, he selects the file and opens it.

"Sir, Agent 4004 has no discernible immune response to EV.

There is no evidence of a recent or current infection of any sort. No righting protocol," Ashton reports.

"To the other matter then," Draeger replied, no hint of reaction to this first piece of information.

"Yes, um, there is indeed foreign DNA in the sample. Unfortunately, I am not set up in the present quarters to conduct the genomic and proteomic sequencing." A bead of perspiration surfaces on Ashton's upper lip.

"Tell me then, Mr. Ashton, where the required infrastructure is to be acquired. And when," Draeger commands.

"Well, sir, I can requisition the computer programming and lab equipment today, but that will take some time. The fastest way would be to have the Halimand-Castonguay lab disassembled and brought here. It was designed specifically for the task at hand."

Draeger considers for a moment and then looks down at Ashton, who retreats so far back into his chair as to cause it to recline.

"Mr. Ashton, the fastest way is to convey your person and the project to the Halimand-Castonguay lab at the Midwest campus. In fact, you can leave today."

Jackson settles behind the wheel of the black sedan for the return trip. Ashton climbs into the comfortable back seat, resigned to his fate.

I really should consider moving there, he tells himself, *or at least getting a permanent dwelling there.*

He does not, however, find his current situation terribly vexing. This assignment will allow him to flex his substantial intellectual muscles in his capacity as a doctor and a scientist. Being Draeger's wingman has its perks, but Ashton relishes the opportunity to exercise his skill in the lab.

Jackson is quiet, so Ashton takes in the passing scenery, mile after mile of forested lands dotted with lakes and the occasional eagle's nest high up in the majestic red pines that loom over the landscape. His mind slips back to an all departments conference some years ago where the Environmental Department's Solid Waste Division presented a slideshow with a cheeky title, "The Litter Legacy," demonstrating the ancients' ravenous consumption of material and convenience goods and their flagrant disregard for the environment as millions upon millions of tons of refuse were strewn along highways, under bridges, and in ditches, parks, woodlands, and waterways. The agents flashed photographs from the ancient archives of a woodland deer choking on a plastic bag, a black bear chewing on a plastic water bottle, a caribou with human refuse ensnared in its antlers, fish trapped inside plastic bags, birds being strangled by sheets of discarded cellophane.

It took the Waste Division years and years to recover the debris, one highway, one lake, one river, one park at a time. Meanwhile, EV did her magic. The typical righting protocol for littering is a variant EV15 infection, the ancient Norwalk virus. Not terminal but embarrassingly evident and sufficiently uncomfortable to deter further transgression. Ashton admires the miles of pristine, unsullied landscape. A most private thought creeps into his conscious, one never to be repeated aloud.

Is she really so bad?

We are outside on the front porch. It's a cool but sunny autumn afternoon. Tucked against the house, we are somewhat sheltered from the fall breeze.

Grandmothers are so perceptive, it's uncanny. No one in my family even suspects I am in turmoil, but Grams never misses a beat.

"So," she begins simply, "what happened with the young man then?"

My eyes go wide. I try to recover, but she's caught me. I sigh.

"It just didn't feel right somehow, Grams."

I try to leave it there, but she knows I'm only telling half the story. Grandma sets her lemonade down on the little table between us and tries again.

"Ah, the heart wants what the heart wants, now doesn't it?"

She's always dropping these aphorisms. She seems to have one for every occasion.

"So, Evey, what is it that your heart wants if not young Matthew?"

Oh boy, I can't lie, at least not completely. She will see through me in an instant.

"Well, I did meet someone from my department."

I don't want to elaborate. Not satisfied, Grandma probes further.

"And this boy works in the equine program or the lupus program?"

She almost got me on this detail, but I remember Jake telling me about his program before the oval lab.

"Actually, his purpose is with the canine program."

"Tell me, Evey, what is it about this young ..."

"Jacob, Jake," I fill in for her.

"... Jacob, that has caught your eye?"

I think about this for a minute. How can I explain how tethered I feel to Jake, connected. And how to explain how lately he won't let me touch him, won't even let me inside his personal bubble? That should make for interesting conversation.

Instead, I go with, "It's kind of weird, actually. He is almost the opposite of Matt. He is handsome, to be sure, but he doesn't know it, doesn't try. He's actually a little scruffy but in a charming way. Our love of animals and our shared commitment to their welfare makes us kind of kindred spirits, I guess. Plus, he is so easy to talk to, to just be myself around him and not have to worry about what he will think of me. He doesn't judge at all."

I leave out some pretty pertinent details like how we share a common immunity to EV, we discovered a plot to neutralize her, and we are currently holding the key to that plan in the form of a computer file that is now on my laptop computer. Cosmo senses my wariness. He trades his prone position for a sitting one, places his head in my lap, and eyes me with sympathy.

If I thought I got away with my half-truths today, Gram's shrewd discernment of Cosmo's behavior just gave me away.

Jacob and Hercules, his ninety-pound German shepherd, stroll down the sidewalk in his quiet neighborhood, enjoying the mild and sunny Sunday afternoon. Taking their time, the duo stops by the local park to toss a frisbee. The dog never tires of chasing the orange disc for his human companion, which may have something to do with the treats he is rewarded with after each successful retrieval.

"OK, Herc. Time to make for home. Let's get you and me some dinner."

The dog's ears perk up at Jake's voice and his own nickname. The two have been inseparable for the last six years. As they round the last corner that brings them onto their street, Hercules drops his head and his usually sprightly tail drops to the ground. He slows his gait to a crawl, moving now with trepidation toward the house. Jake is baffled. Never before has he seen the dog so defensive.

"Herc, what in the name of the Biodome has gotten into to you?"

The animal allows him to tousle his scruff but never takes his eyes off the house. Jake can just make out someone standing on the porch, talking to his mother in the open entrance way. Tall and masculine for sure, but it takes another dozen steps for his heart to lurch into his throat as the stranger turns toward him. Dr. Draeger, standing inches away from his mother in what appears to be light conversation as though he were an old friend stopping by to say hello.

Now the dog is growling softly. He has his ears pinned back, and the fur between his shoulder blades is standing on end.

"Easy, Herc," Jake tries to soothe the animal, watching his every move. He doubles his hold on the leash, unsure what the dog will do next.

His mother waves, beckoning him to the rendezvous.

"Ah, there he is now. Perfect timing," his mother chirps as he walks into the driveway.

He has the dog firmly in tow. The canine is slinking and grumbling in warning with every other breath. Jake tries to ignore the fire that has just ignited inside his left calf muscle, chalking it up to a muscle spasm or a cramp.

"We are so proud of him, Dr. Draeger. It's so gracious of you to visit us personally with this glowing progress report. It is so encouraging to learn he is finally living up to his potential." His mother is singing his praises as she watches him approach.

Ha, don't you mean your potential, Mother? he thinks.

"Dr. Draeger, what a pleasant surprise, but I can't imagine what would bring you all this way, and on a weekend no less," Jake says, keeping a safe distance, not wanting to invite another handshake. He feels flames licking up the back of his leg but manages to withhold his growing discomfort from his mother and the doctor.

"Dear, Dr. Draeger wanted to give us his personal endorsement. You've been so modest about your contributions to his project."

His mother is being nauseatingly ingratiating, the sycophantic persona completely out of character for her.

"Yes, young Jacob, nice to see you so vigorous and wholesome," Draeger seems almost puzzled as he greets Jake. "I trust you are well?"

There is slight hesitation and inflection in his words that Jacob's mother fails to register but that Jacob knows means the doctor is confounded. The dog is crouched at Jake's feet, still making low grumbling noises in his throat. If Draeger notices the threatening behavior, he says nothing.

"Of course, Dr. Draeger. Honesty, integrity, and purpose," Jacob returns smoothly.

The reference to the Biodome canon disarms the doctor. The heat creeping up the back of Jacob's leg has reached his lower back, but Jake refuses to acknowledge it in the presence of this man.

"I am on my way then." Draeger nods.

After a brief exchange of meaningless platitudes with Maureen Domanso, Draeger climbs into the back seat of his black sedan and the driver pulls away from the curb.

"Well, that was a pleasant surprise. It looks like you're a chip off the old block after all." Jacob's mother manages more self-acclamation than praise for her son. No sooner has she said it than the door behind her closes, leaving Jake standing on the edge of the driveway with his dog, coiled like a spring at his feet.

Finally, Jake reaches for the back of his leg and feels the heat through his joggers. Pulling his hand away, he extends it to Hercules to reassure him that the danger has passed. Jake barely yanks his hand back in time as the animal peels his lips back in a vicious snarl and lunges at his master with powerful jaws wide open.

CHAPTER 18

Life imitates Art far more than Art imitates Life.

— **Oscar Wilde, *The Decay of Lying*, 1889**

ASHTON IS SETTLED IN his new lab within the lab, the former Halimand-Castonguay station, hating the openness of the setting. He feels exposed. There is nothing to be done for it. No matter where he places his chair along the stainless-steel table, his backside is open to the hollow expanse of this odd structure. He docks Castonguay's laptop and opens the genomics software icon in the top right corner—a blue-and-red DNA helix encapsulated in a small white box.

Moving to his right, he retrieves the DNA sample from the liquid handling robot, having successfully extracted the DNA from the blood sample earlier this morning. He moves to the DNA sequencer on the table behind him and flicks the unit to life.

I am taking these back with me, Ashton thinks as he loads the DNA sample onto the glass flow cell and inserts it into the bioluminometric instrument sitting atop the table. Cluster generation takes little time, and soon the sequencing process begins. Ashton feels the tension in his neck dissipate as the familiar routine lulls him, the gentle hum of the sequencer music to his ears, the sound of science in motion.

Jake and I are back on the topic of the blood test. He knows by now that I am not going to let up.

"OK, OK, I'll do it. Today, boss," Jake promises me.

It only took me about fifteen minutes of back-and-forth between pleading and insistence.

"Thank you, Jake. Let's just make sure there is nothing more to this 'routine' health check, as Ashton called it."

"I told you, Draeger even came to my house to make sure I was OK. I'm sure he's doing that with all his team members. I've heard grumblings that the light treatment is starting to cause problems. Ashley says it's harder on her every time she uses it. I heard some of the lab team talking about mild breakthrough infections, EV11 and stuff like that. He's probably trying to figure out a way to upgrade the blue box."

Jake sighs at the unfaltering skepticism on my face. "But I will ask for my test results anyway."

As I reach down to retrieve my backpack, a curtain of hair hides the smile that replaces the skepticism on my face.

I am in my most comfortable lounging pajamas, soft pink fleece bottoms covered in little horses running in all directions and a generously cut, long-sleeve cotton top with a giant grinning horse covering my midsection. I've piled my hair on top of my head in a wild half ponytail, half bun and covered my feet in thick, petal-pink fuzzy socks.

The wind has picked up outside. The chill in the air combined with the ever earlier waning light of day is a sure sign that autumn will soon be moving on. I am sitting cross-legged on my bed, my laptop open to the file that I've practically memorized at this point. I feel a twinge of guilt. I haven't even told Jake that I copied the file before confirming for him that I had indeed destroyed the portable drive.

"Yup, took a good-sized stone to it and crushed it into a mess of broken plastic and a warped little motherboard," I said.

Jake was visibly relieved. I didn't have the heart to tell him that I'd copied its contents to my laptop out of sheer curiosity but also from some deep-seated need to preserve this file for posterity. Jake wouldn't understand and certainly wouldn't like the risks associated with keeping this file. Besides, he seemed to be working through something personal anyway, so I didn't see the need to burden him unnecessarily.

I think back to lunchtime. Jake promised to ask for his test results as soon as he returned to the oval lab. I just want peace of mind knowing that he is not defective, as awful as that sounds. Assurance that his test results look like everyone else's even though he doesn't need the blue chamber. I can never tell him that. He would be mortified if he thought that I thought there was something wrong with him. But if I am being totally honest with myself, I am also being selfish. I want Jake's results as a way to test myself. Because if Jake is defective, so am I.

Ashton connects his laptop to the panoramic screen on the only bare wall of Dr. Draeger's office. Behind his desk is a large triptych oil painting with a bronze plaque centered beneath it that reads *Garden of Earthly Delights—Hieronymus Bosch (1490–1500).*

The left panel of the painting depicts a cartoonlike scene of animals grazing and frolicking in green fields against a blue sky. There is a pond in the center with a unicorn among a host of animals, birds and water creatures in or around the water, and a large fountain in the center. The bottom of the panel depicts a woman standing and a man seated. Both are naked, and in between them is a robed male figure, his kindness bleeding through the canvas.

The middle panel is utterly chaotic, picturing a lush garden with multiple scenes of worldly indulgence—man conquering beast, pleasures of the flesh, an onslaught of encroachment upon nature. Excess, wickedness, sedition. The right panel provides a sharp contrast to the first two, with profoundly disturbing scenes against a jet-black backdrop. It features the same cartoonish figures, but these are depicting grotesque abominations in a tableau memorializing gluttony, vanity, torture, and carnal perversion. The skyline with its whimsical fairy-tale palaces is now fully aflame.

Ashton is so engrossed in the details of the eccentric piece that he fails to register the sound of the door opening and closing behind him. He is startled by Draeger's voice.

"It is indeed the most perfect rendition of humanity, a true masterpiece and a most ancient one, to be sure. A brilliant iconography of the sins of the world as only the ancients could appreciate. But for the Biodome and its pesky little watchdog, man would be free to indulge as man was intended and natural order would be restored on Earth."

It may be ancient, Ashton thinks, *but I'm not so sure it is not better left antiquated.* He forces away all traces of denunciation from his face before turning to Draeger.

"Indeed, sir," is all he says as he repositions himself beside his laptop and brings both screens to life, hoping to curtail any discussion lest his ambivalence reveal itself. "I have significant developments to report," he says abruptly in his typical socially avoidant manner.

Draeger settles into the leather chair behind his ornate ebony wood desk, the delicate black-on-black grain polished to gleaming perfection. Excessive luxury even for the ancients. Like the disquieting work of art framing Draeger's seated form, the bureau is a one-of-a-kind piece carried over the threshold between then and now.

"Begin," Draeger says.

Ashton clears his throat and fiddles with his glasses, his nervous tells on full display.

"Yes, sir." He clicks on a slide.

It features an image of the male human genome: twenty-two Xs side by side, the autosomes, and the last one an X and Y—the sex chromosomes. Spread out among the forty-four autosomes, Ashton has drawn seemingly random black circles at the tips, midway on the arms, and at the base where the strands come together.

"As expected, the existential virus is alive and well in Agent 4004. All thirty-one variants are present and accounted for. No new variants were uncovered in the sample."

Thirty-one circles, each representing the viral gene sequences that every human since the Correction and every human born thereafter carries in his or her genetic code. Humanity's moral insurance policy.

"I see." Draeger's eyes narrow as if trying to answer an unspoken question.

Ashton clicks on the next slide. On the screen is a magnification of the XY chromosomes, the last set in the series. Ashton has circled the tail end of the X chromosome in red ink. Now Draeger leans forward, placing his elbows on the desk and steepling his hands underneath his chin. Ashton takes great pleasure in eliciting a response from the doctor but suppresses the smile creeping onto his face.

"This, however, was quite unexpected. You see, sir, it was my team of research agents from the health department who determined that the existential virus should represent exactly 12 percent of the boy's genome. She is 12 percent of all our genomes, no more, no less.

However, my calculations uncovered that the existential virus is only 11.5 percent of this boy's genome. My numbers are never wrong, sir. So I examined each gene one by one. At the very end of the first sex chromosome, a parasitic genome has been grafted onto the boy's. A combination of intron encoded proteins and junk DNA. This boy has more DNA than he should."

Sweat begins to bead on the little man's upper lip. "This extra DNA has only one set of alleles, one set of genes, which means, sir, that this boy was not born with this genome, yet the existential virus is perfectly intact, so the boy could not possibly have been infected with anything novel since EV does not permit host sharing."

"And the boy is the picture of health," Draeger states as a matter of fact.

"Sir?" Ashton is confused.

Draeger ignores him. "I require the source of that DNA, Mr. Ashton."

Now Ashton begins to fidget. "Sir, I checked the entire Biodome repository. There is no match to this genome. There is simply no way to discover its origin."

"Does this conclude your report, Mr. Ashton?" is all Draeger says in response.

"Er, not quite, sir. The agent has asked for his test results. As you know, sir, we are required, under Biodome Doctrine section 43.4, to accommodate such requests."

"Tell me, Mr. Ashton, of the reason furnished in support of the request by young Jacob."

He knows him by name? Ashton asks himself but carefully conceals his astonishment.

"Agent 4004 stated that his mother is concerned for his welfare and requested the results," he regurgitates the reason furnished to him earlier.

"Then of course we shall provide Maureen Domanso with the

report. She is, after all, an agent of high seniority in the Department of Health Promotion."

"But, sir, she will see—" Ashton begins, but Draeger rolls right over him

"What she will see, Mr. Ashton, is a genomic report with over three billion base pairs and a summary report produced in black and white. No need to draw unnecessary attention"—he nods to Ashton's bright red beacon circling the mystery alleles—"to each one representing an expression of the existential virus."

Draeger continues, "Mr. Ashton, I am well acquainted with Mrs. Domanso. She will not scrutinize the report. She will not even look at it. In fact, she has only requested it for my benefit. Her sycophantic motivations are as evident as her indifference toward her son."

"Oh." Ashton blinks several times, unsure of anything appropriate to say.

"Furnish the monochromatic report to Agent 4004 prior to our departure," Draeger instructs his assistant.

"Um, our departure, sir?" Now Ashton is totally confused.

"Yes, Mr. Ashton. I believe there may indeed be a reference genome in existence for our mystery sex chromosome sequence. The time has come to introduce you to my dear friend Dr. José Castillo."

CHAPTER 19

Gray hair is a crown of glory; it is gained in a righteous life.

—Proverbs 16:31 (ESV)

WE ARE ALL SITTING in the kitchen. Dad is flipping pancakes, and Evander is sneaking the chocolate chips into his mouth when he thinks no one is looking. Mom is flitting about the way Mom flits about, always busying herself with one task or another as we wait for Dad to serve up breakfast.

As the centennial approaches, every department has all hands-on deck. The Bio Web is growing every day. The Bio Web is a map of sorts that identifies the last one hundred years of major milestones from each department and each division within the Biodome, all linked together in an increasingly intricate web illustrating the impact of one department's achievements on another. Dad is especially proud because the milestones from the climate restoration division have an impressive network of outbound links directly supporting developments in agriculture, my department, animal welfare, and Mom's department, Fisheries and Oceans, as well as inbound links from engineering and infrastructure, which, incidentally, also link up with my department. It is a way to help all citizens celebrate their contributions in achieving universal harmony and balance. Every single agent has a spot on the map, a place where they belong. Plus, it's a great school project, as Evander is currently pointing out.

"I have to pick one single division and follow it—inputs and outputs—and create my own inputs and outputs based on what I think still needs to be done, sort of mapping the future, at least the way I think it should go."

"That is really cool, Ev. I'd be happy to assist," Mom says. "So which division have you chosen?"

She is obviously jockeying for Evander to choose her DFO.

"Well, I was kind of thinking of the Department of Elder Care. Grandma and I have talked about it, and she has great ideas about how the Department of Health Promotion, Education, and Research could benefit from the wisdom of 'us old folks,' as Grams calls herself. An underutilized resource, she says."

Mom looks resigned. How can she argue with that? Elders suffered unspeakable horrors in ancient times. Many were relegated to antediluvian government-run facilities with little oversight, atrocities of neglect and abuse rampant in the historical record. Others were left to their own devices on a pitiful allowance after a lifetime of servitude. Many struggled, wondering how they would get through the next season. Some starved or were destitute or homeless. It was an utter travesty of humankind.

Grandma likes to point out that it is one of the richest ironies in ancient civilization.

Biodome archivists liken the current elevated status of elders in the Age of Resolve to the original dwellers, peoples who lived in harmony with nature and held their elders in the highest regard, treating them with the utmost respect and dignity. The usurpers called them savages and spent centuries trying to subvert their way of life. She becomes indignant when she recounts this dark period in ancient history and blesses the Biodome and EV for restoring "us old folks" to their rightful place in the world.

The elderly Steele had a hand in many of the DFO's milestones mapped on the Bio Web.

"That sounds wonderful, Ev," Mom says. "Grandma is a force to be reckoned with. I'm sure your project is going to be a smashing success."

Dad's breakfast is also a smashing success. We enjoy more small talk as we gobble up the fluffy pancakes. We all take one last look at the Bio Web before Dad shuts off the television. The Biodome publishes updates daily for everyone to explore. We can check back at any time.

As Evander and I clear the dishes and get our belongings organized for the day ahead, the Bio Web makes me think of Grandpa. I find myself humming a tune he used to sing as I served as his muse, bringing the little melody to life: "The head bone connected to the neck bone. The neck bone connected to the backbone ... The knee bone connected to the leg bone. The leg bone connected to the foot bone."

Ah, Grandpa, how could the ancients have gotten it so wrong?

Jake makes it a point to arrive early at the oval lab, not wanting to miss his opportunity to speak with Mr. Ashton again about his test results. He was agitated when Jake approached him the first time, almost hostile when he made the request.

"For what purpose, agent?" Ashton blurted out.

Jake had to think fast on his feet. He had not anticipated the reaction.

"Um, my mother would like to verify the results. She is a senior agent with the DHP. She is accustomed to evaluating health data."

Ashton paused at that for a moment. "You are fortunate to have such an attentive mother." The words were spoken with longing. "However, I see no need for your mother to review your test. We are more than capable of accurately interpreting the results." The indignation was once again obvious in his tone.

Jake capitulated in that moment, at a loss to counter Ashton's argument. Now for round two. He has to stand his ground and insist Ashton furnish the report. Everett will accept nothing less. Jake spots Ashton gathering up documents and tucking them inside a large portable carrying case with a long metal handle. His computer equipment has already been stowed away. The lab equipment is now sitting on a rolling cart, it also destined for another location.

Jake readies himself. In physical stature and physical grace, he is twice the man standing in front of him. However, Jake has never been the confrontational type. There is no need to develop dispute resolution skills in the new order, a world of ubiquitous morality. Ashton, however, seems to have retained some of the ancient proclivity for perpetual conflict.

No matter, Jake tells himself. *Just assert yourself politely but firmly and he will see reason. Failing that, we'll go to plan B.*

Jake lengthens his stride, chin held high, exuding a confidence he does not feel.

"Good morning, Mr. Ashton," Jake begins, making the man jump.

"Ah, Jacob is it? You are early today," Aston returns, not unpleasantly.

"Yes, sir. I needed to speak with you about my test results. I must insist—"

Ashton cuts him off. "Yes, of course. You are Agent 4004. You requested your lab results at the behest of your mother, if I recall."

"Yes, sir, that's right. She is quite, persistent," Jake begins once more.

Ashton takes over again, "As she should be. She is concerned for your welfare. That is a most natural maternal instinct."

Ashton is downright congenial. It throws Jake long enough to allow Ashton to continue as he retrieves a green folder from his carryall and hands it to Jake.

"Your test report, as requested."

Jake is replaying their last conversation in his head, wondering if he imagined the acrimony. He regains his mental footing and takes the report from Ashton's outstretched hand.

"Uh, thank you, sir."

"You are most welcome, Jacob."

How, why, what just happened here? Jake's thoughts sputter, but he maintains a neutral expression. *Just a little small talk and then I'll hightail it.*

"Are you leaving, sir?" Jake glances at the cart and the carryall.

"My task has been accomplished. Yes. I will return to my own lab now at main headquarters."

Jake feels a strong sense of relief in Ashton's reply, as though he is all too happy with his imminent departure.

"Well, it was a pleasure meeting you, Mr. Ashton, er, Dr. Ashton, sir. I guess I'll be running along now."

Jake suspects that Ashton wants to say something further, but all he gets is a polite nod. As Jake turns toward the main exit, clutching the green folder, he barely picks up a murmur from Ashton behind him. It's whispered almost remorsefully.

"Yes, Jacob. Run, dear boy. Run."

CHAPTER 20

For everything that is hidden will eventually be brought into the open, and every secret will be brought to light.

—Mark 4:22 (New Living Translation)

WE CAN'T MEET AT our usual picnic spot. The air has turned crisp, and the northerly breeze brings with it a chill that I can't endure for long. For the first time, we plan to meet outside the AW compound on a Saturday. Since I've yet to obtain my driver's permit—I really need to get on that—Jake is going to drive over and meet me at the little coffee house, a regular hangout that won't raise any eyebrows. Simple and quaint with a muted color scheme and nature-themed accents, it is a charming little shop run by the Archour family—Molly, Sam, and their two girls, Sadie and Isabelle, all agents from the Department of Leisure and Recreation.

And here I am, the night before our meeting, pacing the length of my bedroom, my nerves raw with anticipation. What is the big deal anyway? This is a business meeting of sorts, nothing personal. He probably won't even have the report. He didn't sound very convincing earlier this week when we met.

"I'm on it, Evey," he told me when I asked for like the millionth time.

I have pulled out every pair of jeans I own, going through the pros and cons of each pair: too tight, too baggy, too dark, not dark enough. How in the name of the Biodome did I get reduced to this? I finally settle on a new pair of slim fitting bootcuts. Mom said she would take me to the barn after lunch. I've been itching to take Robbie out for a much-needed ride, so my choice of denim works.

I decide on a casual blue flannel button-up shirt, perfect for the cool weather, plus it doesn't look like I'm trying. Which I am. And I don't know why. The fact that it is Jake's favorite color is no coincidence. These past few weeks, Jake has been reticent, maintaining a physical distance between us as though I am offensive to him. I still have no idea what has changed or what I have done to elicit such a cool rejoinder, but whatever I did, it seems to have had a permanent effect.

I haven't even told him about Matt. It's been weeks since I put the relationship on ice. Maybe I've made a mistake. I told Matt I needed some time and space, and I've had both. Now that Jake has repudiated me, maybe I can commit to Matt in the way he deserves. That's exactly what I need to do to get past this little crush. As soon as I am done this meeting with Jake, I will reach out to Matt and open that door. It's just that the connection with Jake felt so … real, so profound. I still can't believe I could be so wrong. A figment of my imagination. I stand in front of the full-length mirror set inside the closet door and chide myself.

Have you made enough of a fool of yourself, Evey? I ask myself. *Seriously, you're practically throwing yourself at him and he is. Not. Interested.*

I stare into my blue eyes and will myself to stop caring. My brain registers the directive. Time to move on. My heart, however, is going to take a little more convincing.

I sleep in fits and starts, Father Time showing me no mercy. Morning comes much too fast. I have to sacrifice some primping time for an extra cup of coffee.

Now we sit in the booth across from each other, and all my insecurities have returned. I finally drifted off to sleep last night convinced that today I would be polished, confident, and polite but emotionally disengaged. Nope. Inside I'm still a puddle of mush. At least I can pretend. My wounded pride deserves that much.

"I told you I'd get it, didn't I?"

Jake is almost boastful. He senses my astonishment.

"Yee of little faith."

"Hey, I didn't doubt you for one second."

We both know that's a fib, but I am enjoying his playful temperament. Juggling my inner turmoil, I just want to keep things light and friendly, nothing more.

"He just handed it over? Just like that?"

I am more than a little surprised. My paranoia is becoming more unjustified by the minute.

"With a smile," Jake replies.

I'm almost feeling silly now.

"OK, hand it over, agent."

I am about to reach across the booth but check myself. I am not up for more rejection today. He senses my hesitation but does not comment.

"Geez, Evey. You really know how to hurt a guy. I drove all the way here. The least you can do is share lunch with me."

Purely platonic, I remind myself. *This is nothing more than a gesture between friends.*

"You are right. This would be the first time we don't eat off the ground and have to share with the ants."

I pull out my Biodome ID card and Jake does the same. This is the universal currency in the Age of Resolve. The Biodome provides for everyone equally. There are no ultrarich or impoverished in the new order. Everyone contributes. Everyone shares in the bounty of a common economy. EV disposed of greed and unscrupulous appetites for wealth when the Biodome discarded man-made currencies.

Grandpa used to say the ancients were their own worst enemies. They had a well-worn saying that money is the root of all evil. And yet, they created a parallel pecuniary universe with competing currencies, which created wealthy nations—the superpowers they were called—so elevated by the value of their currency against other nations, who were left to subsist in poverty and obscurity. As if that isn't bad enough, the ruling classes would debase their very own currencies for their private financial gain at the expense of the citizens they were supposed to be caring for.

I still can't wrap my head around how the ancients came to judge a person's worth by the amount of wealth they accumulated rather than their character, their true intentions, their purpose in society, and their contribution to the health and sustainability of the planet we all share. Just one more reason to be thankful to be living in the Postcorrection era.

Jake and I order our lunches. Mine is a chickpea and spinach salad combination, while Jake goes for a basil and pepper pasta. Two chocolate almond milkshakes round out our orders. We swipe our passes in the card reader, and ten minutes later, Sadie, the younger of the Archour sisters, strolls over to our table with our lunches. She lingers at our table a little longer than necessary. Jake doesn't notice, but I know philandering when I see it. When her coquettish little shoulder shrug and impish grin don't produce the intended results, she pivots on her heel and heads back toward the kitchen. I can't stop the little smirk that ghosts over my face.

We are making small talk and falling into our old easy repartee when I spot the door open over Jake's shoulder. I freeze with a forkful of salad halfway to my mouth. Jake follows my gaze and glances over his shoulder. Matt and Adam Lindstrom walk into the coffee shop. I know they will head straight for the back booth. It's been Matt's table for the past four years. Which means he is about to walk right by Jake and me. And of course, he sees me. His face lights up as he approaches our table and then dims when he sees Jake sitting across from me. He recovers quickly and initiates a light-hearted exchange.

"Hello, Everett. What a pleasure to bump into you today. It's been a while."

Jake senses my consternation without quite understanding the situation. I can feel the heat rising up my face. Some delicate maneuvering is required.

"Hey, Matt. Hi, Adam," I say, casual as a lazy house cat. "Oh, you've probably never met Jake. Jake this is Adam"—I nod to the smaller, dark boy with the tight black curls, chocolate brown eyes, and pouty bottom lip—"and this is Matt." I say it as if it is inconsequential that the two boys who each own some part of my heart are now staring at one another.

Jake takes over, turning on a bromance charm I didn't know he had. "Hey, Adam. And, Matt, you must be *the* Matt, the one Evey is always going on about."

Matt visibly relaxes, his facial muscles releasing some of their intensity.

"Evey and I are just working on a project for the centennial. Since she works in gene pool expansion in the equine program and I'm doing the same in the Canine Division, we were asked to streamline our messaging for the Bio Web. Central AW has so many programs with so many milestones, our mentors are trying to find the best way to cram it all in."

He is so calm and natural. The lies slip so easily off his tongue, it's unnerving. I have seen him do this before with Ashley.

Matt gobbles it up, loosening right up and matching his demeanor to Jake's. "I get it, man. We have to summarize our ecosystem engineering milestones for the Web. It's a lot harder than it sounds."

Matt looks to Adam, who is nodding politely. Now he is emboldened, the perceived threat having been quelled.

"So, Evey, it was really nice to see you. The gang is meeting up at Welsh's Creek for a bonfire next weekend. If you're not busy, it would be great if you joined us."

Clever, using the gang to buffer the invitation.

"Can I get back to you on that, Matt? Let me make sure my mom doesn't have anything planned for the family."

That seems to placate him. I haven't said no, but I've given myself some wiggle room.

"Sure, Ev. Sounds good." Matt turns to Jake. "Hey, man, it was great to meet you. Hope to see you around." He extends his hand to Jake.

Jake looks at the hand and freezes, backing up almost imperceptibly into the back of the booth. But I don't miss it, just like I don't miss the panic on his face, the same look he gives me every time I get close enough to touch him. I don't have time to process it. It's all happening in slow motion, but it's been mere seconds. I swing my hand out clumsily as if I'm about to say something animated and knock Jake's milkshake into his lap, soaking him in the viscous, sticky liquid.

"Whoa!" Matt pulls his hand away, and I use the distraction to Jake's advantage.

"Oh my goodness, Jake. I'm so sorry. I'm such a clumsy oaf."

I pull napkins out of the dispenser, pretending I no longer notice Matt and Adam standing at the end of our table.

"We'll let you deal with that, man. Evey, what a mess. Poor guy's gonna be a walking glue stick."

Matt seems genuinely concerned for Jake. Again, I pretend that their presence is of no import at the moment, and they finally take their leave. Jake is using napkins to soak up the sludge seeping into his lap, but no anger emanates from his person, just relief.

"Geez, Evey. That was an epic little accident. You really got me."

Jake pushes his satchel into the corner of the booth to save it from the mess. I stop moving, I stop breathing, I wait. I wait for Jake to realize that I have gone to stone and look up at me. Only then do I look him straight in the eye and reply with a stern, straight face.

"That was no accident."

I replay the last few hours in my head on the back of my dear Robbie. He is enjoying the attention and my company so much that he doesn't even notice that I am preoccupied. I don't know if I am upset or overjoyed. Confused or relieved. It's not just my touch Jake is avoiding.

Of course, he denied everything, feigning indignity at my accusations. No idea what I am going on about, he said. He expertly turned the tables on me with a line of questioning of his own about Matt and our current estranged status. I found myself stumbling through a weak explanation about how I had asked Matt for a little space and how with everything going on at the oval lab, I was distracted, and it was unfair to him. Besides, I told him, it was putting our little mission in jeopardy. I did not mention that my heart was betraying me. For him. Nope. That part I'll keep under wraps for now.

We didn't even get to the report. I really did make a mess of Jake's lap today. I chuckle a little at the memory of his face as the milkshake splashed across the table. We agreed to meet on Monday on my way to the lupus compound just inside the head of the secret trail. It will be one of the last days I can walk between programs. The temperature seems to be dropping with each passing day. It reminds me that my hands are going numb, the feel of reins disappearing under my fingers. My toes, pressed down against the stirrups, are beginning to lose sensation.

Robbie and I turn the last corner on the well-worn trail and head back for the barn. Sensing a return to his cozy stall, Robbie picks up to a trot. I pat him across the neck, tangling my fingers in his mane. I lie down over my saddle, rest my head against his withers, and sigh.

"If only it were this easy to share my heart with all the boys in my life."

Draeger and Ashton arrive at the university without incident after transferring directly from the airport. There is minimal conversation between the men. Ashton is wholly unprepared for this encounter, having been told little to nothing about the host agents. He dares not ask any questions. Their footsteps echo in the hollow corridor leading to the research lab of the mysterious Dr. Castillo.

The door swings inward almost before Draeger has finished knocking.

"*Sí, sí,* Dr. Draeger. Please come in."

José Castillo holds the door and beckons Draeger and Ashton into the lab. The aging doctor is as disheveled as ever with his uncombed shock of gray-white hair, scruffy chin, and rumpled beige cotton pants that would look dirty even if freshly laundered, which they are not. He wears the same tattered gray cardigan with the patchy elbows. Even his eyebrows could use some taming. But for his sharp, clear blue eyes, he could pass for an ancient lunatic.

Ashton is taken aback by both the man and his lab. The disarray and disorganization are such a sharp contrast to his strict, disciplined approach to person and purpose, it's an affront to his senses. Ashton follows Draeger closely into the lab, standing as far away from the chaos as the space permits. Paper is strewn every which way or stacked in untidy piles that could topple at any moment. Ashton counts five coffee cups and three empty bowls mixed in with the paper. And is that a partially eaten sandwich?

Draeger, tactful as ever, uses the tableau to disarm the doctor. "Dr. Castillo, I can see you are as busy as ever. The Biodome is so lucky to have such dedicated agents as you."

Ashton watched as Castillo is lulled into the trap.

"Ah, *sí*. Yes indeed, Dr. Draeger. We have multiple research programs underway. It can be difficult to keep up with the data." The doctor gives a subdued chuckle. "Pedro was just about to begin filing the records."

"Ah, yes, your young acolyte. We have not been reacquainted as of yet," Draeger returns.

Ashton has been around long enough to detect Draeger's agitation at the mention of this Pedro.

Castillo glances at Ashton. "And this I presume, is your, er, acolyte?" He stumbles and then skips over the young part altogether.

Draeger's reply is tinged with amusement. "Dr. Castillo, allow me to introduce you to Garrett Ashton, my gifted associate."

Ashton feels like a ten-year-old boy who was just patted on the head by his schoolteacher for a correct answer. He lifts his shoulders and rises to his full height. Even stooped over in age, Castillo towers over him as he lumbers over and extends a hand.

"A pleasure to meet you, Mr. Ashton."

Ashton is about to correct Castillo on his proper title, but Draeger permits no more pleasantries.

"Gentlemen, let us get to the matter at hand. Dr. Castillo, we are in need of your research record on the *Tetrapodophis amplectus* file."

Not exactly a command but not a request either.

Castillo becomes visibly uneasy at the mention of the project. "Ah, Dr. Draeger, I am afraid that program has been suspended."

"Go on," is all Draeger says in return.

"Well, you see, sir, we have been unable to locate the specimen. The GPS tracker has somehow failed to transmit the signal since, well, not long after we released it to its natural habitat, I'm afraid."

Ashton looks to his handler, completely oblivious and utterly perplexed.

Draeger pays him no mind. "That is unfortunate."

Ashton discerns no hint of surprise at Castillo's revelation. He realizes Draeger already knew about this development. How he came to know this information is another matter altogether.

"What of the preliminary investigation into the specimen prior its release?"

"Er, yes, indeed. We did do some anatomical cataloguing and some comparative physiological analysis using the ancient artifact, and yes, of course, we completed the genomic and proteomic sequencing that confirmed the genus."

Ashton lights up at the mention of the genome. Draeger gives nothing away, but Ashton intuits that Castillo has said something pleasing to his superior as well.

"That will suffice for now, Dr. Castillo. The file, if you please."

Castillo stares at Draeger for a moment, seemingly unsure of how to proceed. Draeger offers a terse explanation as if lecturing to a child. The condescension makes Ashton cringe.

"Dr. Castillo, as the lead agent for the DAW, it is my responsibility to ensure that the Biodome has an accurate and complete registry of all species discovered on our great planet. Your discovery has sat in obscurity for much too long. Despite this ... setback with your tracking device, I am still obligated to account for the existence of the creature."

This explanation seems to make sense to Castillo, who shares a similar expression of acquiescence with Ashton.

"Of course, Dr. Draeger. Let me find the file."

Castillo looks around the lab sheepishly. There are stacks of files and loose documents everywhere. He's unsure of the location of the file. Just then, the door to the lab creaks on rusty hinges and Pedro enters the room. He looks at his mentor and then to Ashton. Finally, his gaze rests on Draeger. The temperature in the room seems to drop several degrees as Draeger's manner transforms from cordial to ominous.

Castillo turns to his young aide. "Ah, as if by divine intervention, Pedro has saved me from an embarrassing moment."

At the mention of the divine, vehemence emanates from Draeger. Ashton takes a step back, sensing the rage. Either because of his age or his social ineptitude, Castillo doesn't notice the change in atmosphere.

"Dear Pedro, would you please retrieve the *amplectus* project file from its current, um, resting place?"

His gaze darts around the room and back. Pedro looks slowly from his mentor to Draeger and Ashton before walking over to possibly the most orderly stack of files in the lab. He flips through the tabs on the folders and pulls out one of the larger files, which is bursting with documents. He walks over to Castillo and extends the file.

"Dr. Draeger requires the file," the doctor says, looking at Pedro's outstretched hand.

Pedro's expression becomes panicked. "Dr. C., is that wise? We may yet resume the project once we, er, sort out some logistical issues." Pedro seems to plead with his eyes as he stares down the old doctor.

"Yes, well, be that as it may, Dr. Draeger is required to catalogue our findings in the Biodome archive," Castillo returns, embarrassed at his junior agent's mild insubordination.

Pedro tries again. "But, sir, I have not yet prepared the final report. This is but raw data. The analysis and interpretation have not yet been completed. In fact, I saw no need to begin since the project has been suspended."

At this, Draeger seems to relax somewhat.

Ashton steps forward and begins to speak. "No matter. I am an experienced ..." Draeger moves in front of him. Ashton is keenly aware that the curt interruption is a warning.

"Yes, Mr. Ashton is an experienced archivist. He knows precisely how to file inactive projects. Of course, you will inform us when you have resolved your ... logistical issues, and he will change the project status in the Biodome Archive."

Pedro hands the dossier to Draeger, making no attempt to disguise his obvious reluctance. An unspoken exchange between the two concludes with Draeger delicately seizing the file and, in turn, handing it over to Ashton. Castillo pierces the awkward silence by instructing Pedro to check on the progress of the Goliath frog genealogy study. The boy concedes and leaves the lab without uttering another word.

Pedro walks briskly to his cubicle in the research lounge, opens his laptop computer, and drums his fingers impatiently against his desk while the machine lumbers to life. Deftly clicking through files, he lands on his intended target. With two keystrokes, the *Tetrapodophis amplectus* final genomic report is sent from his computer's recycling bin into oblivion.

Before turning in later that the night, Pedro prays to his God for understanding and forgiveness for his mendacities of the day. He sleeps restlessly, fretting over the righting protocol to come. But he wakes the next morning feeling refreshed and with a renewed vigor he has not felt since early boyhood.

The men sit in silence in the back of the black sedan on the final leg of their return to AW headquarters. Ashton is still pouring over the data from the Castillo file, intent on gaining the intellectual upper hand. Of all his personal handicaps, deficits in mental acumen do not figure among them. His concentration breaks with the sound of Draeger's voice.

"Mr. Ashton, I require your assurance that there is sufficient information in the file to develop a genetic profile for comparative purposes." Draeger continues to stare straight ahead.

"Um, well, sir, it looks like we do indeed have the whole genome sequence. However, it is nothing but the raw sequence. The exon-intron boundaries have not been identified. It will be impossible to run the intron prediction algorithms without the original electronic sequence."

He relishes in flexing his scientific brain power, gaining momentum as he pieces together the mystery of the file.

"The best I can do with this data is a manual comparison with our reference sequence. If I can find strings of matching base pairs and align the sequences, I may be able to provide an estimate of the ancestral similitude between the two sequences."

And now the bad news. His insecurity resurfaces.

"But ... However... a high incidence of genetic mutation in one sample or the other will certainly undermine this effort." Doubt creeps into his voice.

Now Draeger glances over at his assistant, askance without words.

"You see, sir, genetic material is susceptible to selective pressure, mutations in the DNA sequence in response to environmental stress to ensure the survival of the species."

Draeger considers a moment. "Survival of this particular species is exactly what I have in mind."

Ashton senses some hidden meaning in this last remark but

remains tight-lipped the rest of the ride to headquarters. Better not to know.

Upon arrival, he heads directly for his makeshift lab. He settles into his comfortable office chair and plops both files in front of him.

What in the name of the Biodome does some lizard have to do with Agent 4004? How could they possibly be genetically connected? Where is he going with this?

Ashton failed to enunciate these questions earlier while he had the chance. He simply nodded and agreed to the ridiculously abbreviated timeline Draeger had assigned. Resigned to a long afternoon that was sure to stretch well into the evening, Ashton eats only a portion of his lunch, leaving the apple and bag of figs for later when he will feel the effects of the drop in blood sugar and fatigue will set in. He opens his file on Agent 4004 and examines the sex chromosome graft. Seventeen thousand one hundred and ninety-one base pairs of unknown origin.

How am I ever going to align the sequences with no reference point and no way of knowing where the DNA is coding and when it is not?

He considers that finding regions with strings of matching pairs for 10 percent of the genome will be a tremendous success. Finding those regions will be like looking for a needle in a haystack.

Well, here goes nothing, Ashton tells himself.

He opens Castillo's file and performs a cursory review of the data—a printout of 17,191 base pairs.

CHAPTER 21

A curse causeless cannot rest upon anyone unless there is a reason for it.
—Proverbs 26:2 (KJV)

I AM JOGGING ON the spot, trying to maintain circulation to my extremities. This is definitely not sitting around weather. I didn't even taste my lunch. I ploughed through it, hand to mouth, not even registering what I ate. I left the equine center with twenty minutes to spare, in such a hurry to meet up with Jake. Now here I am, waiting in the cold prewinter air. I'll have to shuttle bus it between the equine and lupus programs for the next couple of months. Which means today is the last day I will see Jake. And I still don't know why he is avoiding human contact. He can deny it all he wants, but I am certain that something is up with him.

Now I see him bouncing up the trail coming from the direction of the oval lab. He has his bag slung across his chest, pulling against his royal blue bomber jacket. The color against his face only serves to make his eyes even more striking. He is open and cheerful when he greets me.

"Hey, Evey. You look a little chilly."

"You don't say," I return with a mixture of humor and sarcasm. "You, on the other hand, look quite exuberant."

"Well, yes, as I should be. I told you there was nothing to worry about." He pulls the green report cover out of his bag, the same one he had at the coffee shop on Saturday. "I looked it over. I came up aces."

He flicks open the cover and clears his throat as if to orate an important speech. "Agent 4004, existential virus intact, all mutations present in host genome consistent with reference genomes."

The acerbic feeling in the pit of my stomach that I've been carrying around since I first realized I was immune to righting protocols is already starting to fade. If EV is alive and well in Jake, she must also be alive and well in me. I never thought I would be so relieved that I have the existential virus just like everyone else; she's just a little more lenient for me and Jake. Is it even possible that I might be looking forward to my first correction? It seems strange, but oddly enough, I think it is true.

"That's it?" I ask, eyeing a lot more paper than would be required for that single statement.

"Oh, no. Ashton even gave me the genetic report. Well, actually, I told him my mom wanted it, so this is technically for her, but I got the gist of it. A roadmap of where to find EV. See?"

Flourishing the report, he continues, "Each page is a set of chromosomes, and these circles"—he points at the black rings around each pair of chromosomes—"is an EV mutation. And here"—he points at the jumble of miniature print across each page—"are the different strain sequences."

He flips through the pages and lands on the last one. "This one is pretty cool. It's only on one X chromosome. See, that's a guy thing, because I don't have that extra tail on the Y. Cause I'm a cool c-c-cat."

I laugh at that. "*What* are you going on about?"

"See? CCCAT, CCCAT—they're everywhere in my special boys-only mutation."

My first thought is that I don't recall there being differences between boys and girls. EV is EV. My second takes me to the long nights I spent staring at the file. A footnote: *Repetitive sequence units unique to squamate species.*

What? This is nonsense. A flush comes over me, bringing heat to my face, washing away the chill.

"Uh, Jake, can I see that report for a minute?"

"Really? You don't believe me?" Still lighthearted, he hasn't noticed my sudden uneasiness. "Here you go."

He extends his hand, and I retrieve the report gingerly, taking care to respect his personal space. I flip to the karyogram, all of Jake's chromosomes lined up side by side, dyed in the lab so they look like wobbly little earthworms, and numbered one through twenty-two with the last pair marked X and Y. Jake is right. On the bottom right of the X in the XY pair, extending downward, there is a single black circle, an EV mutant embedded in the genetic code. I wonder which one it is. One of the newer mutations, I assume, although I am not sure why I do.

I zoom out, now focusing on the entire image, seeing perfectly paired circles spread out in the genome. One set on the first pair of chromosomes, two on the second, three on the third, one on the fourth, two on the fifth, three on the sixth, one on the seventh, two on the eighth. I see the pattern now. Leave it to EV. The distribution of her genetic code is not random at all but rather a very orderly repeating pattern. It stops with one set of circles on pair sixteen. I am puzzled at first, but when I add them up, one plus two plus three plus one plus two plus three, every three chromosomes represent six versions of EV. It is so mathematically eloquent. Thirty mutations are accounted for by pair fifteen, and one more on pair sixteen accounts for EV's thirty-one mutations.

If the pattern holds true, EV has left herself room for fourteen more mutations in the human host. She is brilliant. My eye travels to the last pair of chromosomes and the lone circle. So what is this then? This does not make any sense. I flip page after page until I get to the XY chromosome. The same picture is at the top left-hand corner and then a string of genetic code, As, Cs, Gs, and Ts, thousands upon thousands of them packed together like sardines, line after line with no spacing. It is dizzying. Spots swim before my eyes. I feel dissociated. I recognize this code. I've seen this code. I know this code. There they are, the CCCAT strings everywhere, the GTAAA strings everywhere. I look to the end of the sequence, at the base pair count: 17,191.

I step back, my blood rushing in my ears and my heart pounding through my chest wall. This makes absolutely no sense. My brain must be scrambled. I am confused. Not enough sleep or too much sleep maybe. Now Jake is alert to my distress.

"Evey, Ev, what's wrong? You look like you're going to faint."

I shake my head and force myself to look at Jake. I need to regain my wits.

"Just losing my mind is all." I chuckle but don't elaborate. Instead, I redirect the conversation toward sane, rational thought.

"You know, Jake, your boys-only mutation cannot possibly be EV."

Now it's Jake's turn to look confused.

"Of course it is, Evey. The report even says EV is alive and well."

"Well, yes, it does, but this last mutation does not fit the pattern, for one. And it's the thirty-second mutation, which makes no sense whatsoever. Unless you've become the host to a new EV mutant." I laugh at the absurdity of my comment. "It's funny. I could have sworn I've seen that genetic code before, though, in the Halimand-Castonguay report. I need more sleep."

Now Jake looks downright feverish. As if he is about to turn and run. From me?

"Whoa, Jake. What in the Biodome? Are you feeling all right?"

"I have to go now."

"Seriously? This again? What is with you, Jake? You claim there is nothing going on with you, but I'm not buying it. If you don't trust me or care about me enough after all this time, after I poured my heart out to you, after everything we've been through …" I don't even finish the sentence. My bitterness and resentment are growing with each word.

I realize my cheeks are wet, yet I am angry and frustrated and extremely disappointed.

"Just go, Jake. Go. I won't darken your doorstep ever again."

I throw the report on the ground at his feet and turn to head back up the secret trail toward the main path. I'm not cold anymore. In fact, I welcome the raw wind against my face.

"Everett, wait."

Jake is still standing in the same spot when I turn around.

"Jake, I've been doing nothing but waiting." I say this with a heavy sigh.

"I know, but you don't understand, Everett." My full name on his lips tells me he is being serious.

"You're right. I don't," I shoot back.

He walks toward me now, speaking softly, "I didn't want to hurt you."

"Well, too late for that." I am being sharp again, but I can't help it in the moment.

"No, I mean I didn't want to *hurt* you," he overemphasizes the verb.

I pause, not sure of myself anymore. "What are you talking about, Jake? You would never hurt me, like *hurt* me hurt me." Now I'm babbling like a fool.

He is standing in front of me now. I look up at him to see tears welling in his eyes. He lifts his hands out in front of him, palms up, waiting. I hesitate and then slowly lift my hands and place them in his.

Jake is dressed in white, in a white room with bricks falling all around him, revealing deadly snakes that fall one by one at his feet. The last snake appears, dispersing the larger, more menacing creatures. The snake periscopes and then compresses its raised body into a tight S configuration. And then it strikes. Jake's eyes snap open and pain rips through his left calf.

For one brief instant I hear his innermost thought: *I remember.*

The images fly by my face as if I am in a time warp. Armed uprisings, insurrections, rebellions, revolutions, hate crimes. The Pinochet Regime, the Rwandan genocide, the firebombing of Germany, Stalinist Russia, the British Empire, the Iraq war. Death, destruction, destitution. And with each image, a jolt of pain, brutal and raw, tears right through my soul as if I am being riddled with ancient bullets.

I jerk my hands away from Jake and stagger backward, my eyes wide open now but seeing nothing. Murky darkness. Slowly, light bleeds first into my peripheral vision, and then I begin to make out the silhouette of the boy standing in front of me, black on white. It takes several moments for the world to come into focus, for the wind screaming in my ears to fade, for the thunder rolling in my chest to wither.

Jake slumps to the cold ground and curls into a ball on his side, holding his knees to his chest, his back to me. I collect myself. Falling apart right now is not going to do either one of us any good. I stare at Jake for a long moment, afraid, actually afraid, to approach him.

"Jake, I, I don't understand," I stammer.

Either he doesn't hear me or he is ignoring me. I am about to try again when he stops rocking and whispers, "I don't understand either, Evey. It was a dream. It was just a dream."

I am utterly dumbfounded. I wait, my breathing still ragged, not sure what to say or do. Jake sits up and starts again, agony written all over his face.

"And now I know I can't cut it out. I can't get rid of it. It's in my DNA."

My mind is reeling. The extra XY sequence, the one that doesn't belong, the one that can't possibly be part of the existential virus. The one I could have sworn I'd stared at a dozen times in my bedroom late at night when sleep eluded me. The repeating sequences unique to the squamate species. Jake removes his left shoe and rolls his pant leg up to the knee. He stands, not caring that his socked foot is resting on the cold soil, and turns around. I see two puncture wounds, side by side, trickling with blood. Slow, lazy rivulets meander down his leg.

"Jake, is that what I think it is?"

My feet carry me backward of their own volition. He turns toward me, the betrayal written all over his face. I understand now why he has been keeping this secret. He knew I would react this way. And I am rising to the occasion, my cowardice on full display. I am ashamed of my behavior.

It's still Jake, my Jake.

I force myself to move toward him, to stand right in front of him, close enough to touch, but I don't initiate contact. His expression changes, softens, as if he is comforted by this meager gesture. He lifts his hands and then brings them back down and holds them unnaturally tight against his side.

"The day we found the flash drive, I had a dream that night. I couldn't remember it, not until just now. I was locked in a room, a white room with no windows or doors. Snakes, all different kinds of terrifying snakes, started pouring out of the walls and slithering around my feet. I couldn't move. I just stood there watching as more and more of them came out of nowhere. Then the last one, it seemed to be the leader because all the other snakes shrank away from it, bit me. But it was just a dream."

I am momentarily stunned. I don't understand how, but I do know why.

"Jake, that's Draeger's snake. *You* are Draeger's snake. Do you know what this means?"

Jake looks me dead in the eye and says with no inflection or emotion in his voice, "It means I am the secret weapon, the tool he needs to annihilate the annihilator."

CHAPTER 22

And they may come to their senses and escape from the snare of the devil, after being captured by him to do his will.

—Timothy 2:26 (ESV)

ASHTON IS PACING, HANDS clasped behind his back, chin low, and grumbling to himself. He's not distraught from disappointment or misfortune but rather from sheer incredulity. And from the uneasiness of knowing that he is about to share his newfound information with a dark man, a dangerous man, a tyrant.

Looking around the office, avoiding the macabre painting behind the posh executive desk, Ashton stops in front of the small library. A collection of texts is neatly arranged on an ornate bookshelf with intricate carvings woven in the corners of the wood. Some of the texts appear ancient; there are leather-bound tomes, volumes written on parchment, and handwritten scripts in calligraphical precision. Epictetus, St. Augustine, Plato, Aristotle, Descartes, Hobbes, Leibniz, Locke, Spinoza, Hume, Kant, Kierkegaard, Nietzsche, Edwards. Ashton notices black satin bookmarks throughout the collection.

Unable to contain his curiosity, he carefully pulls one from the shelf. It shares the same title with seven others, *The Discourses of Epictetus*, and dates back to 108 AD. Like the painting behind the desk, every piece in the collection is original. Draeger would have nothing less.

Sliding his thumb and forefinger down the silk tassel, he gently opens the book to an underlined passage. It reads, "He who is free in the body but bound in the soul is a slave; but on the contrary he who is bound in the body but free in the soul is truly free." He replaces the text and pulls out another, *Plato's Republic*, penned in 375 BC, with similarly marked pages. Once again, he follows the black silk ribbon to "The Allegory of the Cave." A saturnine play of sorts, a conversation between Socrates and Plato's brother, Glaucon, about people shackled by the leg and neck in a deep underground dwelling for their entire lives, staring at a wall with only man-made shadows projected on the cave wall as their reality. Then one is set free. Ashton's Latin is rudimentary, but he manages to follow the freed prisoner's first encounter with sunlight and the real world, his enlightenment, and his return to the cave where he tries to free his fellow prisoners so they may be enlightened as well.

And there, in gentle pencil strokes, is Draeger's distinct interest in the piece.

> SOCRATES: Now if once again, along with those who had remained shackled there, the freed person had to engage in the business of asserting and maintaining opinions about the shadows—while his eyes are still weak and before they have readjusted, an adjustment that would require quite a bit of time—would he not then be exposed to ridicule down there? And would they not let him know that he had gone up but only in order to come back down into the cave with his

> eyes ruined—and thus it certainly does not pay to go up. And the final outcome:
>
> SOCRATES: And if they can get hold of this person who takes it in hand to free them from their chains and to lead them up, and if they could kill him, will they not actually kill him?
>
> GLAUCON: They certainly will.

Ashton feels bile rising in his throat. He replaces the book and moves along the collection to more modern-looking texts. There is an entire section of works by Friedrich Nietzsche that seem to be to Draeger's liking. A number of silk ribbons poke out of eerie titles like *The Antichrist* and *The Birth of Tragedy.* He pulls out Nietzsche's *Gay Science* and the bookmark leads to another underlined passage: "Do we hear nothing as yet of the noise of the gravediggers who are burying God? Do we smell nothing as yet of the divine decomposition? Gods, too, decompose. God is dead. God remains dead. And we have killed him."

Ashton closes the volume and returns it to its resting place on the shelf. He wrings his hands self-consciously in front of him as if trying to wash away some invisible grime. He is still standing in front of the bookshelf when Draeger walks into the room, causing him to flinch ever so slightly.

"Mr. Ashton, I see that you are acquainting yourself with the forefathers of existentialism, the brilliant minds that paved the way for the doctrine of free will."

Ashton composes his features to project mild interest as he turns to face his superior. "Yes, sir. You have quite an impressive collection." He tries for nonchalance.

"It is not the quantity but rather the quality of the anthology that is of import." Draeger roves the shelves with his deep-set black eyes. "Orators of the real truth of the human condition."

Ashton steps away from the books, feeling sullied by their proximity. He walks over to the small table and leans his attaché case against the leg of the table. Draeger settles into his chair and leans on the perfectly polished desk. He says nothing more, observing Ashton through a critical glower, as if suddenly unsure of his character. Ashton clears his throat and projects his best scientific self, removing any hint of emotional strife.

"Sir, I am afraid Dr. Castillo's sample did not yield any fruit in the search for Agent 4004's mysterious graft."

Ashton looks up now, meeting Draeger's gaze, determined to bury any doubts or misgivings he may have planted in the man's incredibly perceptive mind. A wave of reactions passes over Draeger's façade: confusion followed by disappointment and then fury. He rests his elbows on the desk and leans forward, his hands cupping his face as he watches Ashton. A bead of perspiration collects on the assistant's upper lip; he can taste the salt seeping into his mouth at the corners. He suppresses the need to shudder and stands firm in front of his oppressor.

No longer his lead agent or his teacher or his mentor but his enemy. The two men stare at one another for a long moment until Ashton's eyes look to the ancient painting behind Draeger. His gaze lands on the third triptych to the right, Draeger's black hair blending into the black artwork. This elicits the ghost of a smile from Draeger's stony face.

He stands now, moving lazily to the front of the desk, in no hurry. Keeping his eyes trained on Ashton, he closes the gap between them and reaches down to retrieve Ashton's briefcase. Ashton steps back from the table, not daring to object. He watches as Draeger carefully lifts the leather flap and peers at the contents. It takes him but an instant to identify the documents contained in a green file folder. He lifts the file from the briefcase, carefully replaces the flap, and sets the case back down against the leg of the table exactly how Ashton placed it.

Drager returns to his seat behind his desk and places the file, unopened, in front of him. Another moment of painful silence passes, and then he speaks casually, trivially.

"Did you know, Mr. Ashton, that I come from eminent parentage. In fact, my patriarch is still quite celebrated even to this very day. Being descended from this lineage affords me certain advantages when the need arises to, shall we say, manage a situation."

Ashton swallows the thick saliva collecting at the back of his throat and blinks rapidly several times, trying desperately to devise an intelligent rejoinder.

Draeger continues, "No need to respond, Mr. Ashton. Allow me to demonstrate."

He rises regally, with all the pomp and circumstance of an ancient emperor.

"Please," he beckons Ashton closer.

As if his feet are encased in concrete, Ashton forces one foot in front of the other until he is standing at the edge of the desk, twenty-four inches of polished ebony wood separating the two men.

"My paterfamilias is known by many names, but the most endearing moniker that comes to mind in the present circumstance is one of my personal favorites. The Father of Lies."

With that, Draeger reaches across the desk and grasps Ashton's hands in his. Ashton squeezes his eyes shut. Searing pain, blackness, suffering, torture, fire. When he finally opens them, he is inside an illustrious courtroom. Richly stained wall-to-wall fluted mahogany panels and oversized decorative crown molding frame Michelangelo Buonarroti's *The Last Judgement* rendered in splendid detail in a fresco covering the entire ceiling. A lush crimson carpet mutes the echo in the large chamber. Amber-stained lighting is recessed along the perimeter of the wall, and a single red spotlight points directly at Ashton, the light from it casting eerie shadows in the corners.

He is sitting in a fine wooden chair in the middle of the room with no other props. On a dais in front of him sit three bearded, white-haired men, wizened with age. With skin thin as parchment, thick, tarnished gray-white robes, and bare feet, they look more like wraiths than corporeal forms. No one speaks.

The first aged one enters Ashton's mind, seeking the truth, and learns that Ashton has deceived a prince of darkness. Ashton feels the creature leave his psyche, seemingly satisfied with its probe. The second one enters his heart, seeking his true emotions, and discovers that Ashton holds no allegiance to the prince's cause. Ashton's heart flutters, and the weight on his chest dissipates as the specter departs his body. The third penetrates his core, joining with his soul, seeking his greatest fear. Ashton is compelled to reveal his childhood secrets, his longing to belong and to be loved, but buried deeper in the young and now adult Ashton is a more primal need for intellectual superiority above all else, as well as the subsequent fear of losing his perspicacity, his scientific acumen, his gifted status.

The third specter learns that Ashton defines himself by his intellectual curiosity and his computational mastery. His worst nightmare is of himself as academically obscure. Ashton feels the wraith release his soul, as his thoughts and emotions once again become his own. The courtroom remains silent as the wraiths take his measure, each nodding once in turn. By the time Draeger releases his hands, Ashton is reduced to puerility and eternal damnation.

Jake enters the inner oval and walks the aisle between rows of stainless-steel tables. Krista and Danielle are seated together, their faces perched over their electron microscopes, minds deep in concentration. A little farther along, a serious-looking agent Jake does not recognize, a bit older than Jake, sits alone, alternately scribbling notes on a yellow notepad and typing furiously on his laptop computer. He looks over at Jake and nods with no smile and then quickly returns to tapping on his keyboard. There are a few more agents, two more pairs, one he recognizes as Todd and Christopher, and two individuals, Jasmine and Carmen, spread out among the tables, all engrossed in their tasks. The blue chamber is currently unoccupied.

Business as usual, Jake thinks. *Just another day at the oval.*

Nobody stares. There are no displays of concern for Jake's presence. In fact, there is a general indifference toward the transporter among them.

Nobody knows anything, Jake reminds himself. *I am being paranoid.*

He casually approaches Halimand and Castonguay's last lab space, the same one Ashton used until fairly recently. No one has seen or heard from Mr. Ashton in almost three weeks. He was becoming a permanent fixture in the oval lab. His sudden and extended absence of late reminds Jake of Derek and Renee. They, too, were abruptly redirected or reassigned. No one seems to know for sure.

The last time Jake spoke with Ashton, he was moving equipment and packing up his research in preparation for his return to headquarters. He was amicable, even downright cheerful. Perhaps that was it then. Ashton's field deployment is simply no longer required. He is content to have returned to his home base and none too anxious for any more trips to the Midwest campus.

Jake walks between the tables where Ashton was stationed. Scant remnants of his presence remain, including a rather ostentatious black fountain pen with gold trimmings on the barrel, a clean coffee cup at the ready, a recycling bin with paper in it, and a wrinkled napkin. There is also a biohazard bin, currently empty, and a waste receptacle with a single scrunched-up sheet of paper at the bottom.

Odd, since all paper is recycled. Improper disposal is a transgression worthy of a generally mild righting protocol, EV 11 or perhaps 15, just enough to remind agents to be mindful of the environmental impacts of their actions and dutiful in their service to the Biodome.

Jake being Jake, he reaches into the waste bin to retrieve the misplaced paper and put it in the proper receptacle. Suddenly curious, he smooths the sheet with his hands against the tabletop.

Just in case it's something important, he tells himself.

There on the white page is a remarkable artistic rendering of what can only be Dr. Draeger. Perfectly coiffed black hair, tall and lanky form, stylish three-piece suit lightly shaded, complete with breast pocket and black kerchief. Sharp, elegant features are topped off with perfectly shaped eyes colored in darkest black.

Jake eyebrows crease and his heart stumbles when he sees two horns protruding on either side of Draeger's forehead and a forked tail dragging behind him.

We are sitting in a corner booth in the coffee shop. Snow swirls outside the large windows fronting Main Street. The big fluffy flakes hit the glass panes and melt away like tears collecting on the sill.

"You're doing what, Jake?"

I did not see this coming.

"Evey, I need to get away from Draeger. I can't do that if I stay in the DAW. I need this transfer."

Jake is unsettled.

"But, Jake, Draeger isn't even here. He hasn't been back since Ashton left. Besides, he doesn't know anything. We made sure of that."

I don't have to mention the flash drive. Jake knows exactly what I'm talking about. And I really don't have to mention what Draeger doesn't know, the invisible line down the middle of our table that neither one of us crosses is reminder enough of that "what." Jake is not impulsive. He's thought this through. There's more here than he is letting on.

"I just don't feel comfortable there anymore. I need a change of scenery."

Two explanations in one sentence. Without a doubt something is going on.

"Jake, how are you going to transfer now? You are not even on the DAW Midwest register. Agent 4004 is on special assignment."

I am trying to reason with him, but I can tell his heels are dug in deep.

"Well, he's just going to have to release me. I'm just a transporter. There are more than enough of us."

"But they are still doing research in the oval, right?"

Jake mentioned that he saw several lab agents toiling away just last week.

"That's true, but Ashley and Tyler can handle it. Plus, they have Andy from the maintenance team who sometimes helps out."

"If lab agents are still looking, that means you are safe, Jake. We are safe."

Again, I try to persuade him to stay. Is it because I truly think he is safe or because the thought of not seeing him anymore is chewing a hole in my chest? I need Jake in my life. Even though I can't touch him at the moment, I need to see his face, hear his voice. That's good enough for now.

Maybe he's running from me. How do I reassure him that my feelings have not changed? In fact, they may even be stronger now. Forbidden fruit and all that. How do I make him understand what he means to me even though I don't really even understand it myself?

In the midst of my own little internal dialogue, Jenny and Trevor walk into the shop. Snowflakes have settled in Jenny's long brown curls and on top of Trevor's blue striped tuque. Jenny spots me in the corner, but she is not her usual bubbly, energetic self. She appears to be consoling Trevor. I am alarmed. I have been so out of touch with my old gang, I have no idea why they are upset. Now I'm feeling guilty for neglecting my childhood friends.

"Er, Jake, would you excuse me for one second? I just want to say hello to some old friends."

"Of course. I want to look over this recruitment pamphlet. Take your time."

The leaflet in his hand is from the Department of Agriculture, highlighting the Bucolic Farming Program. Obviously he has put a lot of thought into this. He's already looking into other departments and programs. I heard about that program. It does sound quite interesting. Part farmland remediation and part reconstitution of livestock desecrated by ancient industrial farming practices. Massive swaths of land eroded and robbed of all nutrients from monocropping, synthetic fertilizers, pesticides, salinization, acidification—the ancient assault on farmlands was egregious. To say nothing of the abject cruelty bestowed upon millions of farm animals at the hands of the morally corrupt in the name of profit.

With EV and the Biodome came the recognition that sentient creatures have physical, emotional, and social needs much like human beings. Agriculturalists who continued to deny animals their rights and refused to change their farming practices after the Correction were dispatched with EV7, ironically known as the ancient swine flu.

I must admit, I think a rural outdoorsy atmosphere with easygoing, happy-go-lucky dairy cows and quirky barnyard fowl is exactly what Jake needs these days.

"Hold that thought, Jake. I'll be right back."

I make my way over to Jenny and Trevor, who are huddled over their table, talking in hushed tones.

"Hey guys," I interrupt, "long time no see."

Jenny speaks first. "Evey, it sure has been a while."

Ever since I put the brakes on my relationship with Matt, I've been pretty coy, trying to avoid awkward situations for both of us and our mutual friends. Now I can see that Trevor is troubled. His overgrown brown mane is falling into his downturned face.

"Hey, Trevor. Everything OK?" My concern is genuine.

Jenny looks to Trevor, who nods slightly, and then pats the bench seat beside her. I glance over at Jake. His face buried in the pamphlet. I'll just sit for a minute. I slide into the booth beside Jenny but stay out of Trevor's space as if his melancholy is a contagion.

"Go ahead, Jen." Trevor sighs. "Everyone is going to know soon enough anyway."

"Um, well ..." Jenny hesitates as if building up her nerve. "So, Trevor's mom sort of stepped out of her marriage."

I'm not following. Stepped out? What is she talking about? Jenny can see I am confused.

"She had an affair, Evey. With an agent in her department."

Whoa, that doesn't seem possible. Sins of the flesh are as old as time itself. Adultery was eradicated during the Correction. The family is the nucleus of the Biodome. Marriage is a sacred covenant in the Age of Resolve. Many in the new order choose not to marry for that reason. It is as much a commitment to oneself as it is to another.

I already know I want to marry one day. My cheeks flush, and I glance back at my table at this fleeting thought as if Jake can read my mind. In ancient times, marriage was but a trifle. People hopped in and out of matrimony like rabbits with more than half of marriages ending in divorce. Infidelity was the most common cause of these matrimonial failures. Once EV implemented righting protocols on adulterers, marital rates plummeted as the gravity of the marital contract became evident. People now wait much longer to wed, and marriage has become a stable and sheltered institution.

I am afraid to ask what ailment beset Trevor's mother for her transgression. I remember stories from the time of the Correction of a proliferation of EV5 infections, herpetic skin lesions on the mouth and, if the stories were true, even worse ones on unseen body parts. Surely this outward display of infection must be what outed Mrs. Montague. Trying to be tactful and sympathetic, I look at Trevor.

"It will be OK, Trev. Your mom will get better once the righting protocol has run its course. It just looks bad now, but things will settle down."

Trevor shakes his head.

"That's not it, Evey."

Huh? I don't get it. What is Trevor talking about?

Jenny takes over. "Mrs. Montague *admitted* to her indiscretion out of guilt, Evey. She said she was waiting for EV to end the affair."

I am really lost now.

"What are you saying, Jen?"

Jenny and Trevor both look up and make eye contact as Jenny finishes. "The righting protocol never came."

CHAPTER 23

Ask, and it will be given to you; seek, and you will find; knock, and it will be opened to you.

—Matthew 7:7 (ESV)

JAKE ENTERS THE OUTER oval from the southeastern overhead door, carrying a box of lab supplies. The cool spring air rushes in from the large opening, washing over the corner of the oval and bringing a much-needed airiness into the stale space.

As if by radar, Jake immediately spots Draeger perusing the aisles of stainless steel, stopping at each research station as if to inspect project progress. He notices how the agents become visibly tense as he approaches. It's as though a rod has been rammed down their spines. They instantly square their shoulders and stiffen their cores. Draeger stands, hands clasped behind his back, watching for a moment or two, saying nothing, asking nothing, and then carries on to the next workstation.

Jake rolls his eyes at the perpetually overdressed doctor. Today he wears the deepest navy three-piece suit, perfectly tailored as always. His pale gray dress shirt is crisp with starch and emboldened with sapphire cufflinks big enough that Jake spots them even at this distance.

He moves like a cat, he thinks, watching the man glide from station to station with an inhuman stealth. He appears to be distracted, his gaze sweeping the outer oval as if he is looking for something. Or someone. Jake is keenly aware when Draeger's eyes land on him and stay there, watching him without even the slightest turn of his head. A predator locked onto its prey.

Jake is flushed with exertion, his messy dark blond locks blowing into his face from the rush of wind behind him and his pale blue spring windbreaker billowing as if to take flight. Draeger is scrutinizing. Jake feels the weight of the stare, the appraisal. He enters the inner oval, trying to quell the apprehension building with each step. It has been more than four months since he last saw Draeger standing on his front porch. That same feeling of unease bubbles to the surface. Jake watches the imposing doctor from the corner of his eye while he scans the oval, looking for the destination of the lab supplies. He feigns disinterest and walks in the opposite direction toward the front of the oval with his package.

His nerves are raw. He was not expecting Draeger, but now is his chance to ask for the transfer. He had thought Ashton would be the one supervising. He would be much more comfortable asking the podgy little assistant for the transfer. But he is not going to squander this opportunity. While working up the courage to approach Dr. Draeger—the man who makes him downright squirmy—Jake begins rehearsing the ask in his head, coaching himself to be assertive and not pleading.

He gently places the box on the table near a pair of agents and makes to turn around. Only to find Draeger standing in front of him, uncomfortably close. Jake didn't even hear his approach. The doctor stands so close that Jake can see the rings of gold around the irises of his otherwise black, depthless eyes. Jake backs up into the table behind him, the thought of touching Draeger causing an involuntary recoil. The last time he was even near Draeger, his leg had burned with an unbearable fiery pain. He has not had a flare-up in months, and now is no different.

He chides himself for his display of weakness. Collecting his wits, he brings himself to his full height and stands almost eye to eye with the doctor. In the oddest moment of the encounter to come, Draeger bows his head ever so slightly but not imperceptibly and steps back from Jake. His tone is gentle, almost fatherly.

"Jacob, my dear boy, how fortunate I should run into you today."

Literally, Jake thinks.

"And looking so well. Such vitality, such vigor. Why, you are the very picture of health. Truly remarkable." Draeger's comment is laced with a mixture of incredulity and adulation that rattles Jake even more.

"Er, good day, Dr. Draeger. Haven't seen Mr. Ashton around lately. Doesn't he usually do the check-ins with the team?"

Draeger's soft expression dissipates. "Mr. Ashton is presently indisposed. I will personally oversee the project moving forward."

"I see," Jake returns. "I've noticed that we are no longer bringing in specimens for testing. I'm not sure you need three transporters anymore." Setting himself up for the transfer request, he continues, "Mostly boxes of supplies now. Lots of paper. I take it the project has entered a new phase or something?"

He didn't mean for it to come out as a question. So much for assertiveness.

"Very perceptive of you, Jacob. Yes, indeed. The project has taken a most auspicious leap forward."

"That's great news." A smooth lie. "I was thinking now that logistics have died down, I might be able to try a different department. You know, spread my wings a bit."

Draeger considers it for a moment.

"I was not aware that you are dissatisfied with your current role in the department."

Jake backpedals. "It's not that. I am incredibly grateful for the opportunity and have enjoyed my time on this project. I just miss the animals, I guess. I was really enjoying the canine program. I thought maybe the Department of Agriculture would give me the opportunity to interact with different animal species." *No matter what my mother thinks,* he adds in his head.

"Perhaps you would be amenable to returning to the canine program in lieu of a full department transfer," Draeger suggests, much to Jake's delight and surprise.

"I can do that? I thought ... My mom said ..."

Again, Draeger adopts a paternal tone. "I will interpret your reaction in the affirmative. I sense some urgency. Therefore, consider it done. You may resume your agency in the canine program effective tomorrow."

"Seriously?" Jake cannot believe his good fortune. "Thank you so much, Dr. Draeger. I really appreciate this."

Again, Draeger is uncharacteristically warm toward Jake. "It is my great pleasure to see to your needs, Jacob."

Jake's message makes my heart sing. He's not leaving the DAW. In fact, he is returning to the Canine Division, a stone's throw from the equine program. I text back with way more aloofness than I feel: *That's great Jake, but how?*

I wait, drumming my fingers on the hardcover novel resting on top of my bed. I forgot all about it when my phone lit up. I don't even recall reading the last page.

His reply comes in: *Draeger did it for me.*

I don't want to bring it up, but I have to know.

I text back: *So, he doesn't suspect anything then? With, you know, your situation?*

We never say it out loud. We rarely even talk about it anymore. Jake seems just fine despite his genetic stowaway. Of course, we are reminded of his newly acquired condition whenever we are close enough to touch.

He responds: *Doesn't seem so. I think the lab is onto something else anyway. Everything has changed. No more animals, just boxes and boxes of lab equipment, sterile gloves, petri dishes, beakers, vials, and reams of paper.*

Huh. I wonder what that's all about. Why the sudden shift? What are they up to in there? If they don't know that Jake is harboring the antidote, perhaps they've found another way to disable the existential virus. A vice squeezes my insides at the thought. After learning about Mrs. Montague firsthand, I am worried that the rumors swirling around the Biodome are true. EV is no longer protecting us. From ourselves.

Every day I hear a whisper here and a murmur there. Rumors of misdemeanors like petty theft, disorderly conduct, and public intoxication. My parents pretend like its business as usual, but the sheer number of incidents in all manner of transgressions is growing like a wildfire and taking on a life of its own as EV lies dormant. They are pretending for my sake and for my brother's, trying to protect us.

Why bother? We are not blind.

Each day that EV overlooks the trespasses, people grow bolder, no longer fearing her reprisal. As the seeds of amorality sprout among Biodome citizens—a new code of lying, cheating, and stealing—an ancient code reborn.

Our screen time allowance is almost spent for the night. The Biodome provides us the customary five-minute warning. Since we are both close to the administrative complex now, Jake and I agree to meet for lunch in the campus cafeteria tomorrow. It's not scenic like our picnic spot, but the weather is still on the cool side. Besides, that would mean Jake has to trek halfway across campus and back again while I carry on to the lupus compound. I've been relying on the shuttle for several weeks now for that midday transfer. Even though it's early spring, it's just been too cold to hoof it. So indoors it is for now.

I settle back onto my mound of white pillows and try to get back to my book, but it's no use. I replay the last thirty minutes in my head. A complacent and carefree Draeger, a big breakthrough leading to a new project, and no more animal experiments. So, what then, if not a new discovery, a newfound weakness in EV that Draeger and his team can exploit? And why in the Biodome would Draeger just let Jake walk away from the team?

A theory is forming in my mind. Maybe Draeger wants to thin out his retinue. Maybe he doesn't want any unnecessary prying eyes in the oval lab. Could it be that Jake gave him the perfect opportunity and saved him from having to dismiss him? It is obvious now that Draeger has no idea that Jake is hosting the tetra genome. A tension I didn't know I was carrying in my neck eases at this conclusion. Could it be that this is a win-win for both Jake and Draeger? I have so many questions, but one thing I know for certain: I need to get back into that lab and find out what they are up to.

CHAPTER 24

Therefore take up the whole armor of God, that you may be able to withstand in the evil day, and having done all, to stand firm.

—Ephesians 6:13 (ESV)

JAKE IS WELCOMED BACK with open arms at the canine program. His former lead agent, Dr. Corson, seems pleased with his reemergence. He is greeted on this first day back by a litter of excited Labrador retriever pups, nipping and crawling over each other for Jake's attention. Jake hasn't felt happiness like this in months. He lies down on the foam tiled floor faceup, and puppies swarm him, licking his face, tickling his neck, and tugging at his white cotton T-shirt.

The last year disappears in this moment. There are no transporting animals into the lab to meet their end, no disposing of carcasses, no corporeal nightmares, no strange perversion of his DNA. Only one fragment remains. Her face. Her hair. Her laugh. Her longing for him. Her heart rendered to him. Jake climbs up through the onslaught of puppy slobber, grabs a hand towel, and wipes away at his face and neck. He shakes her image from his mind and leaves the puppies to play while he sets to cleaning out the kennels.

Dr. Corson steps into the room with another warm greeting for Jake. "Hello, Jacob. They are quite the rambunctious little bunch, aren't they?"

The puppies are swarming at the doctor's feet. He bends at the knees and indulges the pups with affectionate strokes.

"We'll start genetic screening tomorrow."

The ancients were very fond of the Labrador, which led to prolific breeding by countless amateurs over decades. After generations of irresponsible propagation, the breed suffered from various prevalent hereditary diseases. Hip and elbow dysplasia, retinal dysplasia, retinal atrophy, cataracts, centronuclear myopathy, and exercise-induced collapse. Like the ancients bred these genetic mutations into the breed, Dr. Corson and his team are breeding the mutations out, one litter at a time.

"That's great, Dr. Corson. As soon as we get the all-clear, I will get their adoption documents ready."

"Like you never left." Dr. Corson smiles at Jake. "Would you like to observe the genetic screening process, learn how we sequence the DNA and look for harmful genes?"

Jake's temporary reprieve from his current predicament is yanked out from under him with these words.

"Ah, sure, Dr. Corson. That would be a great learning opportunity."

He tries to remain buoyant, but his inner voice is not to be silenced.

I'm afraid I know more about harmful genes than you will ever know, Dr. Corson.

I'm tapping my foot under the round table, scanning the cafeteria for Jake. I catch myself subconsciously checking my posture, primping my hair, tucking the tails of my gray-and-yellow check flannel shirt, and straightening my collar. Just as I am done fussing, Jake walks in and notices me almost immediately. He weaves his way through the round tables, greeting agents here and there, and stops in front of our table, looking down at me with that heart-stopping grin of his.

"Hello, Ms. Steele. You are looking well today."

He gives a hand flourish and a bow like an ancient aristocrat. I give him a coy smile back.

"You are cheery today. I take it the transition went well?"

"For me, swimmingly. My mom is none too happy, though. After the centennial celebration, I will be finding my own place. It's time."

I forget that Jake is two years older than me. As my eighteenth birthday approaches, Jake will be twenty. The centennial is in ten days. He's so candid about his intentions. I would be a basket case.

"That's a big change. Are you sure you're ready to do your own laundry?" I tease.

"Herc and I will figure it out," he says, referring to his beloved German shepherd. "Not like I can get a roomie or anything, for obvious reasons." He waves his hands in front of him.

He's come to terms with his isolation. The bubble has become part of him. I wonder if that will ever change. I desperately hope time will free him from this prison. Free me as well. I will wait no matter how long it takes.

Balancing our trays laden with a hearty vegetable soup, oven-baked avocado-and-garlic grilled cheese sandwiches, and strawberry rhubarb coffee cake, we head to our table. As I dig into my minifeast, I decide that meeting for lunch in the cafeteria is not such a bad idea after all.

Between mouthfuls, Jake is recounting his morning spent with a band of wayward pups. The oversized flat screen monitor at the back of the cafeteria is projecting a slideshow of spontaneous images of our campus agents from the various programs toiling away. Most of the faces are familiar to me by now. I blush uncontrollably when my own image appears on the screen, grooming one of our yearlings. I remember that day; the little colt was not having it, terrified of the curry comb until I managed to convince him to accede. Not long after my image is replaced with Beth and Sydney in their beekeeper suits, the slideshow cuts off and an "Important Biodome News Update" flashes across the screen. A serious-looking woman with a no-nonsense bob cut that matches her strict comportment appears on the screen. Reading from notes in front of her, she begins to speak.

"Earlier today, the Biodome recorded the first act of murder in ninety-three years. The perpetrator has been apprehended and all citizens are safe. I repeat, there is no danger to any citizen of the Biodome."

As shocking as this news of such a terrible transgression is, I am even more disturbed with the latter part of the message. Why in the Biodome would the assailant need to be apprehended? EV will unleash a fury on this individual the likes of which we have not seen since the Correction. Just as I am about to say as much to Jake, the downcast woman continues.

"This is the latest in a growing number of transgressions where the existential virus has failed to induce the righting protocol. Agents from the Department of Health Promotion are investigating the cause of this temporary interruption."

You could hear a pin drop in the cafeteria. No one is talking. No one is moving. Just wide-eyed stares.

"Jake," I whisper. "Jake," I say again, this time with a harsh undertone.

He looks at me now. No words come out. There's just a blank look on his face, much like everyone else in this room.

"Jake, what is going on in the oval? What are they working on?"

"I have no idea, Evey. The agents are still there, but there doesn't seem to be anymore animal testing." Jake is insistent.

A memory of my first time in the oval flashes across my mind. That awful day in the crate. Derek Halimand talking to his partner.

"I get it, Renee, but we've been at it for over a year now. I'm not so sure she's even zoonotic anymore."

"Jake, what if Draeger has found another way to neutralize her? What if he doesn't need the serpent DNA, your DNA, anymore? What if we failed in protecting her?"

The room is so quiet, I am not even sure I said it aloud. I can barely hear it myself with the ringing in my ears as panic sets in. But Jake heard me. And he sees I'm losing it. He springs into action, willing me with his eyes to follow him out of the cafeteria. He has a dangerous look on his face, one I've never seen before. Fury. We walk as casually as possible out the door and into the chilly afternoon breeze.

As soon as we are alone, he turns to face me. "Do I even have to ask?"

Relief washes over me. I wasn't sure how I was going to tell him. If I was even going to tell him at all. But Jake has never disappointed me, not once, and this time is no different. I should know by now that there is no need to doubt his worth, his fundamental righteousness. I give him a slight nod and shift my gaze toward the main trail.

"Lead the way."

Ashton sits at a small table in the corner of Draeger's office. The nook looks like a child's play center with letter blocks, puzzles, colored pencils, sketch paper, and a whiteboard with markers. Ashton is currently working on a cryptogram. It won't take but a few minutes for him to solve it. His childlike mannerisms and curiosity belie the cognitive processing capacity and eidetic memory of a genius combined with the emotional and social impairment of an idiot savant. He consumes ciphers, crosswords, anagrams, nonograms, and tangrams as fast as Draeger can produce them for him.

Draeger watches his former assistant, emanating an air of sympathy for the man, albeit slight. He rewards Ashton with a "well done" when he solves the cryptogram, which elicits a beaming smile from his new pet.

Referring to himself in third-person toddler speak, the man looks to Draeger. "Ashton do more?"

Draeger hands him a new cryptogram and, verbalizing his thoughts, ponders, "Why Jacob Domanso? Why him? And how is it that he has not succumbed? Where does he find the strength to resist the darkness?"

He looks over at Ashton, who has abandoned the cryptogram and is currently assembling his letter blocks. He spells Jacob Domanso. He stares at the blocks and then looks to his master. Draeger walks over to him and pats him on the head much like a dog.

"Yes, it appears I have given you a new puzzle. I have an errand to attend to. I will be but a moment."

As soon as the door clicks and Ashton is left alone, he begins to rearrange the blocks. Creating anagrams is a favorite game of his. When he is done, he looks at his work and smiles.

Jacob Domanso. Jacob Adamson. Jacob son of Adam.

True to his word, the door handle turns and Draeger reappears in the doorway. Just as he is about to enter the office, Ashton raises his left arm and swings it in a wide arc, connecting with the letter blocks and causing them to scatter across the floor.

When the door opens, Draeger stops for a beat and raises a brow. Ashton tucks his chin to his chest like a child waiting to be scolded. But no scolding comes.

Draeger is uncharacteristically gleeful as he retakes his seat behind the desk. He waves a folio toward Ashton, who is now sliding out of his chair to the floor to collect his blocks. He looks to Draeger with the innocence of a lamb. Draeger begins one of his orations, his jubilation obvious even in Ashton's current state.

"The latest report, Mr. Ashton." He lifts the folio a little higher.

"Order in the Biodome continues to deteriorate. Disorder, disrespect, discourtesy, dishonesty—they infiltrate families and communities like an insidious disease."

A wicked grin spreads across his face. "It is working, Mr. Ashton. The degeneration of society is hastened with each misdeed that goes unchecked. Without the existential virus to maintain universal moralism, the Biodome is quickly being relegated to the ancient status quo. A perpetual battle between good and bad. An interminable struggle for power and prestige. The immedicable oppression of identities and ideals. Where virtue is relative and somehow always justified. The ancients called this freedom. I call this human nature in all its glory."

Ashton registers the missive, his psyche veiled by his curse, his penance. With an affable little shrug that projects total ignorance, he retreats behind the curtain of imbecility and lies in wait. Hiding in plain sight.

CHAPTER 25

For I do not do the good I want, but the evil I do not want is what I keep on doing.

—Romans 7:19 (ESV)

JAKE AND I CARRY four large, albeit empty, boxes between the two of us. Sizeable to distract agents from looking too closely at our faces, which are further shielded by our official gray DAW ball caps, and to blend in with every other delivery of late, which are always packaged in nondescript cardboard.

We walk along the outer oval like we have every right in the Biodome to be here. As we move along the outer corridor, we scan the rows of stainless-steel tables, looking for clues, anything that will reveal the nature of this new research project. Anything to confirm what we both suspect. The lab agents are so engrossed in their research, they pay us no mind. We grow bolder, entering the inner oval and pretending to look for the right station to deliver the boxes.

On our way here, Jake grumbled, "One day. I got one day away from this place. I keep getting pulled back in."

I feel badly for him. I know how much he wants to settle in at the canine program. We scanned the parking lot before waltzing straight through the main entrance doorway. There was no sign of Draeger's black sedan. Jake's agent number is still active, which is fortunate. It saved us from having to sneak in through a back door. Now as we work our way through the inner oval, I see that where there was one refrigeration unit, now there are several identical units lining the east wall of the inner oval. The cages that used to line the underside of the tables to house experimental animals have been removed. I cannot say I am sorry to see those gone. And to my surprise, the blue chamber is gone. No more ultraviolent wash station.

As we continue to scope out the inner oval, Jake suddenly becomes rigid. He beckons me with a slight head toss in the direction of the cold storage units. I am confused at first, but then I see Ashley from the corner of my eye. She's pulling the lever on the half door separating the inner and outer ovals. Now I understand. We hurry our pace slightly, shifting the boxes in our arms to further obscure our faces. As we reach the east wall, Jake pulls the lever on the second refrigeration unit. We step inside and close the door behind us. The change in temperature is a shock to my system, and an uncontrollable shiver starts at the base of my neck and winds its way down my back. The hazy motion-activated blue-white fluorescent light casts an eerie glow in the hollow space.

We unload the boxes and stand back-to-back, dangerously close to touching. I didn't realize I was holding my breath. I exhale slowly and scan the wall in front of me. It's lined from floor to ceiling with narrow steel shelves, each packed tightly with blue plastic trays. The wall Jake is facing is identical.

I reach for a tray and gently slide it out. The tray is filled with dividers, and each little cubicle holds a vial with a rubber top, the kind used for dispensing its contents through a syringe. There must be two hundred vials in this one tray. I feel the bottom of my stomach drop to the floor. We start pulling out trays. Each one is the same as the last. There must be thousands in this one unit alone.

Jake speaks first.

"Well, this explains a lot. The hunt is over. Mission accomplished."

I am still trying to process.

"But how? I thought you were the key. Where did they find another antigen source?"

"I don't know, Evey, but they have, and distribution is well underway. It's no coincidence that EV is down for the count."

Jake and I arrive at the same conclusion.

"Jake, we need to report this to the Ministry of Health Promotion. They need to shut this down."

Jake scoffs. I have never seen cynicism on his features. They twist his beautiful face into something I don't recognize.

"You've never met my mother. Her and those cronies of hers won't shut this down, Evey. They will exploit it. They'll wrestle away ownership of the program, but they will never shut it down. They are way too arrogant and ambitious to give this up. Trust me. I've lived with her and her false pride my whole life."

I can hear the bitterness in his voice, the pain. A mother who never actually saw her son for who he is, selfless, compassionate, humble. All the things she is not.

"Jake, I'm so sorry. Your mom sounds ..."

"Awful," he finishes for me.

I cannot imagine growing up in Jake's house. Where this subject makes me uncomfortable, it just makes Jake bitter. I don't think now is the time to discuss his family.

"What do we do, Jake?"

"The first thing we do is get out of this freezer. I can't feel my fingers."

Leave it to Jake to make a joke right now.

"Right."

I pick up my empty boxes, and Jake does the same. He opens the door just enough to scan the floor. No sign of Ashley. As casually as ever, he props the door open, and we step out into the open space. No one pays us any mind. We start walking toward the outer oval as a lab agent approaches with a blue tray in hand filled with the same rubber-capped vials. He opens the second to last freezer from the end, enters, and reemerges a moment later empty-handed.

We were in the second unit. I do some mental calculations. Assuming every freezer in between is full, there has to be tens of thousands of inoculation doses, not counting the ones that have already left the oval.

Jake narrows his eyes, a new resolve seeming to settle in his bones. As soon as we are outside and well away from the oval, he turns to me and states matter-of-factly, "My mom won't shut this down, Evey, but we will."

Grandma sits at the table between me and my little brother. Dad is at the end of the table, and Mom is about to sit down. She's just put the finishing touches on dinner, a fresh whole grain loaf to complement our sun-dried tomato linguine. It has been five days since the Biodome announced the murder, and everyone is on edge.

"Of course, once the Health Promotion agents discover the problem with the existential virus, things will get back to normal," Mom is saying, carrying on an earlier conversation with Evander.

It's all anyone is talking about these days: What's wrong with EV? Why did she stop the righting protocols? When will she be back on track? No one even surmises that she is being silenced one inoculation at a time. To even suggest that we did this to ourselves is absurd. It must be some type of malfunction within EV herself. As if EV has somehow contracted her own virus.

"Kids at school are saying this is the greatest thing that could have happened. Now we can do what we want." Evander, seeing the looks on all our faces, quickly adds, "Not me, though. I don't think that."

Grandma, who has been quiet this whole time, speaks on the subject for the first time. "Freedom is dangerous. With the existential virus, we have an emergency brake. She keeps us from going over the edge, protects us from our own bad choices. Without her, many will slide into the abyss. Some will fall. Others will jump. That is human nature."

We all stop eating and look at Grandma. Her words whirl around in my head.

"But we do have freedom, Grandma. The Biodome lets us choose our own vocation. We are allowed to change our minds whenever we want. We are allowed to associate with whoever we choose. We are allowed to spend our free time as we choose. We are allowed to marry whoever we choose, or not marry at all if that's what we choose. We can have children if we choose, or not. We can live where we want, move whenever we want. Geez, we are even allowed to sleep in on weekends! I don't understand how that is not freedom!"

I am so confused by this newly rooted notion that without EV we will finally have free will.

Grandma considers a moment. "That is all true, Everett, but with unfettered freedom, we also have the ability to choose to hurt each other, to wrong each other, to profit off each other. We can choose not to contribute to society. In fact, we can choose to consume the common good while hurting it at the same time. This is the dark side of freedom."

Grandma's sobering explanation takes Evander off-kilter.

"That sounds awful, Grams. Why in the Biodome would we want that for ourselves?"

Dad interrupts, seeing his son's growing distress. "Well, it won't come to that. Whatever is going on with EV will get sorted out, the righting protocols will resume, and life will be as it should."

Needing his father's reassurance, Evander pleads, "Promise, Dad?"

Dad has never told a lie in his life. This fact has never been more obvious than in this moment. Grandma is eyeing him tentatively. Mom is looking down at her plate. Dad is squirming in his chair, looking directly at his son with mouth agape, as if he has lost the ability to speak.

I save him. I look directly at my little brother and tell him the truth.

"Evander, I promise you, EV is coming back."

Jake sits in his invisible chair at the dinner table. His mother is going on about her DHP health projects, her DHP agents, her sore feet. Jake's dad nods every few seconds to show he is paying attention. Maureen Domanso is so self-absorbed that Jake is sure she wouldn't notice if he sprouted purple antlers. The thought makes him titter. His father notices and raises one brow as he looks over at his son. The two share an eyeroll as Maureen carries on and on about her day.

Jake never did understand what his father ever saw in his mother. Peter Domanso is a soft-spoken man, a gentle giant at six foot four, bearded, with warm light brown eyes and an openness about him that makes him instantly likeable. Such a stark contrast to his sharply featured, hawklike mother, who is all angles and barbs with piercing blue eyes and pale blond hair that she wears long and severe. She's striking to be sure, but her condescending personality offsets her physical beauty. She's also utterly lacking in maternal instinct. As if she senses father and son are not affording her their undivided attention, she turns to her husband.

"And what, then, do you suppose is behind this EV debacle, Peter?"

Her voice drips with scorn.

Peter is conditioned by years of subjugation at the hands of his overbearing wife. He chooses the path of least resistance.

"I'm sure you're right, dear. There is a virulence adjustment taking place within EV at the moment. Your recalibration theory is obviously the only explanation."

Triumphant, Maureen puffs up in her chair, raises her chin, and nods to her husband in that haughty manner of hers.

"Yes, well, I see you have been listening after all."

Now she looks to her son. She is about to pose the same question when she reconsiders and scoffs instead. "And what could you possibly know about the existential virus? Just a boy who plays with dogs all day long."

It's a cheap shot, intended to remind Jake of her displeasure at him leaving his post with Dr. Draeger. Not rising to the bait, Jake hangs his head, not in shame but in defiance as he mutters, "So much more than you will ever know."

The centennial celebration is going ahead as planned, despite the veil of unease over the Biodome. For the first time in the history of the Age of Resolve, the Biodome has deputized agents from all departments. A brand-new Department of Citizen Safety, the DCS, has been created.

Before the Correction, there were more than twelve million agents charged with upholding ancient laws by apprehending and detaining citizens who failed to conform. In the absence of a moral custodian, thousands upon thousands of these agents abused their positions of authority, and many more were themselves perpetrators of the very crimes they were meant to prevent, operating within a culture of silence that rendered the entire institution morally corrupt. Without the existential virus and her moral authority, the Biodome is becoming dependent on humankind to defend one hundred years of unassailable righteousness. All in the face of a historical track record that predicts imminent failure.

While agents and their families count down the days until the merriment begins, Jake and I hatch our plan. The frenzy of the day will serve as our cover. No one will notice when we slip away from the crowd. The weekend already ensures the oval lab will be empty, but we have the added distraction of the celebration as insurance. The Biodome has declared it a day of gratitude and reflection. All departments are shuttered for the big event.

Jake absconded the key to the northeast entrance as we escaped the lab last week, miraculously undetected. He has been single-minded since the moment we left that freezer. Every day brings news of more appalling behaviors and more brazen acts of sedition throughout the Biodome. It's multiplying like a pestilence.

Jake is scarred by every transgression. Death by a thousand paper cuts. His resolve grows stronger each day. I don't say anything, but I sense reckless abandon. Like a vigilante bent on justice. We want the same thing, but I have not thrown caution to the wind. As I lie splayed faceup on my bed tonight, lounging in an oversize threadbare white cotton T-shirt and joggers rolled at the ankle since they are two sizes too big, I go through the plan in my head. I will head over to the celebration venue with my family. It's being held in our town's largest park space, which covers four city blocks.

The park is currently equipped with food tents, extra picnic tables, kid's games, porta potties, and a large wooden stage where senior Biodome agents will present the Midwestern Centennial Bio Web, one hundred years of achievement. Agents will present their milestones and their connections with other departments and other breakthroughs and examples of us all working together for a better future. Dr. Pines is one of the agents representing the Midwest AW campus. I can't help but feel a twinge of pride at my small part in some of our achievements.

When the concert starts, I will announce to my parents that I am going to catch up with some friends. Then I will head to our meeting spot. Jake's plan is much simpler. He will drive to the southeast corner of the park and wait for me.

When I asked him how he would dodge his parents for the day, he snorted. "Like they'll even notice I'm gone. My mom is presenting on behalf of the Midwest DHP, and my dad will just follow her around all day taking orders."

Every time Jake talks about his parents, I am more thankful for my own.

Sleep is ever elusive. I toss and turn, wondering if Jake and I are truly up to the task we have assigned ourselves. Doubt and uncertainty plague me. I spend the night vacillating between ploughing full steam ahead and abandoning the plan altogether. I wrestle with my misgivings in my semiconscious state until I see Jake standing in profile at a curtainless window, staring out at a lush green landscape. Soft rain falls from a cloudless overcast sky, one solid sheet of gray spreading across the horizon. No wind blows. The rain is in no hurry as it collects on tree limbs, pooling onto leaves and falling to the ground like teardrops. Like the entire world is weeping. I see Jake's face reflected on the glass. The emotion on his face is not one of anger or bitterness. At first, I mistake it for sadness, tricked by the gloomy ether.

No. This is something else, something deeper. Jake turns his head and looks directly at me, and I realize his pain comes from me. Not sadness. Disappointment. I might be able to live with forsaking the Biodome, but I could never live with forsaking Jake.

When I open my eyes, it takes a moment to orient myself. My bedroom is eerily dark with the moonless sky. The nagging doubt I carried with me into sleep is gone. I settle back into my pillows with a steadfastness that calms me to my core. I am all in.

CHAPTER 26

I have been impressed with the urgency of doing. Knowing is not enough; we must apply. Being willing is not enough; we must do.

—Leonardo Da Vinci

THE BIG DAY. IT'S as feverish as I imagined and more. Dad is glued to the television screen. Images of cities around the Biodome flash across it; they're all dressed up as if going to a costume party. Flower wreaths and garland made from native flora from different regions adorn streetlamps, park benches, and doorways. Tiny yellow desert flame mixed in with coiled pink and red grevilleas and tricolored kangaroo paw create stunning showpieces in the far southeastern corner of the Biodome. The green highlands of the southeast are adorned with masterfully crafted adornments made from wild cowslip, red campion, and sea aster, while in the northwest, spiderwort, butterfly weed, and wild anemone create a splash of purple, white, and orange on every street corner. It's a cornucopia of Mother Nature's finest creations and the bounty of one hundred years of harmony and balanced coexistence.

Mom is preparing our picnic basket. It contains a colorful fresh fruit salad complete with strawberries, pineapple, kiwi, blueberries, and red grapes; an assortment of sandwiches cut into geometrically identical wedges; and a roasted red pepper hummus with vegetables cut for dipping and dainty rosemary and olive oil crackers. Evander is filling up the thermoses with ice water. The forecast for our region is perfect for an outdoor celebration, warm but not hot, with a mix of sun and clouds and a light southwesterly breeze.

Dad powers down the television and turns to us. "As soon as Charlie brings Grandma over, we'll head over to the park and find our spot for the day."

There are already a number of families in the park when we arrive. Some are setting up at picnic tables, and others dot the expansive lawn with plaid blankets. Agents stand all along the perimeter of the park, legs shoulder width apart and arms clasped behind their backs. They are all dressed in navy blue fatigues, navy T-shirts with DCS in white bold block letters across the front, and matching navy ball caps that read "Security." So, this the Department of Citizen Safety. My stomach twists. I never thought I'd see the day that the Biodome needed protection from its own people by its own people. It is a stark reminder of just how critical my mission is today, and it extinguishes any lingering trepidation.

Evander is staring at the men in blue, his confusion replaced with sadness as he registers the meaning of their presence. I put a hand on his shoulder.

"It's just temporary, Ev. It's going to be OK."

He doesn't say anything, just looks at me with solemn blue eyes.

By the time Mom lays out the blanket and we get Grandma into a comfortable folding chair, the park is half-full. As I watch these newly minted DCS agents as they scrutinize my family, my friends, my community. I can see just how far we have fallen without EV. I can't wait for the concert to begin.

The morning flies by in a flurry of brief conversations with families and friends as they pass by in search of their own picnic spots. There is no mention of the existential virus or trouble in the Biodome. If anyone notices the constabularies surrounding the park, they stay mum.

We eat lunch as each department presents their milestones and the Midwest Bio Web is unveiled. Dr. Pines is a fantastic ambassador for the DAW, capturing our work eloquently. It does feel pretty good knowing that I had a hand—well, fingers—in achieving some of the milestones Dr. Pines describes to cheering and applause. When the speeches are done and the MC announces that the first musical act will begin shortly, I clear my throat and brace myself. *Here we go.*

"Uh, Mom, I'm going to go hang with the old gang for the concert if that's OK. Jenny and Toby arranged for us to meet up by the stage."

"Of course, honey," Mom returns. "We will be bringing Grandma home soon anyway. Do you have a ride home after the concert?"

This is a lucky break for me. Now I can focus on the upcoming task without worrying about setting of alarm bells if I'm gone too long.

"Absolutely, Mom. Toby will give me a lift."

I hug my mom and then Grandma. I look at Evander, who looks positively despondent. The world he knows has turned upside down with those agents patrolling the perimeter. Dad is consoling him without words, patting him on the back and looking almost as forlorn at his son. While one part of my heart aches for both of them, another turns to ice. I make my way through the crowd, looking back at their disappearing forms and speaking to them from my half-broken, half-frozen heart.

Have faith, boys. EV may be down, but she's not out. I'm going to see to that.

Jake is exactly where he said he would be. He's drumming his fingers on the steering wheel and scanning the park. From this angle, he won't be able to see the band on the stage. They are actually quite good, although I'm really not listening. In ancient times, the entertainment industry was an epicenter of venality and scandal, a breeding ground for capitalist exploitation. Again, with EV came order and legitimacy. Just one more reason the Age of Resolve must not give way to ancient ideologies.

I check over my shoulder one more time. No one has even noticed that I've broken away from the sea of bodies. As I reach Jake's truck, I notice he has a scowl on his face like he's just swallowed a bitter pill. I turn toward the direction of his gaze. He is staring at the back of one of the DCS agents. I didn't see it before. I was too far away and facing forward. But now I know exactly what Jake's eyes are trained on. I have never seen one before, only heard about it from history class. These must have been taken from the ancient archives. I look down the line of agents along the perimeter and confirm what I already knew. Holstered at the waist of every DCS agent is an ancient weapon meant for one man to control another. Or to kill them. A gun.

I climb into the passenger seat and try to soothe Jake. The rage in his eyes is frightening.

"Jake, it's going to be OK. We are going to get EV back."

Jake doesn't break the stare. He doesn't turn to look at me as he responds through clenched teeth.

"And there is no time to waste."

His driving does not match his mood. He pulls away from the curb smoothly and slowly, not wanting to draw any attention. The ride to the DAW is quiet. We are both lost in thought. I am surprised when Jake drives past the main entrance. Did he miss it? No, he knows exactly where he is going, and I decide it's best not to ask questions right now.

A short drive later, Jake turns into what looks to be a large abandoned parking lot. At the far end of the parking lot, another narrow, single-lane dirt road appears, obscured by overgrown trees.

Jake takes the little road, and we emerge on the back side of the oval. Now I understand. This is how agents were getting in and out with everyone none the wiser. A secret back entrance.

"Wait here. I'll be right back."

He is already halfway out the door.

I sit in silence with no objections. A minute or two later, one of the overhead doors begins to rise, and Jake is jogging back to the truck. He jumps back into the driver's seat, puts the truck into drive, and slowly pulls the vehicle into the bay beside a tow motor and a stack of old lab equipment. Once we are inside, he closes the overhead door. I can't help but feel we've just been swallowed whole. Jake seems to lighten up a little.

"Like we're not even here," he comments, whether to himself or to me I'm not sure.

Our first order of business is cutting the power supply to the refrigeration units. We can't reach the power supplies at the back of the units, and besides, there are a dozen of them and that would mean moving every one of them. Jake has clearly thought this through. He grabs a key ring hanging at the back entrance near our bat cave, and I follow him as he walks over to a nondescript metal door. After flipping through the keys until he finds the right one, he opens the door to a utility room, heads straight for the electrical panel, and then puzzles over the right breakers. There are no labels.

"Evey, you'll need to tell me when I've got the right breakers. Listen for the freezers to stop humming. Do you have your phone?"

I pull the phone from my fanny pack.

"Good. When the freezers die, text me. I'll flip the breakers slowly until I get your text."

Feeling useful for the first time since we arrived, I compose the text and then scurry to the inner oval and position myself in front of the bank of freezers. I let my ears become attuned to the hum of electricity and listen intently for what seems like forever. Finally, silence. I hit my precomposed text: "Done."

I open the door to one of the units just to be sure. No light comes on, and the box remains quiet. I see Jake coming toward me at a lope.

"It shouldn't take long for those units to thaw. I think these inoculation preparations are pretty sensitive to temperature, so I would say mission accomplished. Now on to the head of this hydra."

We both look up at the same time to the sound of footsteps coming down the outer oval. My heart is hammering through my chest and judging by the flush racing up Jake's neck and face, I'd say his vital signs are about as unstable as my own. No one is supposed to be here today.

Draeger is setting the pace, his long lean legs swallowing the ground in front of him. Ashton is bringing up the rear, looking up and around the oval with wide eyes and mouth agape, like a child at the carnival for the first time. His clothing—brown corduroy pants, beige sneakers, and a white T-shirt complete with suspenders—make him look even more ingenuous, like some grotesque human hormone experiment gone horribly wrong.

We squeeze tightly against the back of the last freezer, mere inches between us, crouched so our heads don't reach over the half wall. I try to control my breathing, but my heart is demanding more oxygen than I am currently providing it, and my head begins to swim. Jake is completely motionless, coiled like a cat ready to pounce. Draeger and Ashton enter the inner oval and head for one of the lab stations.

"Now, Mr. Ashton, let us see how much of your scientific training remains intact."

Draeger watches as Ashton approaches the high-powered

microscope, fumbles with a slide, and endeavors to place it under the eyepiece with clumsy hands. Draeger looks up suddenly, tilts his head slightly to the left, and draws a deep breath, which he holds for a brief moment before exhaling slowly through his nose. The hint of a smile passes over his face.

"Mr. Ashton, excuse me a moment, but do continue with the task I have assigned you."

Draeger walks slowly toward the bank of freezers on the east end of the inner oval, his extrasensory perception working like a homing device, having no need for sight or sound. He approaches the end of the line of freezers and stands in front of the very last unit with his hands clasped behind his back.

With complete composure, he calls out, "Jacob, what a delightful surprise. Perhaps I could be of assistance with ..."

He trails off, his message clear. Jake and I look at each other in horror. How? We didn't budge, didn't make a sound. With nothing more to be done, we step out from our hidey hole and into the presence of the most beautiful man I have ever seen. Dark, intense perfection.

"Ah yes, there you are my dear boy. And I do not believe I have had the pleasure of your acquaintance." He is looking at me now with intoxicating eyes.

Jacob stands in front of me, partially obscuring me from view, in a protective gesture. As if a spell has been broken, I shake my head slightly, coming to my senses. Jake is as dangerous as Draeger in this moment, almost hissing out his next words. He does not lie.

"Dr. Draeger, this has to stop. The existential virus cannot not be neutralized."

Draeger considers this for a moment and replies without a hint of malice, despite Jake's threatening tone: "It seems you wish to suppress free will on behalf of every living person now and forever. I trust you have considered the consequences of your current quest."

He pauses a moment for effect and then says, "Very well. Allow me to assist you in your endeavor. However, your customary manners are deficient today, Jacob. You still have not introduced me to your friend."

We are both taken aback by his acquiescence and the polite rebuke. It has disarmed Jake, who now seems unsure.

"Er, this is Everett, Everett Steele. Evey, this is Dr. Draeger."

I step out from behind Jake, and without thinking, I reach to shake Draeger's hand.

Jake squeals, "Don't!"

But I have already offered my hand, and now it is in Drager's. He does not shake it, though. Instead, he brings it to his mouth and gently presses his lips to the back of it. In that moment, I am carried to a garden with lush green trees pregnant with fruit—apples, pomegranates, peaches, figs. I'm barefoot and almost nude in a diaphanous white dress with no undergarments, utterly exposed and reveling in the freedom of my nakedness, surrounded by men and women fully exposed in unspeakable acts of eroticism.

I come back to myself when he releases my hand. The intimacy of the exchange brings flame to my cheeks and shame to my heart. Jake is looking between Draeger and I, concern furrowing his brow.

"Evey, are you all right?"

Draeger is looking at me knowingly. His eyes tell me he saw everything. I feel violated.

"I'm fine, Jake," I lie, suppressing the trembling in my hands by sheer will.

"Do enlighten me, Jacob and Everett. I am interested in your remedy for this crisis of conscious developing in the absence of our beloved existential virus."

I defer to Jake, who cuts a commanding presence in his own right in his present state.

"We need to know what goes into making these vaccines, the ingredients."

It's not a request. It's bold and direct, not negotiable.

Draeger seems almost amused. "I can certainly assist in that regard. Please, this way."

He waves in the direction of the lab station where Ashton has an entire slide deck fanned out in disarray. He pays no mind to the microscope but rather is fitting the slides together like a jigsaw puzzle, creating a pattern of slides that reminds me of the ceramic tiles in my kitchen. He smiles at Jake and I as we approach, as though hoping we will commend him on his creation.

Draeger does just that. "Well done, Mr. Ashton. Such artistic flair."

This elicits an even broader smile from Ashton. Jake and I look at each other in bafflement. What in the Biodome happened to Mr. Ashton? He has lost his wits.

Draeger senses I am about to ask and interjects, "Mr. Ashton has met with an untimely righting protocol of his own, I am afraid."

Now Jake asks incredulously, "EV did that to him?"

Draeger thinks for a moment and then replies, "Although I am not partial to jargon, I do believe there is an ancient idiom that best responds to your question, Jacob."

He waits.

Of course, I take the bait. "Which is?"

He actually smiles.

"EV isn't the only game in town."

A long pause follows. The silence is deafening.

If I was uncomfortable before, now I am unnerved to the point of panic. Maybe this was a bad idea. Maybe we should just hightail it out of here and forget any of this ever happened, not the least of which would include this conversation.

Jake doesn't share my angst. His tenacity is on full display. "We're wasting time. You said you would help. Where is the inoculation formula?"

Draeger raises a brow at his tone but does not rebut. He fires up the nearest desktop computer and easily navigates among the folders and locates the file.

"As you wish," he declares, ceding the computer to Jake.

I approach the computer with Jake and click on the file. A multipage document opens with lists of ingredients like a recipe book. It seems there are several vaccines. I can only surmise that each is specific to EV's various manifestations. Each formula is numbered: C2, E4, F1, C8, F9, L3. That was way too easy. The computers are on a shared drive. When I delete this file, the formulas will be gone forever. I turn to Jake.

"I think we should destroy the server, Jake. It's the only way to be sure."

Jake nods.

"The server room is in the back where we came in, but first things first."

He looks at Draeger, who offers no argument. I am just about to hit delete when I glance at the heading beside C2. It reads "Parvovirus." Parvovirus? It sounds familiar, but I don't recall an EV mutation by that name. I continue to scan the names of the vaccines: C3, Distemper; C4, Bordetella; E1, Strangles; E4, Tetanus; F3, Calicivirus; F6, Panleukopenia. My stomach drops.

"What's the matter, Evey? Just delete it. We'll deal with the server later," Jake prompts.

I look up a Jake, mumbling to myself, "C, canine; E, equine; F, feline."

"Evey?"

I push back from the computer, bolt for the freezers, and open the second one in the bank. Trays of C2, C3, C4. I open another freezer: E1, E4.

I turn and shout, "Jake, turn the power back on now!"

Jake is bewildered. He comes rushing toward me. I am on the verge of tears.

"Jake, these are animal vaccines, all of them. They are part of the program."

Draeger is lilting gently from side to side, hands clasped behind his back as he approaches us. He looks bemused.

"Of course they are animal vaccines, fair Everett. This is the Department of Animal Welfare, after all. I cannot fathom what else they might be." He spreads his hands innocently.

Jake ignores him for the moment and turns to me. "Are they ruined? Did we ruin all these vaccines?"

"I don't know, Jake. Just restore the power," I say.

"*Tsk, tsk,*" Draeger admonishes, waving one long slender finger in front of our faces. "Think of all the poor puppies and kittens who will suffer now as a result of this reckless behavior. And, Everett, my intuition tells me you favor horses. So unfortunate that our equine program will be seriously diminished now."

What have we done? We wanted to believe so badly that we could fix EV that we were blind. And foolish. I know Jake is thinking the same thing. His bravado has evaporated.

"It hasn't been that long, Jake. They might be OK. The freezers are sealed."

I know that's not really where his mind is. Neither is mine. We failed. Now we will regress to a time where people will be divided racially, socioeconomically, geographically, and religiously. A time where the strong and the unscrupulous will prosper at all costs, while the weak will grow weaker and the winner will take all.

Now Jake addresses Draeger sheepishly, "I am so sorry, Dr. Draeger. We thought ..."

He seems unsure of how to finish the apology, but there is no need. Draeger is gentle now, almost parental.

"Now, now, children. A misunderstanding, to be sure. However, all will be as it should be. Assuming you no longer wish to destroy these vaccines, that is."

Jake looks up now. "No, of course not. We've been so careless, we almost ruined everything for the DAW."

The guilt is already gnawing at him. I feel terrible, too, but something just doesn't feel right. *"All will be as it should be."*

Not all will be fine, or all will be OK, but rather as it should be. Which is what exactly? A voice in the corner of my mind is whispering to me: *This is what he wants. He wants EV to fail.*

No there's more.

He wants us to give up so EV will fail.

Looking at Jake right now, I'd say he's going to get his wish. Fatalism has already begun to set in.

CHAPTER 27

God had one son on earth without sin, but never one without suffering.

—St. Augustine

AFTER JAKE RESETS THE breakers and we check the inline thermometers, I feel a flood of relief when the formula sheets confirm that the vaccines are still stable.

I try to console Jake. "See. No harm, no foul. Just a little overactive imagination."

Draeger is not the least bit upset with us. I hope his kindheartedness will ease Jake's self-reproach. I, for one, am ready to put today behind us. Dwelling on it isn't going to change anything.

We are just about to make our way back to our covert parking spot when Ashton, who has been playing with the slides this entire time—he now has three boxes splayed across the workbench—begins to hum the alphabet song. Jake and I both glance over at him. I have no idea what transgression he committed to deserve this ... severe punishment is the only way to describe it ... or how it came about.

That is one conversation I do not want to initiate. Despite whatever it is he has done, it's hard not to feel sympathy for the man.

Jake and I lock eyes. I can only shrug. It's such an unremarkable response on my part, but there is nothing to be done. He gives me a couple of shallow nods to acknowledge he feels the same way. We turn our backs on the scene and prepare to wipe away this day with milkshakes and butter pecan tarts at the coffee shop.

Just as we start moving, Ashton begins to sing in an infantile singsong voice that belongs in a kindergarten class: *"A-B-C-D-E-F-G, Jesus died for you and me. H-I-J-K-L-M-N, Jesus died for sinful men."*

We hear a gurgling sound behind us and both turn to see Ashton gasping for air. Draeger has the other man's hands in his own and is squeezing so tightly that his skin has gone white. There is utter madness in his eyes.

His voice has dropped an octave, and his demeanor is as volatile as an erupting volcano. "Mr. Ashton, I must say, expectation is indeed the mother of disappointment. I expected so much more of you, and I am truly, extremely disappointed."

"What, what are you doing to him," I blurt out. Then I shout, "Let him go!"

"This is no concern of yours, Ms. Steele," Draeger warns, maintaining his hold.

Jake stares at the scene. The perpetually unflappable Dr. Draeger has shown his true colors. He half mumbles, "You are silencing him."

Then, seemingly involuntarily, he repeats the verses, *"A-B-C-D-E-F-G, Jesus died for you and me. H-I-J-K-L-M-N, Jesus died for sinful men."*

I watch his face contort with pain. He doubles over and pulls frantically at his pant leg, red seeping through the fabric and bleeding onto his hands. Stumbling backward, he releases the material, turns his palms toward his face, and splays his fingers.

Staring at his stained hands, he whispers, "It's me. It's been me all along. I have brought hell on earth."

I stare at Jake in horror. His pallor is gray, and he is twitching uncontrollably, sweat beading on his face. It has surfaced. After months of peaceful coexistence, it's unleashing a fury on Jake. Draeger is squeezing even tighter. Ashton's eyes begin to bulge, and blood trickles from his nose and the corner of his mouth. Draeger's wrath engulfs the oval. The lights flicker, the computer screens blink, and a blast of hot air washes over me.

It takes a minute to realize that the screaming in my ears is coming from my own body. The light is fading from Ashton's eyes. Right before he slides from the stool and slumps to the floor, he looks at Jake, seemingly willing him to make eye contact. Jake lifts his head briefly and meets the man's eyes through his own suffering. Ashton nods once and smiles. Then he is gone.

Draeger gently lowers Ashton to the concrete floor with a tenderness that belies his murderous rage. He looks at Ashton one last time with an expression somewhere between remorse and insouciance. Clearly, he took no pleasure in executing his former assistant. Now he walks slowly to Jake, who is whimpering from the pain. Moving slowly as though approaching an injured animal, he rests his hands over Jake's from the opposite side of the table.

"There, there, son. Ease your troubled mind."

I watch as the creature relinquishes its hold. The pain on Jake's face subsides like a receding tide. Jake grabs Draeger's hands like a lifeline. I don't perceive the gesture as weakness; it is purely survival instinct.

Draeger soothes him. "All is well now."

I look between the two of them.

"You knew. You've known this whole time." It's not so much an accusation as a statement of fact.

Draeger looks at me now. Jake holds on tighter.

"Jacob is the chosen one. He will be glorified for millennia to come. The Savior."

I can't believe what I am hearing.

"Why, of all the people on this planet, why Jake?" My voice is trembling.

Draeger nods satisfactorily. "That is a most perceptive question, Ms. Steele, the answer to which eludes even me. I had not expected him to adapt so well."

He sees by my expression that I don't agree with his assessment of Jake's adaptability.

"This is a unique circumstance, I assure you." He glances over at Ashton. "Jacob will live a long and happy life, free of any encumbrance."

That is somewhat comforting. So, EV is dead and with her, all the protections from the human condition, our universal morality. It will take some getting used to. It will take time. My tone changes to one of complacency. My immediate concern is Jake's welfare.

"Is he OK? Can I take him home?"

Draeger looks at Jake with the utmost respect. "Jacob is just fine. This was an unfortunate adversity, to be sure, but an isolated one." He gently pulls his hands away from Jake, who looks at him with fear in his eyes. "You are fine, son," Draeger reassures him.

Jake stands motionless, waiting. The pain that wracked his body seems not to return. His relief is palpable.

"Come on, Jake. Let's get you home," I say.

I just want to get him away from Draeger and this crime scene. A crime was committed here. How, I don't know. If I had not seen it with my own eyes, I would never believe it to be true. I feel tainted somehow, unclean. I suppose this is the new reality, and so far, it leaves a sour taste in my mouth.

Jake recovers quickly. He nods and we start our slow march back to the truck.

Suddenly, Jake turns to me. "One second, Evey. Let me make sure everything is OK in the utility room. Just wait for me in the truck."

He throws the keys at me. I catch them reflexively.

"Oh, OK. I guess that's not a bad idea."

Jake doubles back and covers the short distance to the utility room, and I head for truck. I sit in the passenger seat, twirling the keys for what seems like an inordinate amount of time. I step out of the truck and exit the bay.

"Jake, everything OK?" I call out.

When I hear nothing, I make my way back the way we came. The door to the utility room is open, and the lights are still on.

"Jake? Jake?"

I walk into the room. A peculiar smell fills the room. Peculiar but distinct. And familiar. Just like when I paint Grandma's nails on the deck on warm summer days. Nail polish remover. I follow the scent and come to a large cabinet on the back wall of the room. The doors are flung open, and containers of chemicals are haphazardly strewn about the area. Glass beakers, funnels, slides, vials, burners, flints, a couple of broken microscopes tagged for repair, and containers of chemicals ranging from tiny bottles to drums.

I scan a few of the labels: sodium hydroxide, pentanoic acid, hydrochloric acid, trimethylphosphine, silver chloride. The source of the odor is in a large yellow container. The cap has been removed, and the contents are evaporating into the small room. Acetone.

"Jake!" I call out louder this time.

I run back to the bay. The truck remains vacant. Jake is nowhere to be found. Dread floods my veins. I run back to the oval, scanning the inner floor and yet see no sign of Jake. Draeger is still here, standing in the same spot we left him in, but now he is looking up over the strange dull glass into the outer oval. I follow his line of sight and my heart drops.

Jake stands amid the sea of chairs about halfway up and in the northeast corner. I can hardly see him from my vantage point. I scoot out a little farther and then I see him clearly. He is holding a yellow container identical to the one I just inspected. He removes the cap and begins pouring the acetone over the seats, walking the full length of the oval to the southeast corner. He doubles back, stops in the middle, and pours the remainder of the container where he stands. His voice echoes in the hollow space, creating the effect of coming from all directions at once, a disembodied message.

"Draeger." There are no more niceties now. "There is still one more possibility you forgot to mention."

Draeger looks positively despondent. "Jacob, you must come down from there, son. You are not thinking clearly."

"Oh, I assure you, things are crystal clear. As long as I walk this earth, the existential virus will die, filth and corruption will infiltrate the Biodome, and we will be no better than the ancients, raping and pillaging the planet, clawing each other's eyes out for power, wealth, and status."

Draeger implores Jacob, "But, my son, that is mankind's fate, to prosper or perish in a world where man in free to choose his own right or wrong."

Jake pulls a flint from the back pocket of his jeans.

"Not my world."

He looks directly at Draeger.

"And one more thing."

There, on Draeger's face, is an emotion no one has ever seen before in the man. Fear.

Jake finishes, "I'm not your son."

He strikes the flint, and I watch as one single spark falls in slow motion. A wall of flame races north and south from the center of the oval along the row of seats. I scream.

I stand paralyzed, watching the centuries-old hardwood seats, dry as tinder, erupt into flame row by row. Eighteen thousand of them. I can't see Jake for the smoke and fire. The last year replays in my head like flashbacks: our first meeting on the secret trail, our second meeting where he almost burned me alive, when I discovered that EV was under attack, when I asked him to help me stop it, our picnic lunches, sharing stories, sharing pieces of ourselves, laughter, stolen glances, a stolen kiss—the only one that really matters to me—stealing the genome sequence that would neutralize the existential virus, the moral compass that keeps the world right, the moment I realized Jake is carrying that genome in his own DNA, the pain and sorrow of touching him, the bigger pain and unbearable sorrow of not being able to touch him.

This is all my fault. We are here because of choices I made. Choices I was allowed to make that I should never have been allowed to make in the Age of Resolve. Freedom to choose without consequence. And look where we are. Grandma's words come back to me.

"Freedom is dangerous."

No Grandma, I say to myself, *freedom without responsibility is dangerous.*

I am responsible for what happened to Jake. I see it clearly now. I need to run. And run I do. Into the fire. The heat is so intense, it feels like my skin is going to boil off my bones. I get down on the concrete floor and crawl up to the stairs nearest to where Jake was last standing and slither up on all fours. I am screaming his name over and over again, coughing with every other breath. We can still get out. There are clear paths through the flames along the wide expanses of concrete. I am far enough away from the flames, but the heat is burning my lungs.

I get to the row where Jake was standing, where he dropped that one deadly spark and created this inferno. I roll over onto my back against the stairs to catch my breath. I can see the ceiling of this cavern now. Massive wooden beams are being devoured by roiling flame. A shadow crosses over my face. Draeger. Standing above me with not a care in the world for the fire raging around him.

He says simply, "He has chosen. He is gone."

He turns and walks away, leaving me lying on the concrete stairs surrounded by hell. He's gone. I am numb. I need to move. I need to crawl back down these stairs and to safety. *Just one more minute,* I tell myself. I lie there, watching the flames dance across the beams above me. I am mesmerized. The heat is drying the tears that are spilling onto the sides of face and into my hair. I need to blink them away to clear my vision. I close my eyes.

CHAPTER 28

Who gave himself for us to redeem us from all lawlessness and to purify for himself a people for his own possession who are zealous for good works.

—Titus 2:14 (ESV)

I HEAR BIRDS. TINY little songbirds that sound as though they are flitting here and there, trilling as they glide from tree branch to tree branch. I am lying on my back. I sink my hands into soft plush grass that cradles me like a child. I crack one eye open and see the source of the melody: birds I have never seen before. They are stunning exotic creatures—green parrots, blue-and-red macaws, rainbow-colored lorikeets, golden pheasants. Birds of paradise.

I open both eyes now and gently study my surroundings. The beauty of the landscape is breathtaking. Gently flowing waterways and lush tropical plants laden with foliage, some with leaves that could swallow me whole, and all in vibrant shades of emerald. Every animal I have ever seen and some I have not roam passively through the undergrowth, none threatened by my presence.

I lift my head and then slowly rise to a sitting position, waiting for the heat and the pain to come. I remember lying on the stairs, the blaze greedy for every molecule of oxygen. I needed to rest for a minute, to close my eyes. I am dreaming. That must be it. I need to wake up now and get down these stairs to safety. I stand, not on shaky legs as I expect but strong and whole. I am wearing a white sheer dress that almost reaches to my ankles. I realize it's the same dress as the one Draeger glimpsed. It's more modest this time. My breasts and privates are swathed in the softest white linen. And I am wearing sandals this time, which are delicately laced up my calves.

I feel so clean. My hair smells like fresh rain and falls like a curtain down my back. My skin has been scrubbed, and as I rub my fingers along my neck and then my arms, I imagine this is what newborn skin feels like. I inspect my hands. My nails are perfectly manicured and I no longer have calloused palms.

I am surrounded by lions, giraffes, tigers, and beautiful wild horses, yet the fear does not come. I feel peace and tranquility. I feel safe. The way I felt before the existential virus was annihilated. I never realized how anxious and afraid I had become until now. I bask in the freedom I feel now that the burden of that fear has been lifted. There is no sense of urgency here, no imminent danger, no feeling of foreboding.

I walk along a stone pathway, taking in the beauty of this magical garden. I pass over a small bridge, below which I can see orange and yellow flashes in the stream—fish frolicking in the shallow water. Up ahead, a massive tree takes shape, absorbing the skyline behind it. Dome-shaped and covered in millions of iridescent leaves, its color contrast against the horizon is mystical. The trunk of the tree is ten men thick and gnarled with age but vibrant with life. I stop and stare, imprinting the image before me in my mind for posterity. I never want to forget this moment.

I resume my light gait, and a speck midway up the trunk of the tree begins to take shape. At first I saw nothing but a spot on a large knot, my eye drawn to the brilliant white against the bark of the tree, but as I draw closer, my heart takes off at a sprint. My feet take off of their own volition, running toward the tree.

Jake, all dressed in white like me, sits high up in the tree, the embodiment of serenity. And like me, I can see he has also been cleansed. His longish hair is coiled into a halo of silky curls, his jaw is clean shaven, and his complexion is glowing. He doesn't move when he sees me, but his crystal-clear blue eyes smile at me, welcoming me.

"Jake?"

I feel silly asking his name. Now he gives me the grin that has had the same effect on me since the first time we met. I feel my heart melt. A blush makes its way across my cheeks, and my legs turn to Jell-O.

"Evey, come on up. The view is amazing."

He extends a hand to me. I hesitate. We have not touched since he revealed his condition to me. He does not take his hand away but reaches a little lower. I stretch and carefully place my hand in his. Touching him is pure joy. The same intense emotion I felt the first time we kissed comes rushing back. I am greedy for it now. I give him both hands as he pulls me up onto his perch.

"Jake, you're healed," I squeal.

He is serious for the moment.

"When I woke up here"—he looks out over the garden—"I felt different. Whole again. Clean. Like I'd been tethered to an anchor and had been dragging it around everywhere I went and suddenly it was severed and I was free."

I know exactly how he feels.

"Where is here exactly?" I look over at him. Even in profile I can see the serenity on his perfect face.

He is quiet for a few seconds and then, almost in a whisper, he says, "The beginning. We're at the beginning."

I am lost for a minute until I realize he is speaking in the literal sense.

"*The* beginning?"

Now he looks at me and smiles. "Yes, *the* beginning, Evey."

"Wait, if this is the beginning, then you and I ..." I trail off here, feeling my face turning fire engine red.

"Only if that's what you want, Evey. I would never ..." Jake looks suddenly nervous.

"Is that what I want? That's all I've wanted since the day I met you, Jake."

There's that boldness resurfacing. Jake looks relieved. He intertwines his fingers with mine and looks at me. "Very well, but one step at a time, Ms. Steele. We haven't even been on a proper date yet."

My head is spinning. I think my heart is somewhere on those clouds dotting the horizon. A thought intrudes the moment and brings me back to reality.

"But, Jake, what about our families, our friends?" I sputter.

"They are in the Biodome where we left them, Evey." Jake says this as a matter of fact.

"But what happened? Is EV going to be all right? Is the backslide into ancient civilization going to stop now?"

I am a little panicky. He looks back out into the garden.

"I think so. I mean, I took that beast down with me. But it's not in here, not in me anymore, so I can't be sure."

He holds his free hand over his heart as he speaks. He looks solemn now.

"I can't go back, Evey. I made my choice. But you, there is a part of you still in the Biodome. I can feel it. It's not too late for you, Evey. You can go back. If you chose to."

The part that loves my mom, my dad, Evander, Grandma, and Cosmos. The part that wonders if they will be OK without me. The part that wonders if EV is going to restore harmony, integrity, and purpose in the Biodome. I can't deny what Jake has said. But I look at the landscape around me, the utter beauty and purity of it all. Then I look back at Jake.

There is another truth I cannot deny. I love this man. And together we can build a new life here, in this paradise. But won't I always wonder if I sacrificed my family for my own happiness? Maybe EV is back and everything will be as it was before: Mom and Dad will continue as well-respected department agents. Evander will grow into a handsome young man, become an agent, find a nice partner, and maybe marry. Grandma will continue to age with grace and live out the remainder of her life in peace.

Or not. Did the serpent escape before Jake's sacrifice? Will it find another host? Will EV die and mankind be plunged back in time and back onto the path of assured self-destruction? Jake watches me as I wrestle with conflicting emotions, conflicting wants and needs.

"Everett," he says gently, "time is running out. The greatest freedom we have is in choosing our own destiny. I cannot take that from you. I have chosen mine. You have to choose yours."

I will choose. Tomorrow. Jake and I climb down and stretch our limbs at the enormous base of the tree. We wander the garden, hand in hand, for hours, watching the animals roam, graze, and bathe in the pristine waters. We talk about our early years, drawing parallels to the simplicity of this world to that of a child—the innocence, the sincerity, the feeling of security.

When the sun begins its decent in the west, we forage at the forest's edge, collecting blueberries, hazelnuts, mushrooms, wild roses, and mullein, which we steep in water from a hot spring for tea after fashioning cups from bamboo shoots. Our dinner is simple, yet I have never felt more nourished. We settle in the soft grass at the base of our tree. I have christened it *our* tree already. One by one, the animals settle down around us. There is no predator and prey here. Jake and I lie on our backs, looking up at the stars that dot the clear sky, our shoulders touching and hands clasped.

We talk well into the night, our conversation punctuated with fingers pointing at the stars when one of us discovers a constellation. Orion, Taurus, Leo, Scorpius—the bear, the bull, the lion, the scorpion. My brain connects the stars, bringing the creatures to life. It becomes a game. Like old times, we start keeping score and making bets on who will find the next one. And then I see it, as if taunting me from the heavens: the giant red star. Almost involuntarily, I follow the tail of stars downward, the Cauda, and then up from the red center point to the head and open maw of the Serpens Caput. I stare at it but say nothing. A shadow passes over my heart. Jake's hand flies up and he points away from my stare.

"Ha! Libra. See there? The scales."

I tear my eyes away and follow Jake's finger.

"You got me."

I disguise my unease with a cheerfulness that I do not feel. I let Jake win the bet. I do not tell him the serpent is watching us from above.

When sleep finally drags me under, I dream of Evander, watching him at the park the day I left, the look of despondency on his face, the hopelessness in his eyes. A serpent slithering at his feet. I bolt upright and gasp for breath. It takes me a second to orient myself. I look over at Jake. His face slack with sleep. His tranquility centers me, and I lie back down on my side, focusing on the blades of grass illuminated by the moon. I stay that way, refusing to look at the stars, until my body slowly disappears and sleep takes me away once more.

The next morning, I wake to the sounds of wildlife, the mewling of cubs, the rustling of the grass as antelope and oxen graze side by side, the trilling of brilliant birds calling from tree to tree. I am still on my side on the bed of grass. My back is to Jake, who, judging by the rhythm of his breathing, is still asleep. I watch the animals, observing their unprocessed behaviors in their natural habitat. Is this not what we were trying to achieve in the Biodome? Giving them back what was rightfully theirs to begin with? Before the ancients desecrated the earth in their never-ending quest for more. I see now that we were on the right path, with the help of the existential virus to keep the new order from falling into the gluttony trap of old.

Jake stirs. I roll over to face him, and a smile slowly creeps onto my face. I have never been this close to anyone ever. The intimacy of waking up beside him sends a shiver down my spine. He opens his eyes slowly, and we lie there, watching each other.

Finally, he breaks the silence. "Good morning, Ms. Steele. Did you find the accommodations to your liking?"

Leave it to Jake to crack a joke at a moment like this. I punch him lightly on the shoulder.

"He saves the world, but he's still a goofball."

He laughs out loud and pulls me into a hug.

I cannot imagine anywhere else I would rather be in this moment. All the anguish from just yesterday is rinsed away as though it is a thousand-year-old wound that has long since healed and scarred over. We stay like this for a long while, frolicking, bantering, and embracing each moment.

After we've washed up in a nearby stream and collected an assortment of berries and fruit that hang in abundance throughout the garden, we sit at the base of our tree for breakfast and continue our conversation from last night. We never seem to run out of things to talk about. We flip-flop from serious discussions about the Biodome and the state of the universe to silly chatter like an impromptu trivia match and "guess how many fruits in the tree" challenges and back again as if it were the most natural thing in the world.

By midafternoon, we sit at the edge of a small lake, watching the birds glide on and off the surface of the still water. Suddenly, Jake becomes serious. He looks at me and takes my hands in his.

"Evey, that day in the oval when you kissed me"—my heart starts to stammer—"I have never wanted anything more in my life."

Oh. I wasn't expecting that.

"There were just too many things in the way, too many obstacles. I thought it would be best not to overcomplicate our already complicated situation."

"I see," I reply, enunciating slowly.

He continues, "And then when, well, when I got bitten and the snake highjacked me, well, there was just no way."

He's watching me. I don't look away. I ask one simple question.

"And now?"

He does not answer with words. Instead, he cups my chin in his hand and pulls me gently toward him. When he brings his mouth to mine, every doubt I ever had dissolves away. Maybe just one more day. I can decide tomorrow.

CHAPTER 29

A shadow leaned over me, whispering, in the darkness
Thoughts without sound;
Sorrowful thoughts that filled me with helpless wonder
And held me bound.

—Alfred Noyes, *The Shadow*, 1923

THE HEALTH PROMOTION AGENT is changing the fluid bag and checking the central line. Most of the medical equipment in this room was retrieved from the ancient archives or from the Department of Elder Care and assembled specifically for this unique case.

An eighteen-year-old female was left at the main entrance of the Department of Health Promotion's Midwest campus on the afternoon of the centennial celebration. It is presumed that she was trampled when the crowd in the community park became unwieldy during the afternoon concerts. Department of Citizen Security agents eventually brought the situation under control, but not before a number of people were injured as overzealous youth rushed the stage. What was supposed to be a day of commemoration for the Biodome became a harsh lesson on the precariousness of the Age of Resolve in the absence of the existential virus. It was a stark reminder of the fundamental contribution of EV to the new order.

In the short time she was listless, countless shameful acts and flagrant displays of dishonor and disrepute were committed throughout the Biodome. One hundred years of rectitude had eroded in a matter of months. When EV returned to her full glory on the day of the centennial, it took no time at all for the abhorrent behavior to cease. It was nothing but a blip. Harmony, integrity, and purpose have been restored, and so has the collective sense of calm and order.

Now Everett lies in this bed, connected to an ancient ICU monitor, her heart rate and rhythm on full display and her blood pressure, body temperature, and oxygen levels monitored around the clock. An agent from the Department of Elder Care enters the room. It seems odd to Everett's mother that an EC agent should be tending to her daughter, that is until she witnesses the agent's deftness as she applies pressure cuffs to Everett's legs and engages the sequential compression device. The machine inflates and deflates the cuffs. The serial compression of her leg muscles and veins will prevent blood from pooling in her lower limbs while she lies unconscious.

Gordon Steele walks into the room while the agent is in the middle of the compression series. He looks to his wife. "How is she doing?" he asks, hopeful.

"Same," is all Sandra Steele offers in response.

The health agent, now finished with the central line, moves to the EEG electrodes attached to Everett's scalp, ensuring they are affixed properly. Dr. Amadio ordered another EEG this morning. These are performed several times daily, so the electrodes have become a permanent fixture. The health agent attaches the input ends of the wires into the monitor and begins the procedure. A paper printout of what Gordon and Sandra are watching on the screen pools beside the machine. Dr. Amadio walks in and smiles when he sees the monitor.

"A happy, active brain. A very good sign," he reports.

He addresses Everett's parents now. "Her vital signs are excellent, her heart is strong, her organs are perfusing without assistance, and her brain activity is, well, exceptional. Wherever she is, she is quite content. There is no sign of distress. Medically, she is quite stable. It's all up to her now. She has to decide to wake up."

Gordon and Sandra clasp hands. Brave smiles are pasted on their faces.

"Thank you, Dr. Amadio," Sandra addresses the medical agent while Gordon walks over to his daughter and brushes his lips against her forehead.

"Did you hear that, honey? You can come back to us now. You're good as gold." He lingers a moment longer, breathing deeply as he works to control his emotions. The distinct smell of smoke in his daughter's hair still lingers after thirty days in this bed.

Vladimir Draeger stands over the prone form, staring into the pale face of the sleeping girl. It had been a challenge to extract the child from the inferno. The building had begun to collapse in on itself just as he lifted her into his arms and made his way down the stairs, into the maintenance bay, and eventually outside. He had stood holding the girl, repositioning her against his body to protect her limp neck, and watched as the roof bowed and then sank inward.

The fire never breached the outer walls, which were made of twenty-four-inch-thick concrete block and sheets of inch-thick tempered glass. The structure withstood the onslaught. Now the oval looked like an ancient coliseum, a lifeless shell. The roadways circling the oval protected the surrounding forest from the heat and any fugitive sparks. Eventually, the flames died, and the remnants of the lab sat smoldering. Ashton, his former assistant, lay somewhere in that rubble. The boy lay somewhere in that rubble.

He had looked down at the girl in his arms. Her lungs and airway were likely seared, but her body was whole, intact. He had lain her gently in the back seat of his black sedan and driven in silence. Five days later, a concrete slab was the only evidence that a building ever sat on the former site of the secret lab. Or that two people ever perished there.

Now he watches the girl, her hair fanned out on the pillow, her eyelids fluttering, the rhythmic in and out of her breathing as she lies insentient. He looks at her hand nearest him where it rests on the bed, an IV line inserted just below the wrist. His gaze follows the drip as it trickles from the bag and down the clear tube to its final destination.

Whispering almost apologetically, he addresses Everett. "I must learn of the fate of the boy and what has become of my kin. I suspect you may hold this information. I have waited some weeks for you to recover. However, time is of the essence. It is best that you do not resist. This will take but an instant." He reaches for the hand and gingerly places in it in his own.

A battle of wills.

She is strong, even in sleep. His attempts to penetrate her formidable defenses are met with resistance, barring the intrusion. Sweat beads along her hairline, and the bleeping of the monitors increases in intensity as her pulse quickens. She jerks uncontrollably, spasms wracking her body.

Once her physical body is finally overwhelmed, Draeger reaches into her mind, probing her memories. Images of the girl's life flash before him. He discards them like trash, rifling through her innermost moments without a care for the violation. Slowing his assault as images of Jacob Domanso flood her psyche, the secret is eventually revealed. He extracts the information without touching her mind. A small mercy then.

He releases her hand, places it back at her side, leans in close, and whispers softly. "Well done, child. Sleep."

The bleary-eyed nightshift agent comes running into the room and skids to a stop at the girl's bedside. The ICU monitor shrieks alarms: tachycardia, BPM 167, and hypertensive crisis, blood pressure 180/120, both accompanied by involuntary muscle spasms that animate the girl's body. The agent is frantic, searching for the cause of the sudden upheaval. The monitor leads are intact, the central line is secure, and the fluid levels and drip rate are exactly as they should be.

In the chaos of the moment, the agent barely registers the dark form that sneaks out the door behind her. As suddenly as it manifested, the crisis passes and the girl returns to her quiet slumber. The health agent later chalks up her faint recollection of a what was surely a male figure slipping out of the room while she tended the girl to nerves and fatigue. Afterall, visitation hours had long passed. No one would be visiting the girl at 3:00 a.m.

Pedro sits in his cubicle, pouring over the latest data on the migratory patterns of the *Tyrannidae* family of birds, native to the southwest central Biodome. So engrossed in his analysis, he doesn't even notice the small bell-shaped icon shaking in the toolbar below his open document. Even when he does finally register the alarm, it takes him several seconds to process the message. He closes his *Tyrannidae* data file, scrolls over to the alarm, and double-clicks to open the program. He sits for a long moment, staring at the screen, a mix of excitement and dread filling his belly. He jumps up from his chair and runs the length of the hall toward Dr. Castillo's office. He knocks twice but does not wait a polite amount of time before turning the door handle.

Castillo appears to be napping. His half-eaten lunch is abandoned on the corner of his desk, now spoiled by two roving flies. Pedro watches his mentor, mapping the lines on his leathery face, the creases at the eyes and around the mouth. He is a man who has laughed. Well past retirement, tired, no fight left. Changing his mind, he is about to back out and close the door when Castillo lifts his chin and straightens his rumpled form. He has that bewildered look of someone lost partway between a dream and reality. He gains his bearings and focuses on Pedro standing in the doorway.

"*Sí*, Pedro. What is it, *menino*?" he asks, slipping between languages.

"I should not have disturbed you, Dr. C. I just wanted to update you on the migration data. You will be pleased."

"*Sí, rapaz.* I will be down shortly."

Castillo straightens up, brushing away breadcrumbs from his stubbly chin. Pedro closes the door behind him and walks slowly back to his cubicle, deep in thought. Choosing to lie to his lead agent should earn him a severe righting protocol now that EV is back on course. Pedro is willing to accept the consequences. Just as he is willing to accept the fight. He strengthens his resolve with scripture.

Even though I walk through the valley of the shadow of death, I will fear no evil, for you are with me; your rod and your staff, they comfort me.

Arriving at his desk, he sits back in his tattered old chair and shakes the mouse attached to his laptop to bring the screen back to life. He sits watching it for a long time. A little red beacon on a topographical map. A long-lost signal from the ancient Ceará. The tetra is back.

EPILOGUE

I chose well. And so to the selfless act of one young man do you owe your salvation. Your second chance to chart a path toward unity, peace, and prosperity for all. Do I have faith that you will do the right thing? That you will live the life I have given you the way I intended? Let's just say I have a plan B. A second beginning. One that starts with a boy who never abused the freedom I have granted him. A boy with untarnished integrity. And one girl. A girl with the unfettered liberty to make her own choices and who, up until now, has not disappointed. One girl of two hearts. I chose. He chose. And now she must choose. A choice that will decide the fate of humanity.

Printed in the USA
CPSIA information can be obtained
at www.ICGtesting.com
BVHW040930020823
668099BV00010B/31

9 781663 244772